The Boy Who Made Good

The Boy
Who Made Good

A NOVEL BY

MARY DEASY

An Atlantic Monthly Press Book

BOSTON · Little, Brown and Company · TORONTO

ATLANTIC–LITTLE, BROWN BOOKS
ARE PUBLISHED BY
LITTLE, BROWN AND COMPANY
IN ASSOCIATION WITH
THE ATLANTIC MONTHLY PRESS

Published simultaneously in Canada
by Little, Brown & Company (Canada) Limited

PRINTED IN THE UNITED STATES OF AMERICA

The Boy Who Made Good

I

THE fall I went East to college for my freshman year, my father made a remark to me that I have never forgotten since.

"Never let it bother you," he said, "if other people seem to get all the glory in life. Remember it's not always the kid everybody is watching who gets the brass ring and the free ride on the merry-go-round."

I suppose he was thinking at the time that he was a good case in point himself, which was certainly true. I may as well say at once that my father was Pat Donlon, who—as you may know if you live in the general vicinity of the Mason and Dixon line, only west of the Alleghenies, and can remember back twenty years—had a hand in making a good many politicians in those days. So he knew all about glory—the dime-a-dozen varieties that he had helped to manufacture himself, and that could be counted on to fool people just long enough to win an election, as well as the rare, spontaneous, genuine kind that no one knows how to manufacture at all. Parnell had that, he told me; Napoleon had it; Joan of Arc had it—"and in the end," he said, "in one way or another, the world destroyed all of them for having it. Maybe it was because people saw something for once that was bigger and higher and brighter than anything could ever be in their own lives, and they were afraid of it, or jealous of it, or they wanted to prove to themselves that all it really belonged to was an ordinary human being like themselves. Anyway, for whatever reason it happens, just remember that it does happen, and that you can get as much satisfaction, and probably a hell of a lot more happiness, out of life if you sit back and let somebody else have the limelight, as long as the hard cash is going to you."

I was eighteen at the time this conversation took place, and I suppose it was given to me, along with a few more pieces of advice on the pitfalls that might logically beset a young girl living away from home for the first time, as a necessary part of the educative process by which the middle-aged gently seek to destroy the more dangerous illusions of the young. Looking back at it now, I can see that in one respect my father was underestimating me: most of the illusions that ordinarily trip up young girls had already been destroyed so thoroughly for me by that time that I had had to construct a whole new set of my own, with the result that I looked at the world from behind a code of rules somewhere between the Girl Scout handbook and Machiavelli's advice to ambitious politicians.

On the other hand, there are certain things that no one can learn except from experience, and so it wasn't till almost two years later, when the Ivor Kelly affair was over, that I really began to understand what Father had meant when he had talked to me about the advantages of obscurity. As usually happens, of course, it was too late by that time to do any good, but at any rate I could look back and see that someone had tried to warn me of the kind of catastrophe that is likely to occur when you involve yourself too closely in one of those destinies that is ringed around by the transient tinsel of human applause.

Not that I would do it differently, even now. But I might have saved myself some of the bad moments of riddled hope; I might have sat, like the driver of a car going ninety miles an hour toward a curve it cannot possibly take even at fifty, and foreseen with the satisfaction of mathematical certainty the smash-up that was going to shatter my intact little world.

My father was the second-generation product of the Irish who came to this country in the latter half of the last century, settled down wherever the railroads they built left them, and raised their sons—the luckier, more ambitious ones—to be businessmen, lawyers, politicians, and priests. The particular railroad my grandfather Donlon helped to build was one that ran south through Queensport after the War Between the States, and he ended up there with a white-collar job and a house on Lexington Street that he bequeathed to my father at his death, along with the valuable piece of information that the man who votes right and cultivates the right connections gets ahead. The house turned out to be mortgaged, but the information was pure coin of the realm; like the "Open sesame!" of a fairy tale, it raised Father in less than a dozen years from a small-time lumber salesman to a big-time contractor with a lot of valuable state

[4]

business. By the time I was fourteen we had a genuine imitation old Southern mansion in Fort Paris, on the La Fayette Pike outside of Queensport, a stable with a pair of real horses in it, and a finger in every political pie in the state. That was in 1929; after the crash and still more after the death, in 1933, of Lucius Pennefather, who had been Father's political fairy godfather, things weren't quite so good. But there still seemed to be enough to send me East to Bryn Mawr that year, when the time came for me to go to college.

At Bryn Mawr I learned how to be an outsider, which is a valuable experience at my age, but particularly so at the age of eighteen. As a result, I found that I was able to look at myself with a certain detachment at a time when most girls are still immersed in the security of a group, and to see the people and places I grew up with in the kind of perspective the ordinary person doesn't usually gain till much later in life. It was a peculiar experience, in many ways; somehow it was just as if I had never seen any of those people and places before that time. And it was almost the same way with myself. For eighteen years I had been inside a girl named Betsy Donlon, and nothing about her had been unfamiliar to me; but now suddenly I was standing somewhere outside and looking at her the way you would look at a complete stranger. And this girl, the one who was Betsy Donlon now, even looked different from the one I'd used to see when I'd looked into the mirror at home. She was taller, and her face was longer and prettier, and she had let her hair grow—it looked perfectly black, and she wore it smoothly back from her face and in a low knot on her neck—and there were black flecks in her eyes that made the blue look bluer. I used to look into the eyes in the mirror and it didn't seem possible to me that the thoughts in my mind were the same thoughts that were going on behind the eyes in the mirror.

By the time my sophomore year began, though, I had another kind of problem to think about. Father hadn't said anything to me during the summer vacation, except to drop a few dark hints, but I'd noticed he'd suddenly discovered that half a dozen building lots could be carved out of the land on either side of our house, and that we didn't have to have horses to get around with, any more than we had to have two cars. So I didn't need more education than one year at Bryn Mawr had given me to figure it out that we were faced with a problem in economics. That was all right with me—I could remember the house on Lexington Street, where the mortgage hung over our heads almost as tangibly as the roof, and we still managed

[5]

to enjoy life—but I could see what it was doing to Father. I didn't know exactly how to put my finger on it then, but I do now. It's undeserved success that people are so terribly afraid of losing; they know they haven't any way, themselves, of ever getting it back again.

No matter how bad things were, though, he still wanted me to keep on at Bryn Mawr, so I went back in September, but not for long. Right from the start things began to get embarrassing—bills that weren't paid, checks from home that didn't arrive or, worse, arrived and came back marked *No Funds*, occasioning frantic wires and even more frantic explanations from Fort Paris. Finally, in January, I got a long letter from my Aunt Bridgie, who had brought me up from the time my mother had died when I was two; it tactfully suggested that I come home at the end of the term. I say "tactfully" because, as usual, it was impossible to get anything definite out of her letter, which was full of the "had-I-known's" and "sad-though-it-be's" that conscientious young ladies learned to adorn their letters with in the nineties. But she did mention something about my going on with my education a little less expensively at the state university, so I gathered I was to leave Bryn Mawr for good. At any rate, I packed my things and bought a railroad ticket, and one cold afternoon in February I started out for home.

That is where this story really begins—on the Potomac Limited, somewhere between Philadelphia and Queensport, about six-thirty on that February afternoon. I had gone back to the diner shortly after the train left Washington, along with the woman who shared my section, a buyer for a Queensport department store. She was one of those bleached-blonde, fortyish women who seem to think that youth is a matter of bright clothes, make-up, and incessant conversation, and I was already beginning, after ten minutes, to regret our sudden intimacy over the dinner table when somebody came up behind me and spoke to me. I looked around: a solid, compact young man of about thirty, with quick brown eyes and an Irish-looking face, was standing in the aisle beside my chair.

"You're Pat Donlon's daughter," he said to me.

It was more a statement than a question; he looked at me as if he were challenging me to deny it. I recognized Kirby Hays, one of Father's political friends, and smiled and put out my hand.

"Hello, Kirby," I said. "I didn't know you were on this train." The steward was hovering politely; I looked at the empty chair at our table. "Would you like to sit here?" I asked.

"Thanks, but I can't. I'm with some people." Kirby glanced back momentarily over his shoulder at the door of the diner. "Here they come now," he said to the steward. "We'll want a table for four." To me, he went on: "How is Pat?"

"He's fine."

"And you—" he said. "What are you doing, going home this time of the year? I thought you were at some fancy college."

A group of three men was coming past him down the aisle. The first, a cheerful, oldish-looking young man with a disappearing chin and an obvious penchant for the collegiate in clothes, clapped him on the shoulder and said, "Hey, Kirby, share it—share it!"—looking at me.

"I'll be along in a minute," Kirby said. "The steward's getting you a table."

The second member of the group, a stout, balding man of fifty-five with the look of a self-important baby, took the collegiate young man's arm and led him, protesting, back past our table. Last of all, and seemingly disengaged from the rest, came a dark man in a dark suit—a strongly marked face, black-browed, sensitive, broad-cheek-boned, that caught my attention suddenly with a vague familiarity. The woman opposite me at the table—her name was Carr—put it into words for me in a startled murmur: "Isn't that Ivor Kelly? I thought he was *dead*."

"If he is, he hasn't heard about it," Kirby said. He added kindly, to Mrs. Carr, who was still registering disbelief with a pair of straw-colored brows: "He was sick quite a while; you probably heard about that."

"I heard he was dead," Mrs. Carr said positively. "I remember reading it in the newspaper. It was an auto accident, a couple of years ago—"

"That was his wife," Kirby explained patiently. "They were both in the accident; you've got it a little mixed up, that's all."

She shook her head, her earrings moving sharply, in little definite jerks.

"Well, all I can say is, I *read* he was dead. And he might just as well have been, for anything you heard about him after that. You know how he used to be all over the papers."

Kirby gave up; he said he would see me later and went on down the aisle of the car to join his friends.

"Who is he?" Mrs. Carr asked. "A politician?" She looked back over her shoulder at the group. "They look like a bunch of politicians."

"He's a lawyer."

"Um-m. A lot of them are. That's how Kelly got his start too, you know." She began to eat her soup, looking critically at the noodles. "I used to see his picture in the papers when he was running for Congress. It's no wonder he got elected; he was as good-looking as Valentino or Wally Reid in those days."

I looked down the car at the table at the other end where the four men sat. Ivor Kelly was sitting facing me, not talking, looking out the window mostly, but turning his head now and then to smile at something one of the others said. Once his eyes rested on me, and for a moment I felt him walk into my world, look around at it with a reassuring understanding, and then lay it gently aside again. It was a strange feeling: I remembered those eyes—different and yet the same—from old newspaper photographs that had haunted my adolescence. It was like seeing a dream become reality—changed somehow, but still identifiable.

"He's gotten heavier since then," Mrs. Carr said. "He must be forty now, if he's a day. And looks it, too, if you want my opinion. You can't live that kind of life without its showing up on you sooner or later." She decided against the soup, pushed it away from her on the table, and studied the group behind her again over her shoulder. "They say in the twenties he and that wife of his used to go on parties that lasted a week," she said; "everybody in town knew about it when they were back in Queensport. Once he drove a new Mercedes right into the lobby of the Savoy Plaza Hotel over in Corioli. It never got in the papers, but I had a friend who was night clerk there, and that's how I know all about it."

She looked at me as if, in case I expressed any disbelief, she was prepared to document her story with details of the weather, her friend's vital statistics, and a written statement of the damage done, so I tried to erase any appearance of skepticism from my face. But I wished I had come into the diner alone; I wanted to be free to watch what was happening at the table at the other end of the car. It was obvious that a certain disagreement was developing there: the collegiate young man was in the cheerfully belligerent stage of wanting to communicate with everyone; the stout, self-important man had begun to frown; and Kirby, looking noncommittal with his eyes bent on his plate, was washing his hands of the whole affair. It looked like the kind of dinner that would degenerate in a minute or two into a definitely unpleasant occasion, with unguarded words spoken, offended feelings, and the attention of the rest of the car aroused by raised voices and indiscreet gestures.

"His wife's father was some big Hollywood director," Mrs. Carr, happily unconscious of what was going on behind her, continued. "They say she was plated with money when she married him. They went through it all like that—" she snapped her fingers. "At least, that's what I heard down at the store, and they ought to know, because they had plenty of trouble collecting on their bills."

I thought it was fairly unlikely that Mrs. Ivor Kelly, whether she had been plated with money or not, had patronized the store Mrs. Carr had announced she worked for, but my companion seemed to be enjoying herself, and I was watching the other table, so I only smiled politely and let her go on talking. What was happening down there was enough to absorb all my attention, anyway; I was seeing in action something I had heard about only as a legend—the operation of Ivor Kelly's charm. All at once, just when it seemed the situation would get out of hand, he had joined the others—or, to put it more accurately, he had abandoned his attitude of civil detachment and suddenly engaged himself intimately in their problems. Of course I couldn't hear a word of the conversation, but I could see the effect—the immediate relaxation of the tension, the gradual process by which he apparently convinced the others that he was entering sympathetically into each of their grievances, above all, the manner in which he seemed to promise them that they were actually doing something interesting and amusing, instead of something unpleasant or dull. Even the solemn waiter was smiling now as he hovered over the table, rearranging dishes.

"His name really isn't Ivor Kelly at all," Mrs. Carr announced suddenly.

I looked at her, a little startled.

"What is it?"

"Mike. Mike Kelly. Call him that sometime and watch him jump. I know a girl who went to school with him in Queensport. Then he went to California and came back married to this Stella Blair, and that was when he changed his name."

She sounded so convincing that for a moment I almost forgot that Father, who had also known Ivor Kelly in those early years, had never spoken of him as "Mike" in his life, any more than he had pronounced "Ivor" with the long *i*, as Mrs. Carr was doing now. I didn't intend to argue with her, though; if she wanted to tell me that Ivor Kelly owed money to every department store in Washington and Queensport, and ran for office under a different alias every two years, it was none of my affair. I answered her with "yes" or "no," and after a little she began to tell me about her sister's divorce, and we got off the subject of Ivor Kelly for good.

When we had finished dinner she wanted me to go on into the club car with her, but I said I was tired and was going back to my seat. She was a little disappointed; I think she had designs on the collegiate young man, and was figuring on my acquaintance with Kirby to give her an entering wedge with him. Kirby looked around and waved as I got up, but I only waved back and went on out of the diner. They all seemed completely happy now at the other table, and I thought, between admiration and envy, as I walked forward through the swaying train, of the social gift that could weld a group like that into a satisfied unit.

When I got back to Car 7 it was quiet there, with most of the other passengers still in the diner or the club car, and I sat and read a magazine for a while. About nine-thirty Kirby came in and sat down in Mrs. Carr's empty seat, opposite me.

"I've been looking for you," he said. "Your friend's having quite a time for herself in the club car."

"She isn't really my friend," I said. I didn't know quite how to talk to him; he made me feel very young because the last time I had seen him, over a year before, I had still been "the little Donlon girl" to him, and I wasn't sure he didn't think of me that way now. "She only has the section here with me," I said; "I never saw her in my life before I got on the train." I added: "She's told me some amazing stories about your friend Mr. Kelly. All in the past tense. I don't think she's completely convinced yet that she isn't dealing with a ghost."

"I noticed she seemed to have some definite ideas on the subject."

"She says his name isn't Ivor Kelly at all. I'm to call him Mike and watch him jump."

"That's his middle name."

"Is it, really? I'm glad. Then she didn't make it all up." I wanted to go on talking about Ivor Kelly, but I didn't want Kirby to imagine it was on a personal basis, so I added carefully: "He looks terribly interesting, as if anything she made up about him would fit in somewhere in the things he's done."

"It probably would." His eyes lit on me suddenly. "Look here," he said, "you're not getting any ideas, are you? He's way out of your class; the last time I saw you, you were playing with dolls—"

I could feel myself coloring up. "I don't know what on earth—" I began.

"Besides, he's got a girl. I happen to know. A beautiful girl with money and charm and a figure and—money. You ought to get interested in somebody like me. I'm safe; I haven't got any beautiful girls. You'd be the very first one."

"I still don't know—"

I was used to the vocally indirect but actively unmistakable approaches of boys my own age; Kirby's, made without the prelude of so much as a touching of fingers, while we sat on opposite seats in a Pullman car, left me confused. The porter came by.

"Make up your berth, miss?"

"Yes—please."

I jumped up—I was glad of the chance—and went over to sit in an empty seat across the aisle. Kirby followed me, but didn't sit down.

"You're not interested in my proposition?" he said. "What's the matter—doesn't Pat give me a good character?"

"He gives you a wonderful character. He says you're going to run the whole Democratic state committee some day, when you learn to play the sure things instead of the long shots."

"What else does he say? Does he tell you I'm a sterling character, kind to my old mother, and to be trusted to pay the monthly bills?"

"I like your mother," I said. "I remember going to your house with Aunt Bridgie one day when I was about ten, to deliver Sacred Heart League leaflets, and she had a whole kitchen full of cats; it nearly broke my heart when Aunt Bridgie wouldn't let me take one of them home with me. She talked about you all the while we were there; I wasn't sure when I left whether you were the President of the United States then, or were going to be elected the next November."

A pair of women came past him down the aisle; one of them, as the train swung round a curve, clutched sharply at his arm, righted herself embarrassedly, and, trilling apologies, went on through the car. Kirby looked down at me again.

"You still haven't told me what you're doing on this train."

"I'm going home," I said. "I'm going to transfer to State next term. It's a long story—"

"Don't tell me if you don't want to. Did you get fired?"

I laughed; it was a new experience to see a disapproving expression on Kirby's face.

"No, I didn't," I said. "If you must know, it's nothing more interesting than money."

"Pat's not in any trouble?"

"Isn't everybody? We're going to do a little economizing, that's all; we've decided I can be educated just as properly at State as at Bryn Mawr."

"Then you'll be around," he said. "I'm glad to hear it. I think we two ought to get acquainted."

"But you've known me ever since I was born—"

"I knew a skinny kid who used to wear middy blouses and moon around under the back porch with books she oughtn't to be reading and darn near killed me once jumping out of a tree when I happened to be innocently walking under it—"

"I *fell* out. You probably saved my life, being there."

"You ought to be suitably grateful, then. Grateful enough—oh, to be home some weekend in a fairly amenable state of mind if I happen to call you—"

I laughed again. It was queer having Kirby talk to me like that, after all the years of his living in another, grown-up world, different from mine; now he was suddenly inviting me into his. It was an interesting world, but I didn't think I would ever really belong there. There was nothing of myself that I wanted to share with him; we only had other people in common, in whose lives we could both live for a while.

"I may be there," I said, "but if Father gets hold of you first, it won't make any difference to you whether I am or not; you'll be too busy nominating congressmen and winning elections."

"We'll forget all about future congressmen. Even about future governors—"

The word—the way he said it—gave me a moment's intuition.

"Is that what he is?" I said—"your friend Mr. Kelly? A future governor?"

"He might be, if we can convince enough of the right people that it's a good idea." Kirby shook his head, moving aside again in the aisle to let another group of people pass. "How did we get back to that subject again? You can vote for him; you don't have to talk about him."

"I'm not old enough to vote—don't you remember? Besides, you're with him—you're going to work to elect him, I suppose; don't you like him?"

"I don't like playing nursemaid to a time bomb."

The train swayed round a curve, and I caught the look on his face as he steadied himself: not dislike—a sort of worried and reluctant admiration, the kind of expression you might see on the face of someone watching a reckless acrobat going through an impossibly difficult routine on a high trapeze.

"A time bomb?" I said. "But why—?"

"First place, because he only cares fifty per cent of the time about making the right impression, and it's a well-known fact that our civilization is going to fall to pieces the day people stop caring about making the right impression. Second place, because—"

He broke off; I saw his eyes fix themselves suddenly on the door at the end of the car. When I looked in that direction too I discovered the collegiate young man from the diner; he simultaneously discovered Kirby, and came forward with determination down the aisle.

"Here you are," he said. He looked several degrees less happy than he had in the diner, but still kept his cheerfulness to the extent of a rather placative smile that he fixed alternately on Kirby and me. "*Cherchez la femme*," he said; "isn't that right? I thought if I could find this young lady—"

"This young lady is Pat Donlon's daughter," Kirby said. "And this interfering idiot," he went on, to me, "is Ken Baggott. Now, blast it, will you get out of here?"

"I can't," Baggott said. He turned his gaze, half-alarmed, from Kirby to me. "I was sent. You know Mr. Whiteley wants a fourth for bridge."

"I don't like bridge," Kirby said. "Tell him I'm reading an improving article in a magazine—'How to Avoid Your Traveling Companions on a Train.'"

"He'll take Ivor for his partner," Baggott offered helpfully. "We can win fifty bucks off them if we both stay awake."

"I'm not that hard up. Pick up somebody in the club car; there're always a couple of people there who don't mind what they do for fifty bucks."

He turned his back pointedly on Baggott, who lingered, however, looking at me as if he were appealing to me to intercede for him.

"Why don't you go and play bridge?" I said to Kirby. "I'm going to bed anyway, and Mr. Whiteley looks like a very important man—"

"He owns half the town of Ashbourne, and another half over in Leesburg—Whiteley Bricks, you know," Ken Baggott said seriously. "And he has to get off at Leesburg sometime around three o'clock in the morning; it makes it very inconvenient for him if he hasn't something to keep him occupied till then—"

"Oh, for God's sake—!" Kirby said. "Go on; tell him I'll be there in a minute."

"Honor bright?"

"If you say another word—" Kirby began.

"All right—all right." Baggott retreated, alarmed, up the aisle. From a safe distance he pleaded: "But make it quick, will you, Kirby?"

Kirby watched his reluctant tweed back disappearing through the door.

"I declare to God," he said, "there goes the biggest fool this side of the Rocky Mountains."

"He's in politics too, isn't he?" I asked. "I think I've heard Father mention his name—What on earth do you do with him?"

Kirby shrugged. "He has his uses. For one thing, he keeps everybody happy; they take one look at him and say, 'My God, what a moron,' and right away they begin to feel superior and successful. When a man feels superior and successful, he'll do anything for you."

His concentration on me, I was glad to see, had been distracted; after a minute he said he would see me in the morning and went on out of the car in the direction Ken Baggott had taken. My berth was made up by that time, so I went back to the dressing room. It was full of purposeful women in various stages of undress, each of them seriously engaged in the performance of her own particular beauty ritual, and regarding her own face, in a mirror that reflected a half-dozen others, with a single-minded devotion to duty. One of them, a middle-aged woman with an expensively preserved figure, broke ranks long enough to observe with horror that I washed my face with soap and water—"My dear, do you know what you're going to look like in another ten years if you keep that up?" The remark drew the attention of two or three other women, who looked at me disapprovingly, as if I were a sort of renegade to my sex, so I quickly finished my preparations for the night and headed for the privacy of my berth.

It was a while before I went to sleep. There were the usual night noises of a Pullman car—people going audibly up and down the aisle, the porter's subdued, cheerful voice, the steady, monotonous rhythm of the wheels—but it wasn't that that was keeping me awake. I kept thinking about Kirby, and Ivor Kelly, and the bridge game that was going on in a drawing room somewhere up ahead; then I was trying to remember a remark I had heard once, a year or two before, about Ivor Kelly, something to the effect that if that auto crash hadn't put him out of political circulation when it had, he would have succeeded in doing the same thing for himself before very long. "*Sure* the guy's a genius, but he only works at it every other Friday and on holydays of obligation. This isn't 1926 any more; people like their politicians sober these days." The conversation had gone something like that.

I tried to remember more, but it began to get mixed up with a dream about the bridge game, in which Mr. Whiteley insisted on paying his losses in bricks instead of money, so that the table at which he was playing was gradually piled high with mountains of bricks that reached in precarious rows to the ceiling. That must have been the last thing I had in my head before I really fell asleep, because hours later, when the crash woke me, I thought for the first instant it was only those stacks of bricks that had come unbalanced and were toppling down together all at once.

That was for the first instant; the next moment I was really awake —awake enough to realize that the train had come to a sudden stop and that my berth had been violently tilted sideways, so that I was lying uncomfortably on what seemed to be the window-blind. I tried to sit up, and bumped my head sharply on something hard; at the same time I heard women's voices beyond the curtains screaming shrilly for the porter, and a man's voice, sounding awed and sober, very close outside, as if its owner were sitting in the aisle: "My God, I think I've broken my leg."

I decided suddenly that I was dealing with a train wreck, and made a new attempt to disentangle myself from the shambles of my berth. Strangely, my first emotion was not one of fear or of shock, but of violent indignation against someone—the engineer, the railroad company: I couldn't decide which at the moment. As I groped in the pitch-darkness, my hand touched something smooth and soft— the fur collar of my coat. I held on to it firmly, pulled it around my shoulders, and managed to climb the uphill slant of my berth so I could draw aside the curtain and look out. There wasn't a light any- where. It was like walking into a darkened movie-theater out of bright sunlight; you knew there were people all around, but you couldn't see a thing.

If you couldn't see them, though, you could hear them—thirty or forty men, women, and children all talking, or crying, or screaming at once. Apparently it was the people on the other side of the aisle who had had the worst of it; when on our side we had only been thrown against the windows, they had been hurled out of their berths onto the floor. I sat there for a moment, listening to that pandemonium—even in the darkness I could recognize Mrs. Carr's voice above me, calling frantically for the porter—and then all at once, before I had really made up my mind what I was going to do, I was crawling experimentally out of my berth, clutching at curtains, and finally landing on the slanting floor in a tangle of other people's arms and legs. At the same instant somebody somewhere turned on a flashlight. It would have been funny if nobody had been hurt—the electric beam of light darting quickly over the grotesque confusion of the car. I couldn't help thinking that it looked like the room in the fun house in an amusement park where they put out the lights and the floor tilts and everyone goes sliding down into a heap at one end. Only now everyone was in pajamas, to make it even worse, and there were clothes and luggage strewn all over everything.

The flashlight, though, had an immediate and wonderful effect on everyone. A tall man with a booming voice suddenly announced that we'd all better "get the hell out of here—women and children first," in the finest chivalric tradition. Somebody else tried the door, found it could be pushed open with the aid of two or three assisting shoulders, and sent back the report that it was cold outside—"Everybody bring out some clothes or blankets." A solemn-looking boy of about my own age, with a bloody nose, turned up abruptly at my elbow and asked me if I was hurt; when I said I wasn't, he insisted on seeing me safely outside.

"But I want to help," I protested. "There are people hurt here—"

"You heard what the man said: 'Women and children first'—" He had an earnest Deep South accent, and he was desperately serious; I thought he must have had a nasty blow in the face, and he looked as if he were trying hard not to cry.

"Look at yourself," I said to him. "You need somebody to look after you more than I do."

"It's just a little blood. Not enough to hurt anybody—"

All at once I realized how silly it sounded, the two of us standing there arguing with each other in the crazily tilted aisle, and I capitulated.

"All right," I said. "But my suitcase—" I looked back at my berth. "I ought to have some clothes—"

The suitcase was under the berth; a few minutes' struggle brought it out battered but intact.

"Have you got some shoes in there?" he asked me. "They say there's snow outside—"

I nodded, following him down the aisle. The door was propped open now and people were climbing down before me to the ground. It was a dark night; there was a faint powdering of snow on the earth. I felt the freezing air through my pajamas and pulled on my coat, shivering.

"All right," the boy said. "Down you go—"

He held on to my hand as I half-jumped, half-slipped from the platform of the car. I was still barefooted; the first thing I did when he handed my suitcase down to me was to open it and find a pair of shoes. A tall girl in a blue robe appeared suddenly beside me.

"You're lucky," she said. "I was in an upper berth; my suitcase just seemed to disappear."

I had a warm sweater in my bag; I gave it to her, along with a pair of heavy socks that she pulled on under her slippers. While she sat on the suitcase, putting them on, I looked for the first time at the train. Up ahead the locomotive, black against the white snow in the darkness, lay on its side in a cloud of steam, with the cars sprawled irregularly out behind it like the cars of a child's toy train that the child flung down and deserted when it grew tired of playing with them. Some of the rear cars were still on the track, and from all of them an antlike stream of people was pouring. It didn't seem at all impressive or dangerous; it was hard to think that people had been hurt, perhaps killed, in there.

By this time at least half the people in our car seemed to be outside; I saw the man with the broken leg carried out awkwardly and laid on blankets on the snow, but no one else appeared who looked seriously hurt. One woman was hysterical—she had a cut on her head, and she thought she was going to bleed to death—and there was a small dark intense young man in striped pajamas who kept wringing his hands and saying, "Seventy uncut diamonds—my God —seventy uncut diamonds—" as if it were some kind of litany he was repeating. He wanted to go back into the car and look for them, but

[17]

they were still bringing people out, so we all tried to dissuade him; besides, there was only one flashlight, and it was needed for the people who were hurt.

While we were standing there arguing with him I suddenly saw Kirby Hays; he had come up to one of the men who had been in our car and was asking him if there was a doctor in our group—"or anyway a nurse," he said urgently. The man said he didn't think so, and Kirby was turning away when he saw me and stopped and came back again.

"You all right?" he said. "My God, I'm glad to see you."

"I'm fine."

He was dressed just as he'd been when I'd seen him hours before, in a gray suit and a blue shirt and tie, and he looked so ordinary and sane standing there in the midst of all our grotesque, snatched-up costumes that I wanted to hold on to him.

"Where are you going?" I asked. "I'll go with you—"

"I'm trying to find a doctor. We've got a man badly hurt back there; nobody seems to know what to do for him. The conductor's out cold somewhere—" He focused on me abruptly. "Look, I want to keep an eye on you. Go up forward two cars and find Ken Baggott; tell him I said to look out for you till I get back."

He was gone again before I could say anything. It occurred to me all at once to wonder for the first time what was going to happen to us—how we were going to get away from there, and who was going to look after us all: there was nothing in sight but the wrecked train, the snow, and some hilly fields, with what looked like a road cutting through them up ahead. And there were those people lying there in the snow—I had a sudden feeling that the least I could do would be to start walking and keep on till I found a house or a telephone. I picked up my suitcase—somehow it seemed to make me feel more as if I were still on a trip instead of in a nightmare to have it along—but I hadn't gone ten steps before Kirby came by again and grabbed my arm.

"Where do you think you're going?"

"Somebody's got to go for help—"

"That's all been taken care of." There was a tall thin man in pajamas and overcoat with him; Kirby motioned him ahead. "Right over there—the man lying on the ground—" He still had hold of my arm. "You're coming with me," he said; "I won't let you out of my sight again."

[18]

We followed the tall man across the thin snow.

"Is he a doctor?" I asked.

"Yes. Anyway, he's a nose and throat man—that poor guy's got it in the chest. We got him out of the locomotive; I guess he's the engineer—"

I watched as the doctor knelt beside the dark figure on the snow. Somebody was talking to him—Ivor Kelly, he too dressed just as he had been in the diner, hours before. Kirby turned me around.

"Don't look at it. You can't do anything."

"Are you sure somebody's gone for help?"

"Ivor found a guy who lives around here; he knows where there's a house with a phone." He laughed suddenly, the sound queer against all that confusion: it had seemed to me as if no one would ever laugh again. "Now I know why they made him a captain during the war," he said. "He should have been a general; he had us all organized within thirty seconds of the time that train went off the track."

Somebody came up to us; it was Ivor Kelly.

"Kirby—" he said. His eyes went over me briefly and kindly; even at that moment I wished I weren't standing there in a coat and pajamas, with my hair in braids like a fourteen-year-old. "We're going to see about getting some of these people back to the cars that are still on the track," he said. "It may be a while before they get any ambulances here; there isn't a town of any size in miles—"

"What about him?" Kirby asked. He nodded toward the figure on the ground.

"He's got it pretty bad, I'm afraid." He dismissed that problem—not unsympathetically, but with decision; he had done all he could along that line, and now there were other things to be attended to. "Suppose we set up a sort of first-aid station in the first one of those cars that's on the track," he said. "Get anybody that needs medical attention back there right away, and any doctors or nurses you can round up from the other passengers—"

"Can I help?" I asked.

"You might pass the word."

I doubt if he had really seen me; I was only somebody standing there, healthy and in one piece, whom he could use in this emergency. But Kirby didn't like it.

"You stay right here, where I know where to find you," he said to me. "I don't want you wandering around in this mess."

I started to protest, but Ivor Kelly cut that short, speaking to Kirby.

"All right. Don't stand there. She'll be here when you get back."

"She'd better be."

Kirby started off, and for one additional moment I had Ivor Kelly's undivided attention. He was frowning at me slightly, trying to remember something.

"That's right," he said suddenly. "You're the girl Kirby spoke to in the diner—Pat Donlon's daughter. We'll have to take good care of you."

"I don't really—"

I didn't know what I was starting to say—something to the effect that I didn't belong to Kirby, and that I could go wherever I pleased. But he had stopped looking at me as a person again, and was simply fitting me into the reorganization of this chaos.

"Why don't you go over there and see what you can do for that woman with the children?" he asked. I noticed he was a little absent already, his mind a jump ahead of what he was saying. "She has three of them—at least two too many for her to handle."

He was gone before I could protest. I went over a little reluctantly to the woman he had indicated. She was young and bewildered-looking, dressed in a sweater and skirt because she had been traveling in one of the coaches: she had been visiting her family in the East, she said, and was on her way back home. All the children were under five; she had the baby in her arms, and I took the next oldest, a girl, and tried to comfort her for the loss of her pink rabbit and a bump on the head. The oldest of the three, whose name was Pete, was showing a propensity to wander off into the crowd that had his mother on tenterhooks, so I finally fished a pair of belts out of my suitcase and invented a game in which he was alternately a watchdog on a leash and a horse being saddled and bridled in a stable. I remember thinking at the time that if anyone asked me afterward what you did in a train wreck, I would have to say that I personally had spent my time playing children's games. It didn't sound very heroic; I wished Father had insisted that I take a course in nursing the summer after I'd graduated from high school, instead of one in stenography.

I don't know how long I stayed there; you lose track of time when everything happens so fast. After a while it began to get light—not a real dawn, just a faint graying of the darkness that kept spreading farther and farther till I could see what was going on around me. I realized then that the people who had been lying in the snow had all been taken inside, and that headlights were beginning to flash in and out of sight as automobiles came down the winding road ahead. It seemed that we were all going to be safe, after all; I wanted suddenly to cry. That was when Pete slipped away from me again, and I ran after him, and when I came back with him there was Kirby.

"Hello," he said, as if he hadn't seen me before. He looked happy and relieved; he needed a shave. "Are you all right?"

"I'm fine. Kirby, what's *hap*pening? Those cars—"

"It's all over but the shouting. There are a couple of doctors here; there'll be ambulances and some busses in a little while—"

"Was anybody killed?"

"The engineer's in pretty bad shape; he seems to be the worst." He shook his head. "My God, what a night! It's just occurred to me that we ought to feel damn lucky to be alive."

Somebody shouted at him suddenly, and we both looked up and saw Ken Baggott standing a little way off, beckoning to us. Kirby turned back to me.

"Listen, youngster," he said, "do you want to go on to Queensport with us? You can wait here and take a bus with the others if you want to, but it's going to be a pretty slow business, probably, and Ivor's lined up a car—"

"A car? To drive you to Queensport?"

"Matter of fact, I think he bought it. It looks like it'll hold together for the trip; it's only about a hundred miles."

"Did he ask *me?*"

"I'm asking you; there's plenty of room. What's the matter—don't you want to go?"

"Oh yes—I do. Only my clothes—"

I hugged my coat around me, suddenly self-conscious in my pajamas.

"You've got things in that suitcase, haven't you? We'll stop somewhere so you can dress."

He picked up the suitcase; before I knew it, I was walking along with him beside the tracks.

"What did you do—sit up all night playing bridge?" I asked him.

"Harvey Whiteley only got off an hour or so before the wreck. It didn't seem worth while to go to bed. We started a poker game;

I'd have won forty dollars if that car hadn't gone off the track when it did."

We joined Ken Baggott, and the three of us walked down to the road together. There, in the midst of a suddenly busy stream of traffic—where did it all come from, at dawn in this lonely end of nowhere?—we found Ivor Kelly standing beside an ancient black Ford, looking critically at the tires.

"I think it'll make it," he said to Kirby. "We'll have to take a chance." His eyes fell on me; he had a way of looking at you as if you were the only person he really wanted to see just then, and as if you had done him a particular favor simply by being there. "Hello," he said. "Are you coming with us?"

"Kirby said—"

"Kirby has some fine ideas."

The dark morning-stubble on his face made him seem younger and more approachable, as if it were a disguise he was wearing, behind which he could act just as he liked. A serious young man came up to Kirby and spoke to him.

"I'm from the Alleghan *Globe*. You people been in the wreck?"

Kirby said firmly: "We're curiosity-seekers. Tourists from Topeka, Kansas. They told us there was going to be a train wreck here, and we drove all night to try to catch it. It just so happens that we were half an hour too late."

He slung my suitcase into the car.

"All right, wise guy!" the serious young man said. I saw that he was frowning uncertainly, looking at Ivor Kelly as if he thought he was someone he ought to know.

"Who's going to drive?" Ken Baggott asked. He got in behind the wheel. "Oh boy, I haven't driven one of these babies since 1926."

"Well, watch your step," Kirby said. "We're all believers in moderation here; only one wreck a day, is our motto."

"Do you want to sit in back with Kirby?" Ivor Kelly asked me. I wished he would stop being so considerate of me and Kirby, or that I could come straight out and tell him I wasn't Kirby's girl. We all got in; he said, "All right, Ken; let's go"—and we backed around and started up the hill. Just as we did, the serious young man started to run after the car.

"Hey, wait!" he called. "Wait a minute! Aren't you—?"

The rest of it was lost in the distance. Ivor Kelly turned gravely around to Kirby.

"I take it you think this is no time to meet the press."

"We look like a lot of bums," Kirby said. "It'd make a swell picture if somebody happened to have a camera; Ed Dodd would have it nailed up on every telephone pole in the state. Complete with Betsy in pajamas—"

"I've got to change," I said with conviction. I had a confusing feeling of being mixed up in some sort of plot, and of not knowing my lines or what I should be doing at any given moment. "Maybe I oughtn't to have come at all—"

"We'll take good care of you," Ivor Kelly assured me. When he looked at me, it was worth it—the wreck, the cold, the inconvenience, all of it. He had dark eyes that trusted you, under those black Irish brows that didn't trust anybody, and you saw everything that happened to you reflected back to you from them with understanding. It didn't seem to make any difference in the way I was beginning to feel about him that he was a lot older than I was, and tired, and not even particularly good-looking any more: his face had the used look of something you've decided not to wear any longer, and tossed into a wastebasket—only then you find you've got to wear that or nothing, so you take it out again and try to fix it up so it's presentable. "You're not *afraid* of us, are you?" he asked me, and then, as if he didn't expect me to answer that: "Kirby called you Betsy. I'm going to call you Betsy too. I knew your father when he was just about your age."

The car was at a crossroads. Ken peered right and left at the gray winter landscape.

"Is this the main road?" he said. "What the hell—I'm lost."

"You go right," Kirby said. "Or at least I think so—all these damn hills look alike. I haven't been around this neck of the woods since Jack Turlow was running for state treasurer two years ago—"

"You lost that one, all right," Baggott said, with cheerful conviction. "Boy oh man, you'll have to do better with this one or Harvey Whiteley'll have you served up for breakfast the day after the primaries. On toast. He wants to ride a winner."

"Nobody ever heard of Jack Turlow before I started running him around the state," Kirby said. "That's not one of our problems now."

"Just the opposite. Our problem now is that they may have heard too much."

I saw Kirby throw half a glance at Ivor Kelly, decide to say something, and then say something to Ken instead: "Why don't you just shut up and drive?"

Ivor—the others called him that, and I was beginning to in my mind too—looked as if he hadn't heard. He turned half around to speak to me.

"I'm afraid we're boring you," he said. There was that automatic thoughtfulness again; I wished I could believe it meant anything, but I knew he was only being polite. "We ought to talk about something that would interest *you*," he said. "For example—oughtn't you to be at school?"

"I was a sophomore at Bryn Mawr, but I'm going home now." All at once a wild idea came into my head; I forgot all about next term and the state university and said: "I'd like to get a job. I've had a year and a half of college, and I took a course in stenography two summers ago—"

I don't know what I expected—that he would say without hesitation that he needed a secretary, and that he knew of no one more qualified than I was for the job: you get some queer ideas when you've been up half the night and in a train-wreck and have just met somebody you know you're never going to be able to get out of your life again. But then I remembered my braids and my pajamas, and my total lack of even a trace of lipstick; I wouldn't have blamed him if he had told me to go back to playing with my dolls. He didn't, of course; he was too nice for that.

"Pat ought to be able to get you something," he said. "I don't know anybody any more; I've been away too long—Only I think you ought to finish college," he added suddenly. "People talk a lot about education's not being important for girls, because they'll get married anyway, but I don't see it that way—"

It was the first thing he had said that made him sound naïve to me—when you're nineteen every general idea sounds naïve if you've heard it before. But I didn't mind it in him; it made him seem more accessible, somehow, as if there were some area at least in which I was wiser than he. That means a good deal when you're nobody in particular and are trying to think of a reason for somebody important to look at you twice—and there was always that alarming shadow, besides, of the girl Kirby had mentioned on the train, the one with money and charm and a figure and—money. I needed something to bolster my faith in my own chances, otherwise it was too much like trying to win a race when you aren't even able to walk to the starting line.

Kirby said to me suspiciously: "I thought you told me you were going to State."

"It isn't all settled."

"Is Pat that hard up?"

"Oh, it's not that—really." I wanted to stop him; he was ruining it all. "It's only—I want to *do* something—"

"If that's all you want, why don't you just marry somebody? Me, for instance—"

I couldn't help laughing; maybe it wasn't a bit funny, but it seemed so public for him to say it there in the car in front of everyone, with the wreck just behind us and me in my pajamas and all of us looking so awful. It was like starting to laugh in church: you know how terrible it sounds, but you simply can't stop. Then suddenly I realized that they were all looking at me very solemnly, and that I wasn't laughing at all—I was crying. I was shocked myself; I stopped and said guiltily: "Oh, I'm sorry—"

"You're hungry," Ivor Kelly said decidedly. "I know exactly how you feel. We'll stop the very first place we come to and have some breakfast. Then we'll all feel better."

Somehow it made me feel worse to have him so tactful; it was as if he really hadn't expected anything better of me.

"I don't do things like this," I said. "I'm perfectly all right—"

"It was my fault," Kirby said. He looked at me. "I'm not up to my usual form at the crack of dawn. You have to make allowances—"

I wanted to explain to him that the way I had behaved had no real connection with what he had said; it was only a combination of circumstances—the wreck, the people lying back there in the snow, the fact that I was tired and cold, the ridiculous irony of the wrong man's suddenly deciding to take a violent interest in me. But we were coming to a town; it seemed better to let the whole thing go. Ken pulled in at the first gas station and, amid some voluble explanations on his part about the wreck—the proprietor hadn't heard of it, and he seemed to think we were a decidedly queer quartet—I took my suitcase to the ladies' room and did a hasty job of making myself presentable.

When I came back Ken was still explaining, and a boy of seventeen or so had joined the audience; he was standing there beside the proprietor, mirroring his unconvinced expression. The proprietor spoke to me as I came up.

"Young lady, I'd like to hear your story about all this," he said. "Any of these fellas relatives of yours?"

"They're friends of my family," I said. I glanced at Kirby and Ivor Kelly, alarmed. Kirby looked angry and Ivor had a polite, detached, reckless expression on his face; he seemed too much interested in the possibilities the situation presented to step in and do his usual job of smoothing things out. "We've been in a train wreck," I said; "they're driving me home to Fort Paris. It's perfectly all right—"

"You're sure you're not runnin' *away* from home?" the proprietor put it to me shrewdly. "Runnin' away with one of these fellas?"

"Now, look here—" Kirby said.

"I'm not askin' you; I'm askin' her."

"Well, you can ask me," Kirby exploded, "because I'm telling you. There's nothing illegal in what we're doing, unless it's illegal for people with a little common sense to be caught within the limits of this town. What do you think we're doing—kidnaping her?"

"It's *really* all right," I assured the proprietor.

I looked at Ivor, appealing to him to do something, and he stopped being a spectator and said to me gently: "Why don't you call your father now? He'll be worried when you don't turn up on time and he hears about the wreck." He spoke to the proprietor. "Is there a telephone we can use?"

The proprietor acknowledged that there was. He led the way inside—I could see him reluctantly relinquishing his idea of telephoning himself for "the authorities"—and amid a dismal clutter of tools, old automobile tires, and Coca-Cola bottles I picked up the phone and put in a call to Fort Paris. It was Aunt Bridgie who answered. She said Father had already gone to the station to meet me, and had heard about the wreck there—"They said there was nobody killed, but we were worried half out of our minds. Are you sure you're all right?"

"I'm fine," I said. "I met Kirby Hays on the train, and I'm driving back with him and some friends of his. I ought to be home in a few hours."

Aunt Bridgie's voice crackled on over the phone. "Are you *sure* you're all right? Where are you now? I'll have to get in touch with your father right away, and you know how he is: if I can't tell him exactly where you are and what you're doing, there won't be a minute's peace around here today."

I looked over my shoulder at the proprietor, who was lingering, obviously within earshot, at the door.

"Could you tell me the name of this town?" I asked him.

"This town? Tunbridge."

"I'm phoning from a gas station in Tunbridge," I repeated it over the wire to Aunt Bridgie. "We're going to have breakfast and then we're driving right through to Queensport."

The telephone operator interrupted to tell me that my three minutes were up, and I asked her the toll; it wasn't till that moment that I remembered that my purse was somewhere back on the train and that I hadn't a cent. It didn't make any difference, of course; Kirby was delighted to pay for the call, counting the coins out into the proprietor's hand as if each one of them were a personal vindication. In the middle he paused.

"Maybe you'd like to call Fort Paris yourself," he suggested. "Check up on us?"

The proprietor looked silently regretful that he hadn't had the pleasure of seeing Kirby personally escorted in handcuffs from his gas station.

"I'd be glad to pay the call," Kirby offered.

The horn sounded impatiently outside.

"They're waiting for us," I said. "Kirby, *please—*"

I wanted to get away; I had had enough trouble for one day. Kirby followed me outside, where we found the others, and then we all went across the street to a small dingy lunchroom that seemed to be patronized only by morose truck drivers who were disinclined to be sociable over their morning doughnuts and coffee.

"This is a terrible place," Ivor whispered respectfully. "Don't you like terrible places, Betsy? Places where you know there are roaches under the counter and rats in the garbage pails out in back?"

Now that everything about the wreck was slipping behind us, I could feel us all sliding down from our emotional peak into a subdued and reckless irresponsibility; we were like shipwrecked mariners who had made it to shore, rescued their companions, and then collapsed in undignified and hilarious celebration. We found a booth and sat down, facing each other across a litter of stale coffee cups, eggy plates, and catsup bottles, and picked up the menus with their purple-printed legends:

[27]

> *2 eggs any style, donut and coffee*
> *Wheat cakes sirup, donut and coffee*
> *Ham and 2 eggs, donut and coffee*

"It's no good to you if you don't like doughnuts," Ivor said. "I wonder what they serve for dinner—*Filet mignon and donut?—Lobster à la Newburg and donut?*"

"Don't speak slightingly of the doughnut," Kirby said. "The doughnut is a Great American Institution; no man has ever been elected to public office who spoke disrespectfully of the doughnut. As a matter of fact, we might even put one on your campaign posters—a big picture of a doughnut, and under it: 'Kelly Supports Donuts for All.' The whole thing done in red, white, and blue, of course—"

"What have you people got against doughnuts?" Ken asked seriously. "I'm hungry; you order what you want to, and if you don't want the doughnut, just give it to me." He hailed a passing, harried-looking waitress: "Hey, Beautiful! How about a little service here?"

I wasn't hungry—I was still too tied up in knots of excitement to care whether I ever saw food again or not—but I ordered scrambled eggs and sat there obediently trying to eat them when they came. It wasn't any use; it wouldn't have been even if they hadn't been cold and fried black. I noticed that Ivor wasn't eating either; he drank black coffee and only looked at the soggy mass of wheat-cakes on his plate. For the first time, sitting there opposite him under the pallid electric glare, I realized that he looked ill. It wasn't anything you could put your finger on, just a general grayness, an air of drawing on reserves of energy rather than on a current income. Once—we were all talking about the queer things we had seen in the wreck, and I was telling about the man with the seventy uncut diamonds—he stopped the waitress as she went past and asked her something in a low voice, and I saw Kirby, sitting opposite him, look at him suddenly. When the waitress had gone on, Kirby said rather sharply, but also in a low voice, under cover of my story: "Where do you think you are? You can't get any of that here—"

I flashed a glance at Ivor; he looked patient and ironical, as if he were explaining something to a child.

"I told you you didn't have to worry about that."

"I am going to worry, if you start—"

"Did it ever occur to you that this isn't exactly an ordinary situation? We might all feel—"

They saw me watching them, and broke off.

"We've interrupted Betsy," Ivor said.

"I was all finished."

"So are we." He looked around the table. "If nobody is going to eat any more of this poisonous food, we may as well be on our way."

He stood up. There was something in the way he gathered up the checks—just a faint lift of his brows as he glanced from one to the other of us—that seemed to put us all back in our places as his guests in some carefully arranged excitement, a diversion for which he was paying, not with money alone, but more expensively with those reserves of energy I have mentioned before. We went outside—the raw morning air feeling good after the haze of food inside—and back to where we had left the car. There was no sun, just gray sky and patches of thin snow on the walks, a perfectly ordinary dreary winter day. But I felt as if I were going to a party—the kind of party where you desperately want to be a success; there was the same feeling of heady anticipation, along with the hollow, anxious feeling in the pit of the stomach. I don't know what I thought was going to happen, but of course nothing at all really did. We only drove to Queensport, with all three of the others putting themselves out to be nice to me, but not Ivor especially, so that it didn't count.

It wasn't a long drive, but the roads were bad and the car was temperamental, and it was well past noon when we got to Queensport. The others were all staying in town, but they drove me down to Fort Paris and dropped me off first. I stood on the walk saying good-by while Kirby got my suitcase out of the car.

"I'm afraid you're sorry you came with us," Ivor said. "I didn't know it would be so cold."

"I enjoyed it." Standing there looking at him, his eyes kind and expectant on me, as if it were as important to him as it was to me that we meet again, I knew that this was my last chance; a minute more and it would be too late. "I really meant it, you know, about wanting a job," I said. "Even if I go back to college now, couldn't I do something this summer about your campaign? I mean, you *will* need people who can type, and ring doorbells, and make themselves generally useful."

He considered it. "I don't see any reason why you shouldn't. We'll get Kirby to fix it up. Kirby has a lot of influence—"

"Who—me?" Kirby said.

"—and he won't mind using it, just to keep his hand in. That's the way it is with influence, you know; if you don't use it all the time, people will forget you have it. It's very wearing."

"You ought to know," Kirby said. "What have you been doing all this past week in Washington?"

They looked at each other, ready for more of that sharp interchange, but then both of them saw me watching them and stopped. Kirby picked up my suitcase.

"Shall I bring this in for you?"

"Please don't bother."

I said good-by and took the suitcase from Kirby and went on up the walk to the house. At the top of the gallery steps I looked around and waved to them as the car turned and headed back up the Pike. While I stood there I wished the house had been painted that year; I wished I hadn't dressed as if I'd been going to a fire; I wished the people in that row of practically identical miniature Southern mansions that had sprung up on either side of the house had had time to get their lawns in before the cold weather came. I knew none of it would have made any difference, but it wasn't the picture I wanted to leave. I wanted it to be perfect; I wanted it to be like something you read about in a book; and above all I wanted to look like the heroine of that book, and not like one of those supernumerary characters you meet in the first chapter and then forget.

It felt queer and flat to be home—the color all washed out of everything suddenly, the excitement gone. Father wasn't there, but Aunt Bridgie was, and I sat around talking to her for a while. She was a brisk, pretty woman of fifty who had never stopped being eighteen years old inside; sometimes she dressed as if she were that age, and she usually talked as if she were. If she had ever had any common sense she had long ago decided that it was silly to carry such a burdensome commodity around with her—but she had a serene faith in the impossibility that anything disagreeable could ever happen to her that seemed, on the whole, to serve her just as well.

Finally, around two-thirty, I went upstairs and took a hot bath and then lay down in my room to try to nap for a while. Before I had time to doze off, though, I heard Father's automobile roar up the drive—no matter what kind of car he drove it always sounded, when he was at the wheel, like one of those big yellow trucks of his, with PATRICK J. DONLON, GENERAL CONTRACTOR in black letters all over it. A minute later the front door slammed in the middle of his entering shout:

"Is Betsy home?" I got up and called over the balustrade that I'd be down in a minute.

"Are you sure you're all right?"

"Of course I'm all right."

I put on a sweater and skirt, brushed my hair into a knot, and went down. Father always made me feel young and safe; it was a good feeling, after everything that had happened that day. He was dark Irish, not tall but rugged—though at forty-five he'd begun to put on weight—and he had blue eyes and a good sense of humor that worked except when his emotions were involved. When it came to emotions, he was pure Irish. He still worshiped the memory of my mother, who had been dead for seventeen years, and he had a way of attacking any problem as if it were a knockdown battle between him and the circumstances, animate or inanimate, that had caused it: he hadn't the slightest consideration for anything except coming out the winner. Afterwards, of course, he was usually ashamed of the tactics he had used. When we lived on Lexington Street we had a parish priest who used to say that the Act of Contrition had been invented especially for people like Father, but that he oughtn't to feel on that account that he had to take out a personal patent on it.

Father was in the living room when I went down. He had the afternoon paper, which, he said, had an article on the first page about the wreck, with my name among the local people involved, only spelled wrong—*Miss Betty Donlen.*

"Are you sure you're all right?" he asked me again. I'd come over to kiss him, and he took hold of my arms and stood examining me suspiciously, as if I were a piece of merchandise that looked all right but might fall to pieces the minute you touched it.

"Nothing at all happened to me," I said. "Our Pullman just tipped over on its side; it was all over before I even woke up." I stopped suddenly to consider: "I never did find out what really happened. Does it say in the paper? It just seemed like an act of God, somehow—like an earthquake or a flood."

"An act of God?" Father said. "I can tell you one thing, God had nothing to do with it. It's pure damn carelessness—I'll sue that railroad for every cent they've got if there's a scratch on you." He slammed his hand down on the paper. "You can't pick up one of these things any more without reading about somebody getting killed in a train-wreck or a plane-crash or a bus smash-up. We ought to go back to the horse and buggy if that's all the better we can manage these things."

He was excited, and I loved him for it. I had felt rather desolate, lying there in my room and realizing that I was starting out on a long emotional journey with nobody but myself to care whether I ever reached the place I was trying to get to, and I wanted to stay a while longer where it was safe and people cared very much what happened to me. I suppose I would have begun to get sentimental in a moment, but the telephone rang just then out in the hall, and we heard Aunt Bridgie answering it; immediately afterward she came into the room and told Father it was for him. I noticed that she looked a little upset and indignant, and that she closed the hall door carefully behind Father when he went out.

"What's the matter?" I asked.

"It's nothing. Nothing at all."

It didn't sound like nothing at all, and she had a familiar look on her face, so I put two and two together and said: "Who is it? Lucille Hurley?"

Aunt Bridgie looked at me as if I had just said a couple of four-letter words.

"I don't see how you can say it so calmly," she said. "At your age— if anyone had told me at your age that Pa was—had a—But of course Pa would never in the world—"

I went over to the mantel and smoothed my hair before the glass; I wasn't nearly so nonchalant about it as I sounded. As a matter of fact, thought Aunt Bridgie and I had often talked *around* the subject of Lucille Hurley, we'd seldom talked directly *about* her, in spite of the fact that I'd known she existed for almost four years now, ever since I'd quarreled in high school with Helen Reed, whose family had moved across the river from Corioli to Queensport that year. And what I didn't find out then—or didn't believe—I found out very definitely the night after I graduated from high school, when I went on a double date with a boy from Corioli who drank too much at The Castle and started taking a violent interest in me instead of in the girl he was with. When I didn't co-operate he turned unpleasant, and tried to line me right up with Lucille Hurley; the boy I was with finally quieted him down, but not before I had the full outline of what the situation was between Mrs. Hurley and my father.

I'd never told anyone about either of these incidents, though. Whatever disagreements Father and I had had about the way I ought to be brought up, we'd always cared a good deal about each other, and I think I must have decided somewhere in my mind that even if what Helen Reed and the boy from Corioli had told me was true, it wasn't *really* true—not the way it sounded, at any rate. You know how it is: there are always two ways of looking at everything— the case for the prosecution and the case for the defense. I was very definitely for the defense.

I remember I'd even tried to make a romantic story out of it for a while; after all, this had been going on for years, and they couldn't marry because Mrs. Hurley already had a husband floating around somewhere. I used to imagine her as a frail blonde—a sort of composite of all the long-suffering heroines I'd seen in plays or films— till one summer afternoon when I went shopping up in Corioli with Aunt Bridgie. On Fourth Street we passed a perfectly ordinary-looking woman in her early forties—blonde, all right, but in a soft, faded, comfortable way, and with a face and figure that would have looked a lot more at home in a kitchen cooking dinner for a family than in a boudoir. I wouldn't even have noticed her if Aunt Bridgie hadn't pulled me past her as if we were on our way to a fire, and then dragged me into Corliss's so she could sit down over a cup of tea and weather the shock she'd received. Of course I guessed right away what was the matter with her, and I can remember sitting there at one of those little tables in Corliss's, drinking a Coke, while another of my illusions dropped neatly to the floor and shattered there without out a sound. That was the day I decided that I didn't understand sex; what I was really discovering, of course, was that in any long-standing relationship between a man and a woman glamour is never a very important factor.

This afternoon Father stayed out of the room only a minute or two; almost before he had gone he was back again, opening the door ostentatiously and looking a little flushed and guilty as he came in. "Damn people can't let you alone for five minutes," he said. "That was one of the girls down at the office—" Aunt Bridgie and I looked at each other, but Father was already plunging back into our interrupted conversation. "Bridgie says Kirby Hays drove you home," he said to me.

"Yes. Well, it wasn't exactly his car. He was coming back from Washington with some people—Ivor Kelly and a man named Ken Baggott—and Mr. Kelly bought the car from someone—"

I saw the startled expression on Father's face.

[33]

"Kelly?" he said. "With Kirby Hays? Did you see him?"

"I told you, I drove home with them."

Father sat down and took his head in his hands. "Oh, my God," he said miserably. "That has-been boy-wonder—What in *hell* does Kirby think he's trying to pull?"

He looked so dejected that I shot a glance at Aunt Bridgie; this was no ordinary mood. She wasn't any help, though, so I said tentatively to Father: "Is anything the matter—?"

"This is a terrible state," Father said gloomily—I doubted, though, that it was in answer to me. "Anybody who gets mixed up in politics here ought to have his head examined. There are forty-eight states in the Union, and this is the only one where a fool like Kirby Hays can bring in a drunk like Ivor Kelly and run him for governor—and probably win with him too, if he can keep him on his feet till November."

"What difference does it make to you?" I asked, considerably more coolly. I'd been meaning to ask Father about Ivor Kelly, but if this was the sort of thing he was going to tell me, I didn't particularly want to hear it.

Father looked up. "The difference it makes to me," he said violently, "is that if we don't put somebody in the governor's mansion in November that I can do business with, I'm going to be *out* of business. And we'll all be out of this house; we'd be out of it now if I could sell the damn thing—"

I can't say I wasn't shocked. Of course, as I've said before, you don't grow up in the kind of household I'd grown up in and keep many of the ordinary illusions, but I'd somehow always managed to think of Father as a reasonably honest businessman who happened to have a lot of political friends, and of the governor of the state as somebody who was elected to serve the citizens of that state, and not just to see to it that Father stayed in business. Put it this way: I'd always known there was a connection between Father's prosperity and the fact that he had friends in political office, but nobody had ever drawn a blueprint of that connection for me before. Well, I was growing up now; at nineteen, apparently, you weren't supposed to be shocked at anything.

I think Father realized, though, that he had said the wrong thing; he got up right away and began trying to cover it over with some fast conversation about times being hard everywhere, and people having to look out for their own interests first, before they could afford to think of the next fellow.

"We'll get along all right," he said to me. "You go on down to La Fayette and forget about it, and next year, if you want to go back to Bryn Mawr—"

"I don't even want to go to La Fayette," I said. "I'm perfectly well educated now; I could get a job."

Father looked at me in horror. "And have everybody saying I can't afford to support you?"

"You couldn't affort to support the horses; nobody said anything about that."

He shook his head darkly. "When people think you're slipping, is the time you've got to look out. You go on down to La Fayette; tell people you're changing schools because the climate's better for your health."

I couldn't help laughing at that; I hadn't been sick for more than a day since I'd had the measles when I was twelve. If I had any ideas of arguing with him about it, though, I didn't have a chance, because Ester, our colored "girl," came in just then and said there was a man outside to see Father—"Say' his name Judson—you want to see him?" she asked him. She had a rather uncompromisingly gloomy expression on her face herself; I wondered suddenly if Father had been paying her with the same kind of overoptimistic checks he had been sending me at college.

"Judson? What Judson?" Father said. There was a look of genuine surprise on his face. "Not a tall skinny hillbilly—looks like a preacher?"

Ester nodded. "Say' there's some trouble out on the job, an' he got to see you—"

Father's face changed. "God Almighty," he said.

He didn't even sound upset; he just sounded resigned. He went out of the room after Ester, and a few moments later Aunt Bridgie and I heard him talking to someone in the back hall. We couldn't catch everything—just the flat, innocent, opinionated twang of a hill-country voice against Father's sharper interjections: "Well, tell him he'll get a check the first of the month"—"I know I owe him for that last lot"—and then, "What do you mean, he won't leave it unless he gets the cash? I've been doing business with that s.o.b. for ten years."

I looked at Aunt Bridgie; she had picked up her knitting and was inspecting it critically, apparently paying no attention to the conversation in the hall.

[35]

"Does this go on all the time?" I asked. "Maybe I'd better not go down to La Fayette after all."

Aunt Bridgie glanced up at me, surprised.

"Why, Pat says it's perfectly all right," she said. "He says it's only temporary; everything is going to be perfectly all right by the end of the year."

"After the elections, I suppose," I said.

I looked around at the room; all at once it had taken on the transient, insubstantial effect of a stage set that was going to be "struck" any minute now. What happened, I thought, to houses that were supposed to rest firmly on a solid foundation of money, when all there was left to hold them together was a desperate piecing of promises, bad checks, and unpaid bills? Didn't they simply collapse silently some night, like a house of cards, and blow away to old brick-yards, pawnshop windows, and secondhand stores?

Father came back absently into the room.

"I've got to go out," he said. "There's something I have to take care of."

He was concentrating on something else; he didn't even see us, though he looked at us as he walked through the room to the front hall to get his coat. We listened to the outer door close behind him.

"It's that woman, of course," Aunt Bridgie said disapprovingly. "She might at least have the decency not to call him here while you're home. You *might* accidentally answer the phone—"

She frowned over the knitting, disturbed over some inaccuracy in the stitches.

"I don't think it's that," I said. But she wasn't listening. "Aunt Bridgie—" I said.

"Yes, dear?"

"Who *pays* for things around here?" I asked. "I mean the grocer, the butcher, the milkman, Ester—"

She looked up at me. "Now, you're *not* to worry, Betsy," she said. "It's only for a short time, and you know I have a little money of my own—"

"You lost all that two years ago, on that Canadian copper stock," I said. I sat down ruthlessly opposite her, where I could face her directly. "You may as well tell me," I said.

"Well, there really isn't anything to tell." She was perfectly serene about it, going on with her knitting again. "I don't like to bother your father about it now, when he has so many other things on his mind, so I simply went down to one of those loan companies—The man was really very nice; he went to school with my husband, he says, and he took such an interest in explaining everything to me—"

This was worse than I had expected; the house grew even less substantial around me while I listened, and the furniture, gnawed at by the unseen rats of interest and hidden charges, seemed too shaky to trust oneself to any longer. I made up my mind.

"I'm going to tell Father," I announced.

"You won't do anything of the sort." Aunt Bridgie looked up at me again, astonished. "Why, it's all working out perfectly beautifully; I'll tell him myself as soon as he's had a chance to straighten things out in his business. It just isn't that important, dear."

I might have argued with her about it a while longer, but it suddenly occurred to me that even if Father knew nothing directly of Aunt Bridgie's stratagem, he must have realized that she was getting money somewhere; he simply didn't care, it seemed, as long as he didn't have to cope with it now. For a moment I saw him quite honestly—his badgering charm, his ruthless weakness, his peremptory blindness to things as they were—wondering at the same time how much of each of these qualities I had inherited from him myself.

This was my homecoming, then—a jigsaw puzzle of problems, doubts, and dreams shaken out before my eyes for me to try to put together a logical picture, something I could learn to live by, like a map with nice, specific lines on it to show me exactly where I ought to go. Unfortunately, the only specific line I could see was the one that led down to La Fayette and the state university; it wasn't one I particularly wanted to take, but as long as Father insisted and there was nowhere else to go, there didn't seem to be anything else to do but follow it. Only temporarily, of course, I thought, for at nineteen hope is an infinite thing.

So I went down to La Fayette. . . .

I I

FORT PARIS was burgeoning with spring when I came up from State for the Easter holidays. The house was still there for me to come back to—as solid as ever, apparently, with real honeysuckle greening round the white pillars in the April sunlight—but I found out within half an hour that you couldn't lead a normal life in it any more. There was too much of a sense of the strain of Father's frantic efforts to hold it together; he made me think, with the violent activity of his movements, of those characters in animated cartoons that you see appearing frenziedly in a dozen different places almost at the same moment, trying to accomplish some impossible task. I felt at loose ends, and spent a lot of my time going around with people I didn't much care for so I wouldn't have to stay home and think about what was happening there.

One morning, when I was up in Queensport doing some shopping for Aunt Bridgie, I ran into Kirby Hays; I was coming out of a drugstore on Monroe Street, and he invited me to go back in and have a Coke with him.

"You're just the girl I wanted to see," he said. "Fate threw you in my path. I called you three weekends running after that wreck, and your aunt kept saying you were down in La Fayette."

"I don't usually come home weekends," I said.

"I hoped it was true; you look like a very truthful girl, Betsy. I didn't think you would deliberately lead your aunt into the paths of iniquity by asking her to tell a lie."

He was excited; everybody I knew seemed to be overreacting a little these days.

"What's the matter?" I asked him.

"Nothing's the matter. I'm just glad to see you; that's all." He looked at me absently—we were in the drugstore then, in a booth

[38]

near the door—and I knew he wasn't telling me the whole truth. "How's Pat making out these days?" he asked me suddenly.

"Why—" Remembering Father's admonitions, I stopped, confused. "Haven't you seen him yourself?"

"Oh yes, I've seen him. I just thought I'd get your reaction." He looked, still absent, at something over my head. "I like Pat," he assured me. "I've always liked him. All he has to do is to say the word, and that's all there'll be to it."

"All there'll be to what?"

Suddenly he came back to me again. "That's right," he said. "I promised not to talk politics to you. That wasn't what I wanted to say to you, anyway. I wanted to ask you to go out with me Saturday; I've got a couple of tickets for a show—"

Saturday?"

I considered it, not in a mood to say *yes* or *no*; things seemed just to happen to me lately, and I had stopped thinking of myself as the one who decided. This time it was Kirby who made up my mind.

"Good," he said. "That's all settled then. I'll either be celebrating by that time or drowning my grief, so after the show we'll go to the most expensive place we can find. Do you like champagne, Betsy?"

I smiled. "I've got very simple tastes. Father made his money just at the wrong time for me; I was too old for it to seem like something I had to have, and too young to be impressed."

"You're a jewel of a girl."

All at once he was really beginning to concentrate on me, but an uneasy-looking, apologetic little man appeared in the aisle beside our booth and Kirby excused himself and got up to talk with him for a few minutes at the door. When he came back I said: "You're busy; I'm not going to take up any more of your time."

"I won't be busy Saturday." I got up, and we walked together to the door. "You won't forget?" he said. "I always worry about that with college girls; they have so many things to remember."

"I haven't a thing."

I looked back at him as he walked away down the street; I liked him, but I didn't know why I was doing this, except if it was because I hoped he might talk to me about Ivor Kelly. And after a couple of months down at La Fayette, I'd thought I had that in perspective again. After all, you couldn't go along all those weeks believing in the same kind of wild possibilities that had seemed perfectly logical on the day of the wreck.

[39]

Kirby came to the house around eight on Saturday. I'd seen the newspaper headlines that day, so I knew the sort of mood he'd be in. Even the house seemed anchored more firmly to the ground that evening, and Father had the resigned, peaceful look of somebody who has made a decision and doesn't intend to let himself even consider whether it was the right one or not. In explanation, I might say that what he had made up his mind to was to throw his fortunes in with Kirby and Harvey Whiteley behind Ivor Kelly's candidacy for the governorship. I didn't know how he'd arrived at that decision; all I did know was that Lucius Pennefather's death, a year or so before, had left a power-vacuum in the state Democratic party that two factions were now trying to fill. Apparently Father, who had somehow slipped between the two, had finally decided to ally himself with the one that seemed at the moment the more likely winner, and his judgment had already been vindicated to a certain extent: the state organization had made public that day its decision to support Ivor Kelly in the August primary.

On the other hand, though, the opposing candidate, a man named Ed Dodd, who had been a power in state politics for fifteen years, was known to have a majority of the rank and file politicians on the county level firmly committed to him, which meant that whatever victory Kirby and Father and Harvey Whiteley could claim was on a field strewn with the ghastly souvenirs of internecine war. So I could guess at Kirby's mood—triumph tempered by cold-sober reflection on the battles still before him.

When he came in that evening Father, for once, was at home and sitting quietly in the living room. He didn't even get up when I brought Kirby in—just sat there looking at the two of us with that resigned, unhopeful expression on his face. Kirby went over and clapped him on the shoulder.

"What's the matter with *you?*" he asked.

Father shook his head. "I don't know. I feel like the devil." He stirred himself up a little, doubtfully. "Maybe I need a drink. Would you like a drink, Kirby?"

"If I'm going out with Betsy, I'd better start sober."

"Betsy?" Father looked startled; I'd told him about Kirby, but he couldn't seem to connect the two of us. "Oh, yes," he said then. "Betsy mentioned it. Well, in that case you'd better start sober and stay sober too; I don't want you getting her mixed up in anything.

Betsy wasn't brought up like a lot of girls are these days, you know; she's had good Catholic home training—"

He was suddenly, embarrassingly paternal; I was glad when Aunt Bridgie came into the room and asked Kirby how his mother was.

"She's fine," Kirby said.

"I suppose you're feeling very pleased with yourself today." Aunt Bridgie patted his arm, looking around for her knitting. "I don't know anything about politics, but Pat says you're going to make Ivor Kelly governor."

"We're certainly going to try."

"Well, I do hope you know what you're doing. I'm not quite sure myself—I never did trust a man with such black hair."

She sat down with her knitting. Kirby only grinned—he was used to Aunt Bridgie—but Father said suddenly: "I wouldn't trust him if he was blond as a Dutchman. He's not dependable; he's likely to blow up right in our faces some day."

"That's all over," Kirby assured him. "I felt the same way at first, but he hasn't had more than two drinks a day for six months."

"I don't mean that." For a moment Father had the expression of a man looking back reluctantly at a fool's paradise he had inadvertently stepped out of, but it was too late to go back now. "He's just—not reliable," he went on, with that determined, despairing emphasis. "You know what I mean: you get a funny feeling, just looking at him—like it didn't make a damn bit of difference to him whether he's governor or not."

"He wants to be governor, all right. Even if he doesn't, Harvey Whiteley wants it enough for both of them."

"And besides that," Father started off on another tack, "what makes you think that Ed Dodd's going to sit there on his tail while you bright young geniuses walk all over him? He'll pull the rug out from under you before you know it."

"We've got it nailed down."

"You haven't got anything nailed down. You've got too many people sitting on that rug who're wondering right now whether they aren't making damn fools of themselves, being there at all."

"Including you?" Kirby said.

Father considered it. "All right," he said miserably, "including me. Don't get me wrong, Kirby; I said I'd go down the line for Kelly, and I will. But if I don't get a winner this time, I may as well go out and slit my throat."

[41]

"You've got nothing to worry about," Kirby said. "There are enough politicians in this state who hate Ivor's guts to fill the Rose Bowl, but the voters love him. He could beat Ed Dodd at the polls even if Ed handed out five-dollar bills with every ballot."

Father still looked unconvinced; I could see they had the makings of an evening's argument there that wasn't going to do anybody any good. I looked at Kirby.

"I thought we had a date," I said. "But if you want to stay here and talk politics instead—"

"And waste that beautiful blue dress?" Kirby said. "You're going out and be admired, young woman. Besides, somebody *gave* me these tickets; I hate to waste something I didn't have to pay for."

We might not have got away even then, though, if the telephone hadn't rung at that moment out in the hall. It was for Father—Lucille Hurley, I gathered, from the hurried way he got rid of her as Kirby and I stood saying good-by to Aunt Bridgie at the door.

"No, I can't talk now—No, I said I couldn't—All right, tomorrow then—No, my God, don't do that; I said tomorrow—"

He slammed the phone down just as Kirby and I went out the door; at least, I thought, something had been able to rouse him from his misery.

Later, when we were driving up to Corioli, I tried to get Kirby to explain the fine points of that conversation he had had with Father, but he passed it off as a joke, and said two enterprising young people like us ought to be able to find something better to talk about than politics.

"I thought college girls were interested in practical things," he said. "Like getting married—why don't we talk about getting married? Besides, all the women I know who are interested in politics look as if they'd rather be right than President."

"I suppose that's because they know they've got a better chance—"

"What—?"

"Of being right."

Kirby shook his head at me. "Don't they teach girls in college any more that they won't get a husband if they cap their young men's bright remarks? What's the use of a lot of history and economics if you neglect the essentials—?"

"We don't neglect anything. It's just that I'm not working on that right now."

"I'd make a swell husband," Kirby argued. "Go on, tell me one

[42]

thing I haven't got. Money, brains, character, a sweet disposition—I'm even human before I have my first cup of coffee in the morning."

"That's the trouble," I said. "A girl doesn't feel up to all that perfection."

I never knew how seriously I ought to take what he said, but I was getting over feeling uncomfortable about it; if our relationship was going to progress through a series of wisecracks, it was all right with me. It was a good enough background, anyway, for seeing a gaudy musical comedy that neither of us was much interested in; we sat far down front, and looked up at lines of long sleek black legs waving with rhythmic caterpillar-precision over our heads, and commented on the fact that actors always sound so proud and impressed with their stage-profanity—"You can make love without conviction, but you can't swear without conviction," Kirby said. "Not and sound as if you really meant it—"

After the show we drove back across the river to a place on the La Fayette Pike where there was a good orchestra. There was only a fair crowd, even though it was Saturday night, and the waiters hovered over you respectfully; but Kirby said he could remember, back in the twenties, when people practically had to breathe in unison on the dance floor, and you had to be a first cousin to a prize-fighter or a congressman to get a drink. The twenties had been my childhood years—the "jazz age" was already over by the time I was fourteen—and I had the mixed emotions about them that most of my generation had. We regretted them a little, because they had been promised to us as children and then, when the time came to make good on the promise, they weren't there, and at the same time we felt superior to them, harder and better able to deal with life as it really was. I sat there listening to Kirby talk about the way things had been ten years before, and it was like listening to somebody tell about a party you'd been too young to be invited to—it sounded glamorous but unreal.

We'd been there only about ten minutes when there was a stir at the door that made us both look over, and that was when I started to be glad I had come. Or sorry—I couldn't tell which, in that first moment. Because what I saw when I looked around was Ivor Kelly in a crowd of other people at the door, and among those people was a tall girl with a cool smile who very definitely was with him. She had shoulder-length hair, ash-blonde—that's how sure she was of herself: she didn't even bother to bleach it—and one of those high-cheek-boned faces that were on every movie screen in the country about that time. I recognized Kirby's girl with "money and charm and looks and—money" without a moment's hesitation. She might have been eight or nine years older than I was, and she'd used every one of those years to the best advantage; she had all the self-possession and knowledge of her own good points that you only pray for at nineteen.

The whole party stood there for a few moments in the doorway, while the headwaiter ran up and people all over the room turned to look and the orchestra, which had been playing "Something to Remember You By," broke it off abruptly and went into a fast performance of "Has Anybody Here Seen Kelly?" I watched Ivor; he looked polite but detached, as if he had only happened to walk in while all these things were going on. Then applause broke out in the room and he waved one hand.

"See that?" Kirby demanded. "They eat it up. It's just what I told Pat; he can't lose."

"Is that the girl?" I asked—"the one you told me about?"

"Sure. Polly Conway—Harvey Whiteley's daughter. The rumor is, they're going to announce the engagement as soon as Ivor wins the nomination."

I watched her sitting down at a big table across the room. There were six or seven people in the party—only one other woman, a stout, white-haired, expensively vulgar-looking dowager who was having a wonderful time. I saw Ken Baggott and Harvey Whiteley and a couple of men I didn't know, one of whom—tall, fifty-odd, with an impressive manner—bore a faint but startling resemblance to President Roosevelt. It was nothing you could put your finger on—like a poor imitation that makes you wonder how you can tell who it is that is being imitated—but it was there. Kirby saw me looking at them.

"Do you want to go over?" he asked.

"Oh, no. I don't know those people." I felt panicky, watching Polly Conway; it was too soon to adjust myself to the idea of matching myself against that. "Is it *Mrs.* Conway?" I asked Kirby.

"Her husband accidentally stepped out a window of a very tall building a year or so ago. She tried being heartbroken; it didn't suit her."

I looked at her again. "She's not exactly—beautiful," I debated it.

"Baby, she doesn't have to be. What do you care how the guy looks

[44]

who wins the auto races up in Indianapolis on Memorial Day? You only want to see if he gets killed, that's all."

"But I don't—"

"I mean she takes chances," Kirby explained it to me. "With what she does, what she says, what she wears, where she goes. That's what Ivor sees in her; that's what she sees in him—"

"He doesn't look as if he would particularly care for reckless people.

"Maybe he doesn't. Not any more. But he's playing a game with himself; he's playing that the last seven or eight years never existed. So he's got himself a poor man's Stella Blair to keep up the illusion— You ever see Stella Kelly, Betsy?"

"Only in photographs—"

"*That* was a girl. She and Ivor went up like a couple of skyrockets the year they hit Queensport together, back in the twenties; you could see them from anywhere you stood, and when they were up there the moon and the stars took second billing."

This was worse than anything; it was bad enough to realize my own shortcomings alongside of the live attractions of Polly Conway, but when the perfections of a dead woman were added to the list of what I had to compete with, it seemed time for me to take myself out of the running altogether. If I had ever been in it in the first place, of course—which seemed more improbable than ever now, even when I saw Ivor leaving his friends and coming across the room toward Kirby and me. It was Kirby, I was sure, who was bringing him; if he had never laid eyes on me before, he would have come just the same.

Kirby said, "Hail, the conquering hero—" when he came up, and Ivor gave him the same polite, pleasant look he'd given the applauding crowd, as if he weren't quite sure any of this referred to him.

"I *thought* it was Betsy," he said to me. "You look all grown-up and different."

"It's the dress—and you've never seen me with lipstick on—"

I could feel things happening to the way I breathed when he looked at me, just as they had the night of the wreck; it wasn't any use pretending I couldn't. He said to me and to Kirby: "We all want you to come over. We're having a celebration—at least it started out to be a celebration, only after the first hour there didn't seem to be anything in particular to celebrate—"

"Don't be so modest," Kirby advised him. "You're playing the part wrong; this one calls for the Confident Young Executive." He got up.

"Coming, Betsy?" he said. "Only, listen, Ivor, on one condition—everybody understands that Betsy's *my* girl."

I still didn't want to go; I wanted to less than ever after Kirby had said that. But it wasn't any use. They were both standing there waiting for me, so I got up and went over and was introduced to Polly Conway and Mr. Whiteley and Mrs. Hirsch and Mr. Devanter and Mr. Anonymous—that wasn't really his name, of course, but it was the nearest I could come to it in the general confusion.

"*Pat* Donlon's daughter?" Mrs. Hirsch said. She might have been giving the party; she wanted to be in on everything, with inquisitive exuberance. "You're not anything like him—I'd say a gazelle, wouldn't you?" she asked, turning to the others for confirmation. She explained to me: "We're playing a game; you name a person, and somebody has to say what animal they remind you of. Harvey's a porpoise, and I'm a fat white hen, and Polly's a greyhound, and Ivor's a black panther, we *think*, a rather seedy-looking one who's been traveling around too long with a second-rate circus. Do you mind being a gazelle? *I* think that's flattering; don't you think that's flattering?"

"They haven't found an animal for me," Ken Baggott said comfortably, and Kirby suggested, as we sat down: "Maybe they're just too polite to name it."

"We're not being polite this evening," Polly Conway said. She had the kind of voice to go with her appearance—low and self-assured and not in any hurry, if you know what I mean. I felt like Miss Anonymous, as far as she was concerned; she hadn't bothered to give me more than a glance. "If you want to say 'donkey,' Kirby, go on and say it," she told him; "we'll think of something just as uncomplimentary for you. How would you like 'jackal,' for example?"

Kirby flushed; it was the first time I'd ever seen him look like that. There was one of those thunderously embarrassing silences, and then I said quickly: "Kirby's a wolf; I can vouch for *that*. And aren't my eyes the wrong color for a gazelle's? If it's any help, I once played the front half of a giraffe in a school play—"

It wasn't particularly funny, but everybody laughed, and Ivor smiled at me across the table.

"And the headwaiter—" Mrs. Hirsch demanded our attention again, "is a seal. Do you *think* we could ask him to balance something for us on his nose?"

Mr. Whiteley, ignoring her, leaned across the table to me and asked me impressively how my father was.

"He's very well," I said, feeling queer to be so formal again all at once.

"Three Pink Ladies," Mrs. Hirsch was saying. "One for me and one for you and one for Pat Donlon's little girl. All balanced on a tray on the tip of his nose—"

The owner of the club, a tall man of fifty in an aggressively immaculate dinner jacket, came up to the table to ask if everything was all right.

"Getting everything you want, Mr. Whiteley?—Mr. Kelly? Just give us the word—"

"Three Pink Ladies," Mrs. Hirsch insisted. "And have the headwaiter bring them on a tray balanced on the end of his nose—"

The owner laughed shortly; he had already taken in the mood of the table.

"We don't use jugglers any more in our floor shows, you know. Too old-fashioned."

"Well, I'm just an old-fashioned girl at heart," Mrs. Hirsch declared. She turned to the presidential Mr. Devanter suddenly. "Freddie, come on and dance with me. We'll show them all an old-fashioned waltz."

"But they're playing a fox trot," Mr. Devanter objected.

"Makes no difference. We'll show them a real ol-ld-fashioned waltz."

She got up and pulled him to his feet; we watched them sail grotesquely away across the floor.

"I hope I'll still have it when I'm as old as she is," the owner of the club said, discreetly leaving us, with a wave and a smile for someone across the room.

Mr. Whiteley, his small mouth pursed in the center of his face, looked disapprovingly down his Roman nose.

"Very high spirits in a woman her age. What did you say her husband made his money in?"

"Casks and barrels," Kirby said. "Literally and figuratively—"

"Very influential woman," Mr. Anonymous announced suddenly, surprising us all, and then scuttled back to his modest silence again. He was a dark, insignificant-looking little man who took an intense interest in the conversation, and who seemed always on the verge of making remarks that he decided against at the last moment. Polly Conway glanced at him.

"We're all influential people here," she said shortly. "Isn't it nice

[47]

that all Ivor's friends are so influential? Of course it would be even nicer if they had ordinary good manners too."

This time there wasn't any mistaking it. It wasn't Kirby she was quarreling with, or Mrs. Hirsch; it was Ivor. I might have been only nineteen, but I was female too, and I could read Polly Conway like a book; she wasn't the first girl I'd met who was used to having more money and attracting more masculine attention than any woman in any room she happened to be in. You can get some peculiar ideas when you live in that sort of atmosphere—and tolerance of the presence of people you dislike usually isn't one of them. I gathered that bringing Kirby and me over was simply the latest in the series of mistakes Ivor had been making that evening, as far as she was concerned, and I wished again that I'd been able to think of an excuse for us to stay where we were.

The music ended, and Mrs. Hirsch and Mr. Devanter came back to the table.

"We were sensational," Mrs. Hirsch proudly announced. "Man stopped us, wanted to know if Freddie was a relative of F.D.R.'s." She plunked down in her chair, out of breath. "Told him Freddie didn't have any relatives. Told him if he wanted to see a future President to come over and take a look at Ivor. Isn't that right, Ivor? We'll run you for President one of these days, and you'll end up sitting in the White House, up to your ass in flunkies and second-rate politicians."

Nobody said anything. Mr. Anonymous began a tentative smile, discovered it was the only one at the table, and quickly swallowed it again. After a moment Polly Conway said: "Ivor'll never be President; he's hardly the type. The American people don't ask their President to look dignified every time they see him, but they at least want him to look uncomfortable—"

"Then we'll run Freddie for President," Mrs. Hirsch declared. "He's got the noblest façade since Warren Harding—probably give us the same kind of administration, too." She turned to me. "Wouldn't you vote for him?" she insisted.

"Betsy can't vote," Kirby said. "She's the innocent among us."

Polly Conway looked in my direction, seeing me, it seemed, for the first time.

"I wondered why Ivor didn't want to sit next to you," she said. "Such an attractive girl—But Ivor's so terribly practical."

Ivor was talking to Mr. Whiteley. He glanced around when he

[48]

heard his name, but only included Polly in the general pleasant detachment of his gaze. It occurred to me that he was deliberately standing aside, letting them all do as they pleased—as he had the morning of the wreck, in the gas station at Tunbridge—till a general explosion seemed imminent, when he would step in and with a word put everything to rights again. But tonight it wasn't that simple.

For one thing, we weren't just a lot of people he happened to know —or at least Polly Conway wasn't; I found that out a little later. That was after things had begun to get confused at our table—people wandering in and out of the picture, through a haze of cigarette smoke and persistent saxaphones, with menus for Ivor to autograph, backslappings to exchange with Kirby and Ken Baggott, or embarrassingly fervid protestations of partisanship concerning the coming campaign. The climax to this was the sudden appearance of a truculent but rather helplessly attractive drunk, who planted himself before Ivor and announced firmly: "I'm for Dodd. D'ya hear that, Kelly? I'm for Dodd. Hooray for Dodd! I hope he licks the socks off you." Of course he was packed off by the management before he got any farther than that, but I think about that time Kirby decided the going was getting a little rough for me, and said he was going to take me home. It broke up the party—to everyone's relief, I imagine, but Mrs. Hirsch's—and it was just after that, while I was outside on the club veranda, that I overheard something I would much rather not have overheard.

Kirby and I, I ought to explain, had started to leave first, but near the door he ran into one of his political friends, who drew him aside with the look of someone with a highly confidential communication on his mind, so I went on outside and stood waiting for him on the veranda. It had begun to rain, and it was dark and deserted out there. I didn't realize it, but from the door I must have been invisible behind the pillar against which I stood, because all at once I heard Polly Conway's voice behind me, saying something, it seemed, to Ivor.

"I'm not sorry. Are you angry with me?"

"I've stopped being angry with people. It's wasted energy."

"If you can say it like that—'people'!" And then there was a sudden silence, only the sound of people breathing, and after a moment her voice going on again, altogether different now: "Oh, darling, you *do* love me—"

"We get along, don't we?"

"Oh, *don't* we!"

It all happened in the space of a dozen seconds; I couldn't have let them know I was there before I had already heard too much. I just stood there, frozen, and the next moment the rest of the party, making a loud, cheerful racket, came out the door, and in the confusion I could join Kirby without anyone's having reason to wonder where I'd come from.

It was a fine ending to my evening; I think Kirby thought I was angry about the party, because I hardly spoke to him all the way home. But at the door of the house I kissed him as if I meant it, and he was unexpectedly grateful and careful—I wondered for the first time if he was really serious about all this. It didn't make me feel any better to believe it; I'd never gone in for the theory that half a loaf is better than none.

There was more to that night—not that I knew anything about it at the time, but it turned out to be rather important later, so I may as well put it in here, where it happened. When the party broke up, it seems, Ivor drove Polly Conway to the hotel where she and her father were staying. It was raining hard by the time he left there, and it was past one o'clock, but he didn't go straight to his own place. Months later, when I learned about all this, I learned too that he hadn't been doing much sleeping about this time. The nervous energies that he'd had to call up to meet the requirements of the pre-campaign negotiations had a way of refusing to go away again promptly when the need for them was over; like the magic-working genie who came out of a bottle, they had to be coped with long after they had served their purpose.

On this particular night he stopped the car in front of an all-night diner on Jessup Street—a sudden one-story structure, made of peeling stucco and rusty iron and discouraged neon, in the middle of a block of old brick buildings—and went inside for a cup of coffee. That doesn't sound like a very earth-shaking thing to do; actually, it was one of those accidental occurrences that, nine times out of ten, don't leave even a ripple behind in the lives of the people to whom they happen. But this time, unfortunately, turned out to be the tenth.

Because there was a girl standing in the doorway of the diner— one of those robust, fresh-looking hill-country girls who come up, in a queue of brothers and sisters, to Queensport or Corioli when the land gives out, or the house falls in, or a fabulous tale of city wages or city "relief" reaches the ears of their parents. Her name was Ila May Judson—no Delilah, only a ripe, deep-breasted country girl who looked at least two years older than her actual age of not-quite-fifteen. What she was doing there at something past one o'clock in the morning, alone, was a matter in which before long, over a cup of coffee, she was involving Ivor without any more inducement than her own confusion and his air of considerate attention—an attention that, to her, could hardly have seemed to refer only to his desire of avoiding the horrors of insomnia in an empty hotel room.

The situation, as he gathered it from her, was fairly obvious, one of those ancient little dramas of *Boy meets Girl, Boy falls in love with Girl, Boy induces Girl to slip out at night to continue said meetings,* that have been going on since the Flood. Anyway, this particular drama had ended, as far as the current chapter in it was concerned, with Boy failing to show up at the appointed place to meet Girl as per schedule, and now she was waiting there, in sullen, only half-believing despair, for the rain to slacken so that, in her Sunday finery, she could go home without courting discovery by ruining her clothes.

It was like Ivor to offer to drive her home—a Good Samaritan role that appealed to him for the double reason of providing companionship and postponing the inevitable tryst with Luminal. What pleased him more was that she took his offer at its face value; her obvious inexperience lent a bizarre note to a proceeding that would hardly have interested him if she had taken his assistance less for granted. Only as he deposited her—still sullen, still incredulous—at the front door of the house on Barker Street where she lived, she remarked to him suddenly: "I know who you are. I seen your picture in the paper." But even that was with the unsophistication of a back-country mind, to which the "picture in the paper" was more of a guarantee of superior importance than the writing beneath it labeling him as the prospective governor of the state.

At any rate, the door closed behind her and Ivor drove back in the rain to his hotel; by the next morning the whole incident had already receded so far into the back of his mind that he would have had difficulty in recalling how she looked. He caught the noon train to Ashbourne, with Polly Conway and her father, and I suppose he thought that was that—only Fate, or whatever it is that proves to us where we made our biggest mistakes, had entirely different plans. . . .

I I I

I DIDN'T see any more of Ivor till the end of the term, in June, when I came home from State for the summer. A couple of weeks before, when I'd been in Fort Paris for the weekend, I'd reminded Kirby about the job I'd been more or less promised at Ivor's county headquarters, so three days after I got back I was up in Queensport, trying to learn how to be of some practical use in a political campaign.

I had the idea, the first day, that my arrival on the scene was viewed with resignation, or worse, by the regular workers. As a matter of fact, Martha Madden, who'd been Ivor's secretary during the years he'd been in Washington, admitted to me later that she'd thought I was going to be another of those eager expendables whose idea of working in a political campaign is getting their pictures in the newspapers pinning buttons on prominent people, and waving banners in railroad stations to enliven welcoming committees for important visitors. She told me that at lunch one day, after I'd spent a week conscientiously stuffing envelopes with campaign material and typing interminable copies of form letters, and then she looked at me speculatively and said: "I haven't figured out yet why you really want to get into this. Or—wait a minute, that's right—you're Kirby's girl, aren't you?"

"Is that what Kirby says?"

"He's been known to give that impression."

"Well, it's his impression, not mine. Kirby's a very good friend—"

"Then why the devotion—?"

I knew I wasn't fooling anybody, but I gave her the usual line about Father's interest in the campaign and my wanting to *do* something; that always works with men, who are as trusting as children when it comes to believing you aren't acting from personal motives, but it seldom goes down with another woman. Not with a woman like Martha Madden, anyway. She was a taffy-haired dynamo, touching forty but still good-looking enough in a pleasant, acid way, who'd made her living for almost fifteen years in a business where it doesn't pay to trust anybody's word without first doing some digging of your own.

There wasn't much chance, though, for her to find out anything about my motives in those early days of the campaign, because I hardly saw Ivor then. He was out of town most of the time, and I only caught glimpses of him when he came into our headquarters in the Sadler Building. He'd say, "Hello, Betsy," in that way he had that made you believe you were just the person he wanted to see, and he always stopped a moment to ask after Father, or about how I was getting along—but that was all. I don't mind admitting that I was disappointed, but I wouldn't have thought of walking out. Even if I hadn't had a personal interest in it, the campaign was something by that time that I wanted to see through for its own sake.

I was too much of a novice to know exactly how things were going. Father looked tragic whenever I said anything to him about it, but I didn't think his opinion was a reliable one; he was still afraid that Ivor would manage somehow to throw his prospects cheerfully out the window before the primaries and destroy whatever chances of future prosperity people like Father were earnestly trying to promote. On the other hand, Kirby was as determinedly optimistic as Father was the opposite, and before long I realized that practically everybody who came into headquarters was in one or the other of those two camps: either they relied blindly on the record of Ivor's past performances in drawing the voters, or they were suspiciously waiting for him to make the first false step that would justify all their gloomy forebodings of his unreliability. Martha Madden was about the only one I knew who was somewhere between the two positions; she said it would take a miracle for Ivor to lose the primary, but that he'd managed to work miracles before. And when I protested, "But that doesn't make sense; you sound as if he *wants* to lose"—she only looked at me in a peculiar way and said, "All right. You give me one reason why he wants to win."

Before I could answer, she changed her mind and tried to pass it all off as a joke, but later that day she said something else to me that made me certain she hadn't been joking at all. She'd been telling me about those two years when Ivor had been ill, and she mentioned

that whenever she came to see him he never wanted to talk politics—
"All he was worried about was owing people money that he thought
he might never be able to pay. He had a way of talking about himself
as if he'd added everything up in his life and closed the books, except for that."

I was curious to know if it was his wife's death that had made
him feel like that, but we were in the office, with people going in
and out, and it wasn't the right time for confidences. A few days
after that, though, when we'd been working late and everybody else
had gone home, I brought up the subject of Stella Kelly, and that
started her on a line of conversation that cleared up a lot of things,
though not the particular point I'd been trying to find out. As I remember it, what she told me went something like this:

The first time I saw Stella Kelly (Martha said), was on a March
afternoon in 1922. She was walking down Monroe Street here in
Queensport with Ivor, and she had on a civet coat and no hat, and her
hair was like eager gold light around her face—I thought I had never
seen two people before in my life who looked so absolutely happy
as she and Ivor did. I hadn't seen Ivor for nine years, not since he'd
left Queensport in the middle of our last year in high school, but he
recognized me at once and insisted on stopping to introduce me to
Stella. Of course I already knew who she was; Queensport boys don't
go to California and marry the daughters of famous Hollywood di-
rectors every day.

Stella's family came from Alabama, and she had that trick all well-
brought-up girls from the Deep South have, of seeming charming
even when she wasn't any more interested in you than she was in a
post, so I walked away after five minutes' conversation with her thoroughly convinced that, as far as Ivor was concerned, fairy tales were
as factually correct as the events you can read every day on any
police blotter. I also walked away with his invitation to come and
see him about a job. He was going to practice law in Queensport, and
when he'd asked me what I was doing, I'd answered with the cheerful evasions of the unemployed—you know Ivor well enough to understand what that combination of circumstances meant to him.

Two days later I was sitting in the most impressive-looking office
in Queensport, talking to Ivor, and trying to reconcile my surround-
ings with my memories of the comfortable ham-and-cabbage smell
of the Kellys' little house on Bank Street. Oh yes, Ivor and I grew up

together; I knew both his parents—sober, hardworking, unlucky people, who were always putting a patch on something to keep the rain out of the parlor, or the mice out of the woodwork, or the blessed air of heaven off their own skins. Mrs. Kelly finally died of pneumonia when Ivor was sixteen, and after a year of trying to keep body and soul together on boiled potatoes and bachelor housekeeping, Michael Kelly decided it wasn't worth while not to take the easy way out and die of erysipelas himself.

The day after his father was buried Ivor left Queensport, and I suppose I was the last person in town who saw him before he went. An aunt of his father's had turned up for the funeral—a pious old crone who had her eye on the "bit of furniture poor Mick left—God rest his soul—and what use at all would it be to a calf of a boy who'd have no home of his own for years to come?"—and my mother had sent me over to the house in the evening with a neighborly dish of roast pork and potatoes for her. When I came round from the kitchen door after delivering it, I saw Ivor sitting on the front steps in the half-dark. He was a good-looking boy then, with plenty of charm and intelligence if he'd known how to use them, but he was too full of unpredictable energies to be popular. I suppose I was one of the group that wanted to know passionately on street-corners after school who Ivor Kelly thought he was, on the days when he'd decided he was going to take over some project we were all involved in, and refashion it according to his own ideas.

Anyway, I was going to walk right past him that evening, with nothing but a cool "Hello," when he called after me: "Marty—wait a minute."

I stopped and turned around. He got up from the steps and came over to meet me, looking at me seriously.

"I just wanted to say good-by," he said unexpectedly. "I'm leaving in the morning. I wish you'd tell everybody—"

"Leaving?" I was curious about that; at school we had speculated freely on what was going to happen to Ivor now, and the great-aunt, with her cubbyhole of a flat in Gary, Indiana, was as near as we had been able to come to forming a future frame of reference for him. "Where are you going?" I asked.

He stood there looking at me for a moment before he spoke; I know now that he wanted to try the effect on someone.

"To California," he said then.

"To California?"

[55]

If he'd wanted a response, I gave him one; that was in 1913 and California, to us in Queensport, was only slightly less distant than China.

"Yes," he said. All at once he was on a level of perfect intimacy with me; you know how he can make you feel—as if you were the only person in the world he'd ever tell these things to. Actually, if I hadn't come along just then, he'd probably have gone out on the street and told them to the next stranger who would listen to him; he was that excited, underneath. "You see, I've got a theory," he said, "I mean about doing the things that really count in life. If you're not willing to take extraordinary chances, nothing extraordinary will ever happen to you—"

I took that in; I've always had a practical mind, and this whole thing was beginning to sound highly impractical to me.

"Do you know anybody in California?" I asked him.

"No."

"Have you got any money?"

"You don't understand. I'm going to *work* my way out."

I shrugged my shoulders. "Well, anybody can *say* they're going to California. It seems to me—"

"You have to have faith in yourself," he insisted patiently. "You've got to believe you can do whatever you want to do—"

"That's easy enough. We'd all be millionaires if that's all we had to do."

"No, you wouldn't. Most of you don't even *want* anything for more than five minutes at a time, and if you do, you don't have any real confidence you'll ever get it—"

I was starting to get irritated by that time; he sounded somehow as if he had a direct commission from destiny to lead the kind of life the rest of us were only going to be able to dream about.

"Well, if you ask me—" I began.

"I'm not asking you, Marty. I just wanted to say good-by to somebody—I just wanted somebody to know—"

He stopped, and that was the moment when I guessed at his real feelings—that he was scared and miserable and trying to impress me in order to convince himself that what he was doing was logical and right. At that point I said the only human thing I came out with in the entire conversation.

"Look," I suggested suddenly, "you don't have to go, Ivor. Couldn't your aunt make some sort of arrangements for you to stay here till school ends? You've still got your job at Dinsmore's on Saturdays, and Mr. Clark says you're sure to get a scholarship at State for next year—"

I've often wondered what Ivor's life would have been like if he'd followed that advice. He didn't, of course, but he looked at me with extraordinary gratitude for the simple kindness I'd done him of suggesting that he might be missed. He's always cared so terribly what people think of him, you know; you might not believe it, but even now—

Anyway, no matter what I'd said to him, he left Queensport the next day, and that was the last I saw of him till that March afternoon in 1922 when I met him walking along Monroe Street with Stella. Nobody in Queensport knew much about what had happened to him in the nine years between those two days; the most reliable accounts came from two of the boys he'd gone to school with here, who met him in France during the war. He was a lieutenant in the infantry then—that was before he got his captaincy—and he told them he'd been studying law in California when he'd enlisted. That seemed to put the earlier rumors that had reached us—that he was a fruit-picker, a movie extra, the driver of a sight-seeing bus—in the category of fiction, but you never can tell. He admitted the movie extra part of it to me himself one day when he told me he'd first met Stella Blair on the lot of a studio where her father was directing a picture, but he said he'd taken the job only to help pay his way through law school.

At any rate, after he came back from the war he got his law degree, and right after that a job in the legal department of one of the big studios, and he and Stella were married. He might have stayed in Los Angeles for good if Cecil Blair hadn't died in 1922, in the middle of a complicated battle with his studio; but in the general debacle Ivor lost his job, and crashed some sort of blacklist, I imagine, and that's when he thought of coming back here. Stella had some money—not as much as people here gave her in their reports of it, but enough to see them through some lean years—and they were going to settle down, with nothing but an occasional trip to New York to distract Ivor from his legal career, and live in the country, with horses and cats, in bucolic happiness.

Actually, you know what happened: within a year Ivor hit the headlines and the big money with the Brownway case, and the year after that he was running for Congress. But even before that he and

Stella had managed to make a good start on the kind of reputation that turned them into one of the most publicized couples in the state during the twenties. They had everything it takes to make head-lines—youth, charm, success, audacity, with Cecil Blair and Holly-wood somewhere just behind them, and Washington and Ivor's political future just ahead of them. I used to pick up the morning papers and look at the dark, smiling young man gazing out at me from the society pages and the political news, and remember that miserable, determined seventeen-year-old who was going to "take extraordinary chances" so extraordinary things would happen to him, standing in the front yard of the little house on Bank Street—

Yes, I worked for him all those years, you know; I went to Wash-ington with him and Stella, and I had a ringside seat at the whole thing. I saw the good years and the years when things kept getting worse and worse, when the parties and the bills got bigger and big-ger, and Ivor spent as much time up in Baltimore as he did in Wash-ington, trying to pull himself together enough to act like a capable young legislator, while Stella went through all the frantic evolutions of a woman who's dazzled everyone around her from the time she was fourteen, and is facing the years when she won't dazzle any more. No, I'm not going to talk about that; there were very com-plicated reasons why things went wrong. Most people simply blamed it all on Ivor's drinking, and if you asked them what was behind that, they looked vague and self-righteous and muttered something about "people with weak characters"—My God, I *knew* about Ivor's char-acter; if it was weak, it was only in the department of spending too much energy and consideration on people like them.

Anyway, it all ended that night in 1933 when their car went over an embankment just outside of Washington and Stella was killed. I suppose I thought it was over for good; there were months when Ivor wasn't expected to live either, and I got a job with Senator Hen-derson and made up my mind that life was going to be one dull, placid dream from then on. But a few months ago Ivor phoned me and said he was planning to run for governor—and here I am, back doing business at the same old stand—

We were leaving the office when Martha finished telling me all this. I went off down the hall to the elevator with her, trying to fit it in with what I already knew about Ivor; somehow it was as if my mental picture of him had suddenly gained a new dimension, and I felt confused, trying to adjust myself to it.

"But why should things have gone so terribly wrong for them?" I insisted. "They had everything—"

"Oh yes," Martha agreed, "they had everything. And they were both absolutely convinced that nothing *could* go wrong for them; troubles happened to other people, but not to them. After a bad start, you see, Ivor had found his luck, and Stella had never had anything else from the beginning. I suppose, if you wanted to, you could say that that was what caused the trouble, right there: if you don't expect much of life, you don't run the risk of its not coming up to your expectations."

The elevator came and we got in. With the elevator boy there we didn't talk, but when we stopped at the first floor and got out I said: "You sound as if there's always disappointment if a person expects things to turn out right."

"Isn't there?" She glanced at me as we walked on out of the front door of the building.

"Always?"

"Always." Then she looked at me again, as if it were a joke, and put her hand on my arm. "Don't worry about it. You're a very sensible girl, Betsy; you're not going to expect anything that the odds aren't all on you to get."

"I wish I could be sure of that," I said.

It was a lovely early July day, and when we went outside the sunlight was still and golden with evening; it felt like the kind of time when anything can happen. I thought it was a very bad time not to expect anything of life, but at least I would be sensible and try.

It was only a few days after Martha had told me all this that I came back from lunch to find a note from her on my desk: Joe Gibson, who handled publicity for us, had got himself involved in a minor auto accident on his way to meet some people, and she was taking over for him that afternoon. "Kirby and Ivor have some letters they want to get off today," the note ran. "If Helen doesn't come in this afternoon, you'll have to see what you can do with them. Just for God's sake get the names and the facts straight; anything else can take care of itself."

I hadn't taken any dictation since, in a burst of enthusiasm over finishing a month's course in shorthand the year I graduated from high school, I'd gone up to Father's office and helped out there on a few summer mornings, but I'd been known at Bryn Mawr as "a good aural memory," and with that in my favor I thought I'd get by. Kirby, who came in first, thought it was a wonderful idea, and made some hopeful remarks about the extracurricular duties of secretaries toward their employers before I could get him down to business, but he had an appointment at two, so I managed to convince him before very long that what we were really sitting in an office together for was to work. I can't say I was an outstanding success, though. Kirby's dictation was of the rough-and-ready sort, and I kept interrupting him to protest: "Oh, Kirby, *that's* not how you want to say it"—with the result that we finally had a major argument over a sentence on which we didn't see eye to eye; it ended in Kirby's announcing rather violently that he was glad he wanted me for a wife and not for a secretary.

"I'd make an even worse wife," I said. "I can't cook, but I really am pretty good at grammar."

He looked at me. "Honey, I wouldn't be marrying you for your cooking," he said, and there we were back to that again. But it was almost two by that time, and he had to leave, so I didn't even have to try to change the subject.

Ivor was in the inner office then with one of our county political bigwigs, a man named Scott Brownlee, who was busily engaged, so Kirby said, in playing both ends against the middle as far as the campaign was concerned. I gathered that Ivor's celebrated charm was being requisitioned to try to bring him to see the proper light, but he looked as self-satisfied as ever, and Ivor merely exhausted, when they finally came out of the office together. Ivor walked with Brownlee to the door and then came back and stood by my desk with his hands in his pockets, looking down at the letters I was doing as if he expected to find the answer to something there. It was Saturday afternoon, and there was nobody else around; you could hear Brownlee's firmly spaced footsteps echoing hollowly down the empty corridor to the elevators.

"I can't do anything with people like that any more," Ivor remarked suddenly. "If you don't believe something yourself, you can't make anybody else believe it, either."

He'd never talked to me like that before, and I didn't know anything else to do but sit there, waiting for him to go on, and hoping

I would look like somebody he wanted to talk to when he realized who I was. I didn't, of course; in a moment he glanced up and really saw me and smiled and said: "I thought you were Martha. Isn't this Martha's desk—?"

"She had to see some people. Somebody ran into the back of Joe Gibson's car—"

He gestured with one hand, interrupting me. "Of course. I heard about it. And you're going to do some letters for me." He looked at me gravely. "Do they always make you work on Saturday afternoons?"

"I don't mind at all. I'm not a bit tired." I swung my chair around, facing him. "*You're* the one who looks tired," I said. "Wouldn't you like to wait a while before you begin?"

He deliberated, consulting his watch.

"Somebody's coming around to pick me up at three. That doesn't give us much time, does it? I've got a radio broadcast and a women's club scheduled this afternoon—"

He pulled a chair over and sat down, and I got out my notebook.

"What would happen if you didn't show up?" I asked. "Streets filled with frantic women—radio towers collapsing from the shock—?"

"Well—" He smiled, a little surprised, I thought, by my vehemence. "Candidates aren't supposed to be human, you know."

"They aren't supposed to be sick, either." That was as far as I got before I realized my emotions were showing; I could feel myself coloring up, and to cover it over I said: "You mustn't mind me; I've got an overdeveloped maternal instinct—I worry about stray dogs too. Father says I take it out on him."

"Pat's a lucky man." He asked unexpectedly, after a moment: "What does he think about you and Kirby?"

It was the first really personal thing he'd ever said to me, but it wasn't in the least what I wanted to hear. What made it worse was that that blush carried over, so that he might have thought it was involved in emotions that had to do with Kirby.

"I'm going to give up even saying 'Good morning' to Kirby if people don't stop trying to marry me off to him," I said. "I've been out with him exactly *three* times."

"It's none of *my* business, of course," he apologized.

I wanted to tell him that it was, just as much as he liked to make it, but naturally you can't go around saying things like that. He was embarrassed because he thought he'd embarrassed me, and we started out on the letters without saying any more about it. I had an awful time concentrating; I kept thinking about our conversation, and wishing I'd managed to be more convincing about Kirby. Finally, about three o'clock, an earnest-looking young man in a sports jacket walked in to take Ivor over to the radio station, and said if Mr. Kelly didn't mind, they'd just have time to get to the studio before the broadcast—

"I'll get these out this afternoon, then," I said to Ivor. "Will you be back to sign them?"

"I should have time, around five-thirty. If you want to go on home before that, you can leave them for me—Or why don't you just take them along to Fort Paris with you," he suggested, "and I can take care of them when I'm down there this evening?" I must have looked blank, because he went on, as he followed the earnest young man to the door: "Didn't Pat tell you he'd asked some of us down for cocktails before the dinner tonight? Or have I got my dates mixed—?"

"Father never tells me anything. He thinks woman's place is in the nursery—at least when there's politics in the parlor. Is he picking you up?"

"I think that's the arrangement."

"I'll get hold of him. I've got my car; I can drive you down myself when you come back to sign these."

The earnest young man looked imploringly impatient.

"In a minute," Ivor said. And, to me: "Are you sure you'll still be here?"

"I'm a very slow worker," I said cheerfully.

I watched him go out the door. I thought he looked a little puzzled, which was at least a start; he'd never even seen me before through that impervious gloss of automatic civility. It occurred to me that perhaps no two people ever really began to know each other till they'd made each other uncomfortable at least once.

It felt queer and forgotten in the empty building, with the yellow July sunlight falling solemnly through the windows and the sound of the Saturday-afternoon traffic remote and rather sad in the street below. I phoned Father and told him I was bringing Ivor, and then sat down to do the letters. The elevator came up noisily a couple of times, the elevator boy whistling snatches of "Willow, Weep for Me" in tranced Saturday boredom as he slid the door back and descended slowly again to the regions below; yet outside of a mournful gray-mustached man in a black alpaca suit who came in to leave a pamphlet for Mr. Kelly entitled *Prepare to Meet Your God,* nobody disturbed me for over an hour. Then Kirby came back, signed his letters, and said he was catching the four-thirty to La Fayette— "Don't you want to kiss me good-by?" he asked me.

I stopped folding the letters and looked up at him.

"You and I are going to have to have a serious talk one of these days," I said. "It seems to me you're taking entirely too much for granted."

"I never take anything for granted. It's the secret of my success."

"Then don't take me." All at once I lost my temper. "Oh, darn it, Kirby, I've got to do these letters—"

He looked injured, and went out of the room without saying any more. I didn't think his pique would be permanent, but if it was I didn't particularly care at the moment. At least it might be useful in putting an end to all those rumors about him and me.

It was almost five when I finished the letters. I spent a quarter of an hour making myself presentable, and then waited around rather nervously for Ivor. He was late, and apologetic, but he looked more cheerful than he had when he had left; he told me three absurd things that had happened to him as he signed the letters I had waiting for him.

Afterwards we went down in the elevator and out to my car, a secondhand but impressive-looking Lincoln that Father had picked up as the result of a complicated transaction involving somebody's missed payments and an insolvent finance company. Ivor looked at it respectfully.

"I've never had a secretary before who drove a Lincoln," he said. "Are you sure I oughtn't to have been taking *your* letters?"

"We're poor as church mice; everybody realizes that except Father." He opened the door for me and I got in, sliding under the wheel. "I feel like Marie Antoinette going to the guillotine every time I ride in this car," I said. "With finance companies for the Paris mobs—"

"You're much too young to worry about money."

"I'm not too young for anything. But don't tell Father I told you all this. It's our family secret—the one everybody knows."

It felt strange and important to be going somewhere with Ivor alone. I turned the car south in the late-afternoon traffic, wishing Fort Paris were hours away instead of minutes, wishing above all that now, when I had Ivor's undivided attention, I could think of something to say to him that would make him admit me at once into the inner circle of his life. We passed Bank Street, and he said un-expectedly: "I lived there—as a matter of fact, I was born there."

"Yes, I know. Martha told me."

"One of those women this afternoon wanted to put up a plaque on the house. I told her to wait till I was elected—"

"You will be."

"That's what she said. I told her it still wouldn't do—might interfere with business. The last time I went by there I was *asked* to come in-side."

"You didn't tell her that?"

He shook his head regretfully. "No. I wanted to, but I didn't. I suppose I oughtn't to have told you, either. You're such a *nice* girl, Betsy—"

"I don't know whether that's a compliment or not."

He looked at me kindly. "Of course it's a compliment. When you get to my age, you realize what a rare quality innocence is. Most people confuse it with inexperience, but it's really something al-together different—a sort of ability to expect things of people. And once you've lost it, you have to live in an entirely different world for the rest of your life—"

The streets fell past us slowly: on a front lawn two little girls in pink were having their picture taken by their father; a taffy-colored cocker panted companionably at me out the window of a car that stopped beside us at a traffic light.

"Nobody likes to think they have illusions," I said.

"We won't talk about it," he offered. "You drive awfully well—I haven't felt so peaceful for a month. I don't want to spoil this with an argument."

"You never argue with anybody. I've watched you. After a while people just seem to convince themselves that you're right."

He smiled at me; all at once I was happy, because I knew he was having a good time.

"You have the most remarkable faculty of making me feel like a successful man," he said. "As a matter of fact, I did everything wrong this afternoon—probably lost more votes in two hours than Kirby'll be able to put together in two weeks. I have a terrible time taking all this seriously any more."

"I know. Sometimes I feel as if I were helping to put on some sort of high-school play; you have to keep on pretending even when

[64]

the scenery falls down and everybody forgets their lines and the audience laughs at all the wrong places."

"It's even worse when you're on the road," he said. "The first time I ran for Congress, somebody got some wires crossed and I ended up in a Republican parade in some little town off in the eastern part of the state—Graves, I think the name was. I got in too early, and the other fellow got in too late, and I had the keys to the city before anybody discovered the mistake. They had to hold the parade all over again when he got there—"

We smiled at each other over the story.

"I'd like to go on one of your campaign trips," I said. "Father thinks I've been everywhere because I've been to Palm Beach and Santa Barbara and New York, but I don't know very much about my own state."

"Well, I suppose it could be arranged. We're going to make a swing down through the middle of the state next week; I'll tell Martha to bring you along."

"Will you, really? I'd love to go."

"I can't promise you anything very exciting," he said. "After the first day all the towns and all the people begin to look alike—and I can give you my personal guarantee that all the speeches will sound alike."

"I've never heard you speak," I said.

He considered it. "I used to be a rather good speaker," he decided. "You wouldn't believe it now."

He might have been talking about someone he had known a long while ago.

We were in Fort Paris by that time, and a minute or two later I stopped the car in front of the house—or as near as I could get to it: from the number of cars that were parked out there, you might have thought we were holding a convention inside. Ivor looked at them and sighed.

"Let's drive right on," he suggested. "Don't you think Ed Dodd would make a swell governor, Betsy?"

I pulled on the brake. "You oughtn't to let people make so many engagements for you."

"I like a lot of engagements. When there aren't any, I sit around and begin to think. That's a very bad habit to get into, Betsy."

He came around and opened the car door for me, and we went up the walk together to the house. The windows were open and we

[65]

could hear people talking and laughing inside—the happy, unin-hibited sound of a male gathering with no women around.

"What is this dinner tonight?" I asked.

"Businessmen's club—I'm supposed to demonstrate my Midas touch."

Father was at the open door, watching for us, when we came up the steps.

"How's the boy, Ivor?" He put out his hand, too heartily; he had the soothing, overjovial look of a man trying to appear unconscious of the fact that he doesn't really trust the person he's talking to. "Betsy's chauffeuring up to standard? She drives better than her old man—"

I smiled at Father and went on across the hall toward the stairs.

"I haven't thanked you—" Ivor called after me.

"Put it down as a campaign contribution."

I went on up the stairs; at the turn I stopped and glanced back for a moment. The swarm from the living room had already engulfed Ivor; he was standing there shaking a circle of outstretched hands, and somebody had begun to sing "Has Anybody Here Seen Kelly?" It looked like the beginning of quite an evening.

I V

AT a quarter to six on a bright afternoon early in the following week I stopped the car in front of Father's office on the Pike. The building was a two-story buff brick, all plate glass and horizontal lines and impressive angles—one of Father's pre-1933 extravagances that had never quite managed to get itself finished: you could still open doors on incomplete stairways that led embarrassingly to nowhere, and a discouraged-looking heap of building-rubble waited patiently outside the back windows.

I got out of the car, pushed open the front door, and went inside. There was nobody in the corridor; the building had a deserted, comfortable, after-five look. Halfway back, though, I heard a door close—somebody was coming out of Father's office. It was a woman in a blue voile dress; she came along the corridor toward me and I glanced at her, not recognizing her till she had passed me, when something registered—Lucille Hurley. From the startled look on her face, I gathered that she had recognized me too; I heard the frightened clash of the doors behind me as she hurried through. Walking on, I wondered how I ought to feel; Aunt Bridgie's certainties would have been more comfortable.

Father was absorbed in some papers when I knocked at his door and walked in, but he looked so hot and upset that I suspected the absorption was only for my benefit. As soon as I was inside he burst into apologies for having asked me to stop and pick him up, looking at me anxiously all the while, as if he were trying to read from my expression whether there had been any embarrassing encounters outside in the hall. I managed a noncommittal look. He was so naïve about his deceptions—the whole office was gay with perfume—that it seemed a shame to disillusion him.

[67]

He picked up his hat, and we went outside together and down the corridor to the front door.

"I'm sorry to bother you," he repeated distractedly. "That damn car broke down right in the middle of Monroe Street this afternoon—damnedest mess you ever saw, traffic piled up for a couple of blocks, cops all over the place—It's a damn peculiar thing, if you ask me, that with all these modern improvements we can't produce a car that'll run when you want it to—"

He jumped and took a step backward as he opened the front door; a tall thin man in faded blue work clothes had appeared as abruptly at his elbow as if he had materialized out of the hot July air.

"Judson! What in hell—?" Father recognized him with irritation. "What the devil are you hanging around here for?"

"I never meant to give you a start. I been waitin' fer you—" The hill-country drawl had a familiar sound, but the face was new to me: the flat dark hair, the narrow jaw, the bright blue eyes that looked at you with an expression somewhere between suspicion and innocence. The eyes took me in distrustfully before they returned to Father. "I been waitin' to talk to you—"

"Well? What about?"

The man nursed his idea. "It's kind of private business," he decided.

His bright blue eyes glittered again on me; I felt a little like the Wedding Guest before the Ancient Mariner, but I couldn't help feeling rather sorry for him too: he looked terribly excited, almost sick.

"Can't it wait till tomorrow?" Father asked impatiently.

"I reckon *so*. But I reckon it'd be better today."

"Well, you can tell me about it tomorrow. I'm in a hurry now. Do you understand me? Tomorrow. Come on, Betsy—"

Behind the wheel of the Lincoln, tearing off down the Pike, he exploded: "I'd like to know what gets into those people. You try to act like a human being, and the first thing you know—"

"What's it about?"

"How do I know? I think he's trying to convert me; he's got some sort of religion on the brain—"

I tried not to laugh, but I couldn't help it, and after a moment Father grinned too.

"All right," he said. "Maybe I could stand a little converting. But I'll leave that to my own parish priest, and not to some crackbrained yokel who happens to work for me."

[68]

"Father Dunnigan will be flattered."

"You leave Father Dunnigan out of this; don't you go setting him on me. My God, I've got enough troubles without that."

He brooded over them visibly while he pushed the Lincoln, like a bulldozer, uncompromisingly through the late-afternoon traffic: driving with Father was always a nerve-shattering experience of screaming brakes and sudden close-ups of miraculously avoided fenders. In a few minutes, though, the upset I had given him by almost walking in on him and Lucille Hurley apparently started him on another line of thought. I'd always noticed that whenever he felt guilty about something he had done, he was apt to be particularly worried and severe about my moral state.

This time it was the trip I was leaving on the next morning with Ivor's campaign party that bothered him. Like everybody else, he seemed to have certain ideas about Kirby and me, and I suppose he'd decided that this was all Kirby's plan; at any rate, he started out now to warn me seriously against him. I cut him off before he'd gone far enough to embarrass either of us.

"I'll give you the situation in a nutshell," I offered. "I think he wants to marry me, and I don't want to marry him. Now, does that satisfy you?"

"Marry you?" I could see Father's hackles rise. "What does he think—a girl like you—? Kirby's always been a friend of mine, but I never thought—" He started off again. "Why, a girl like you, with the advantages you've had, the kind of people you've been thrown in with—you could marry anybody you wanted to—"

He sounded so hopeful about it that I had a sudden vision of myself as a piece of merchandise temptingly dangled before a row of wealthy prospective sons-in-law, one of whom was going to solve all our problems for us—but that really wasn't being fair to Father. He wanted me to be happy, not just rich; the only thing was, he didn't see how you could ever be one without the other.

"Besides that," he stated dogmatically, between an oncoming truck and a station wagon that refused to be driven off the road, "he's a dozen years older than you if he's a day."

"People's ages haven't anything to do with things like that."

"I thought you just told me you weren't in love with him."

"I'm not. But his age hasn't anything to do with it."

He shook his head. "You ought to be going with some nice college

[69]

boys," he persisted, "having a good time, instead of getting yourself mixed up in politics."

"I am having a good time."

I smiled at him diplomatically; we were almost home by that time, and I hoped we could get off the subject of my future before he worked himself up to the point where he really began to find objections to my going on the trip the next morning. I needn't have worried, as it turned out; the station wagon we had passed came up beside us just then and cut in before us with a derisive blare of horns, and Father settled down immediately to the duel. By the time we turned off at our driveway he had managed to repass the station wagon, and he went into the house with me in complete good humor; I'm certain he had forgotten all about me, Judson, Kirby, and even Lucille Hurley. There were times, I'll admit, when I envied Father.

The campaign trip I started out on the next day was one of those experiences that can only be represented by a graph that begins at a high point on the left side of the page and ends up, after an uncompromising straight-line descent, as low as it can get down in the right-hand corner. For the first twelve hours it was fun to watch the turnouts wherever we went—the bunting-decked halls, the small-town squares packed with people, the sweating, smiling greeters with badges the size of small cabbages on their lapels, the mayors, the sheriffs, the bands playing inevitably "Has Anybody Here Seen Kelly?" It was fun watching Ivor, in his light summer suit and Panama hat, always the center of attention, always smiling, always with the right word for everyone, handling the never-ending stream of people so that each of them went away convinced that his problems would be the first consideration of the new governor. But even toward the end of the first day the routine was wearing a little thin, and by the time forty-eight more hours had passed I was beginning to feel as if I would never be sane again. Life had turned into one of those unending nightmares in which the same scene occurs over and over again—the same people, the same welcoming speeches, the same smiles, the same handshakes, even the same song, which ran through my mind like a banshee's howl even when we were driving along an empty road:

> Has anybody here seen Kelly?
> K-E-double-L-Y . . .

I got so I could predict the people in the committees and the audiences before I saw them—the fat, sweating, ruddy ones, a generic type whether they were in business suits or in suspenders and straw hats; then the lean, dark, innocent, cadaverous ones, with as many joints as a grasshopper; the eager ones who wanted something of you, and the suspicious ones who were afraid you wanted something from them. I used to wonder how Ivor told them apart, but he knew an astonishing number of them by name, and he listened to the speeches and the demands and the requests with a smiling patience that never seemed to waver.

"The perfect candidate," Ken Baggott said one night—we'd all been to a meeting in the high-school auditorium of a small town down near the southern border of the state, and we were sitting around in the parlor of Ivor's suite in the hotel, too tired or too hot to go to bed. There were Ken and Martha and Freddie Devanter, and a couple of newspapermen who were making the trip with us—the last waiting to talk to one of the local political bigwigs who was across the hall now with Ivor and Kirby in Kirby's room. "Yeah man," Ken said, sailing a paper dart across at Joe Rigney, of the Charleville *Journal*, "the perfect candidate. Brother, has he changed. Ed Dodd may as well save himself some trouble and quit talking right now."

Rigney shrugged. He was a stout man who looked a little like an inoffensive bulldog—not very popular with anyone because he had a way of acting as if he were in the know on everything from F.D.R.'s private taste in ties to the best place to get a drink in Peoria.

"He's changed all right," he conceded. "The last time he was running for Congress, you were liable to have to pour him out for the voters any time after six P.M. What did Harvey Whiteley do to him—muzzle him?"

Martha looked over at him—she was sitting under a burring fan with her shoes off and her head back—and remarked to nobody in particular: "Listen to who's talking."

"All right," Rigney persisted. "I just want to know who gets the credit—Whiteley, or Whiteley's daughter, or God Almighty—"

"You can't go wrong with that one," Martha said. "Why don't you stop right there?"

Rigney lifted his shoulders again.

"I like to get my facts straight before I stop," he said. "What about it, Marty?—you trying to tell me he's got religion all of a sudden? What is it—some new kind of Mohammedanism?—'Harvey Whiteley is Allah, and Kelly is his prophet'—"

"Very funny," Martha said. "Excuse me for not laughing." She yawned without moving. "I think I'll go to bed."

"All right, all right," Rigney said again. "But you know what I think? I think he's putting on an act. And I'm betting it won't last. I've seen cases like that before—"

"You've seen just about everything, haven't you, sonny? It must be nice to be so wise."

"You know I'm right. He's loosening up right now." Rigney picked up the dart and sailed it over to her. It landed on her lap, and she flicked it off without looking at it. "I was watching him tonight," he said. "He got rid of four shots of bourbon without blinking an eye when he was priming himself for that speech—"

Martha closed her eyes. "What are you worrying about? It was a good speech, wasn't it?"

"I've heard him make better." He insisted: "I just want to know what's holding him together, that's all. What does it take to turn a guy like that into Harvey Whiteley's errand boy and make him like it?"

Martha sat up with a jerk. "Now that's enough, Rigney. I *am* going to bed. I don't have to sit here and listen to this."

She got to her feet and marched across the room to the door. We sat there watching her: as she opened the door she came face to face with Ivor and the man he'd been talking to across the hall, said good night to them shortly, and walked off down the corridor without another word.

Ivor came over to us. "What's the matter with Martha?" he asked pleasantly.

Nobody said anything. Rigney decided to busy himself with the local politician, and Freddie Devanter tried the mollifying influence of his secondhand presidential smile.

"We've all had a hard day," he said vaguely. He nodded toward the local politician, who was delivering himself happily to the press. "Did you get our friend?"

"I think he's safe."

"Good boy!" Freddie beamed. "Well, I'm going to get some sleep; we'll have to make Dannelstown by noon tomorrow. What about you?"

"I thought I'd work for a while on that La Fayette speech. Was Martha going to bed?"

"I'm not," I offered. "It's too hot to sleep. Shall I get my notebook?"

He worried about it visibly. "I promised Pat we'd take good care of you. Seems to me you've been up till all hours every night since we started this trip—"

The others were leaving; he interrupted himself to say good night to them. When they had gone, he sat down in the chair where Martha had been sitting. I looked at him: under the harsh electric glare his face was pale with fatigue.

"Do you know there was once a time when I enjoyed all this?" he said.

I got my notebook and pencil out of my brief case.

"Couldn't this wait till tomorrow morning?"

"Tomorrow morning I couldn't even crib somebody else's speech, much less write one of my own."

Kirby, who had gone downstairs for the morning paper, came in, looked at the two of us, and advised: "You'd better both go to bed. We've got a tough day tomorrow." He flipped over the newspaper he was carrying to look at the weather report. "'High of one hundred and two degrees predicted.' I wonder who writes these things—somebody on Ed Dodd's payroll?"

"We'll be through in half an hour," Ivor said. "I've got to put the finishing touches on that La Fayette speech."

"You're wasting your time. If it's this hot in La Fayette tomorrow, they wouldn't listen if you were William Jennings Bryan and Amos and Andy rolled into one."

He went on out of the room, looking hot and irritated. Ivor debated: "This seems to be a bad night for everybody. What was the matter with Martha just now?"

"It wasn't anything."

"You're an awfully poor liar, Betsy. Was it something I did?"

"It was only Joe Rigney. He and Martha had a spat."

I felt so uncomfortable that I was sure he would guess from the way I looked that the quarrel had had something to do with him. I bent over my notebook. He didn't say anything; when I finally glanced up he was sitting there looking at me with an odd, kind, ironic expression on his face.

"Poor Betsy," he said. "I'm afraid we've been disillusioning you."

I tried to smile. "Oh, no. I left all my illusions at home when I came on this trip. I practically never travel with illusions any more."

"Young people nowadays are so wise. When I was your age I

thought everything was possible and most things were important. Maybe they were—"

He looked up at the burring fan as if it were concealing something behind it that he wanted to see, but after a moment he dropped the idea and came back to me again.

"We'd better get to work, I suppose. I don't want to keep you up."

We settled down to the speech. The fan burred on; sleepy moths circled around the white globes of the electric lights. It was one-thirty when we finished and I got up to leave. At the door of the suite I stopped and turned to look at him.

"I'll have this for you tomorrow morning before we start. It won't take half an hour."

He smiled at me, thanking me less with words than with the effort it took to summon up the energies of gratitude.

"It hardly seems worth all this trouble, does it?" he said. "But you see I have to say something, and people have the peculiar idea that they oughtn't to be asked to listen to the same thing over and over again—"

He smiled again and said good night, and I went on down the hall to my own room. I wondered how much he knew about how I felt; if he knew anything at all, the only way he showed it was by being even more considerate of me than he was of everyone else.

When I opened the door of the room I shared with Martha, she was in bed with the light on, reading a magazine.

"Where were *you?*" she asked. "I was almost ready to start phoning people."

"Ivor wanted to work a while on the La Fayette speech."

"Did he say anything about that Rigney business?"

"He wanted to know what happened. Of course I didn't tell him."

"Well, somebody will; you can count on that." Martha threw her magazine on the night table, turned around and punched her pillow, and slid down in bed. "People are so awfully kind to each other," she said. "What makes me so furious is, he was right."

"Rigney?" I couldn't believe it; I stood there in the middle of the room, looking at her.

"You've got eyes, haven't you? He's tired to death, and he's sick, and he's got those damn stupid people yammering at him from one end of the day to the other—You just wait; unless God Almighty decides the time is ripe to pass a first-class miracle or two, you're going to see something you didn't bargain for when you came on this trip."

She turned over and said she was going to sleep; there wasn't anything else to do but let it go. But I lay awake for quite a while after I had got in bed, thinking about what she had said and then about what Joe Rigney had said. Of course I wasn't going to believe either of them, but I think I said a few rather special prayers before I finally dropped off to sleep.

The next morning we were on the road by nine-thirty. Dannelstown, where Ivor was to speak before a luncheon meeting of county Democrats, was only a fifty-mile drive from Wye, where we had spent the night, but he was scheduled to put in a couple of mid-morning appearances at public rallies in towns along the way, so we had to get a fairly early start.

You never remember anything very coherent about a day like that. Later, if you try to put it all together, impressions keep darting into your mind like bits of jagged glass: how hot it was, for instance—people crawling around under that pitiless, cloudless blue sky—or the brassy shout of a politician's voice, "Ladies and gentlemen, I have the honor to present"—and the watching eyes, the faces pale or ruddy with the heat, the slow sweat darkening underarm and shoulder-blade of the dress or shirt before you. Or you remember the smell of fried chicken in a small-town hotel dining room, under the solemnly revolving black wings of a ceiling fan, and the rumble and clatter of voices and dishes unnaturally loud in the stifling air, and how fervently you wanted nothing in the world but quiet and a long cold drink. Nobody in our party had slept well, and we took turns at being unreasonably irritable and pointedly polite; by noon we felt about as cordial toward one another as a collection of wild animals accidentally locked up together in a cage in a zoo. Freddie Devanter and Martha had had a dignified quarrel about the best road to take from Wye to Dannelstown, and Kirby and Ken Baggott an undignified one about a slight slip-up in arrangements, and Ivor had that polite, reckless, detached look that I had seen before, in the gas station at Tunbridge; he looked as if he had removed himself from any sense of responsibility for the whole affair, and would rather enjoy seeing how much of a mess we were going to make of it among us.

That attitude of his extended to his part in the program as well; he looked at the people who came crowding up to speak to him with an elaborate pretense of interest that only missed being obvious because the people he was talking to were too full of their own self-importance to have room for anything else in their minds. I sat next to Kirby at lunch, and he muttered to me under his breath: "Remember I told you way back that that guy only cares fifty per cent of the time about making the right impression? Well, this is one of the other fifty per cent—"

"I feel the same way myself. If one more person says to me, 'Oh, you're *Pat* Donlon's daughter! And how is old Pat?'—I'm going to tell them that 'old Pat' was committed to a lunatic asylum last week, and his daughter is just about to follow him."

"It's all right for you. You're not running for governor."

"It's too hot for anybody to run for governor today. There ought to be a Society for the Prevention of Cruelty to Candidates—"

A small, important-looking man in a linen suit rapped on his glass with a knife and commanded the attention of the room.

"If he talks for more than five minutes—" I breathed, to Kirby.

"Baby, you'll sit here and take it, and at the end you'll applaud —enthusiastically. That's what you came along for."

I looked at Ivor. He was sitting there, waiting for the speaker to finish his introduction, with the patient, unconvincing interest of an adult at a children's party. All at once I began to worry about his speech, and about how many pre-lunch cocktails he had managed to crowd into the quarter of an hour Martha and I had spent repairing the damage of the morning's drive—but when he got up and started to talk, I found that I could relax. It wasn't a very good speech, but it was a perfectly proper one, and fortunately people aren't inclined to be overly critical of what they listen to when the mercury stands at a hundred degrees—not if it doesn't last too long, anyway. When he finished everyone applauded politely, and the sweating band played "Has Anybody Here Seen Kelly?"—and Kirby said: "All right. Round three. He won that one on points. Now if we can get out of here before that mob gets hold of him—We still have a three-hour drive ahead of us."

Getting out of there, as usual, was more easily said than done. There were the average number of people who wanted to develop their own importance by being seen in conversation with an important man, and three of them decided to join our party and go on up to La Fayette for the evening's festivities, so it was quite a while before we got under way again. I was in the front seat of the second car, with Martha and Ken, and it was so hot by that time that none of us, including Ken, who was driving, even had a very clear idea of where we were going. Once, missing the lead car when a truck pulled out between us and it, Ken turned off down a side road by mistake, and we drove for fifteen minutes before we finally ended up facing what looked like a pair of wagon ruts leading nowhere except to the clear conviction that we were on the wrong road.

"They'll wait for us," Ken said hopefully. "They'll pull up somewhere in the shade—"

"Isn't any shade," Martha said. "You might as well look for shade in hell. Come on, you optimist, turn this damn thing around and let's get out of here."

"I told you this was the wrong road," Freddie Devanter remarked helpfully. He was the only one of the men who still had his coat on; it made me so hot to look at him that I wished he'd seen a picture of F.D.R. once in his shirtsleeves.

Martha turned round to him. "You might have been definite about that a little sooner."

"Well, I certainly *tried*—"

The car, backing in a sudden half-circle, left the road and went jolting over the baked earth of the field beyond in a series of eccentric leaps, leaving Freddie's dignified response somewhere in the middle of the road behind it.

"For God's sake, Ken," Martha protested, "you're not driving a truck."

"Sorry." Ken stopped the car, wiped his perspiring hands on his knees, and threw the gearshift into first again. "This sure isn't my day."

"It isn't anybody's day," I said. I pointed off at what looked like a creek beyond a row of trees. "Let's all quit and go swimming—"

"Now there's a brilliant idea."

The car slued onto the road again, and we started back the way we had come. I tried to forget about the heat by looking at the passing landscape, but there wasn't much to see—the same hills and tobacco fields and discouraged-looking cows I'd been seeing all day, with now and then a couple of barefoot kids on a sagging front gallery squinting at you against the sun. We hadn't got far enough north yet to have hit the good land and the big white-fenced estates in the middle of the state.

When we got back on the main road there was no sign of the lead car, and we decided to go straight on; Ken was sure he could catch up with it on the road. As a matter of fact, when we got to Marchfield, about a quarter to four, it was the first thing we saw, parked and empty on the main street in front of the hotel. That was an unscheduled stop, and there was a knot of people on the sidewalk outside that was rapidly turning into a small-sized crowd. Freddie put it into words for us: "My God, you don't suppose there's been an accident—?"

"Waiting for us, probably," Martha said. "Come on, Ken, get this thing parked and let's see what's going on."

We all got out of the car and pushed our way through the crowd into the hotel. It was quite a hotel too, I might say—one of those narrow brick buildings with an old white-on-black sign over the door and faded green half-curtains hung before the dining-room windows and the smell of 1910 dust and cuspidors and salesmen's samples in the empty, wooden-floored lobby. Only the lobby wasn't empty now; apparently all the people who had ever worked at the hotel, and all their friends and relatives, were standing around there, looking curiously into the dining room, where our lost party sat at a center table surrounded by what I took to be local politicians.

I looked for Ivor; he seemed to have picked up some animation somewhere, because he was holding his audience engrossed in a conversation that took top billing even over the heat. I'd seen that happen before—that particular sort of lavish expenditure of a magnetism and attractiveness that could make you believe, for the moment, that the world was a place of infinite possibilities and graceful hopes: as a matter of fact, when you were with people who knew Ivor well you always felt as if they were standing around waiting for it, like people who had seen the curtain raiser and were waiting for the real show to begin. But I'd hardly expected a performance today—not out here in the middle of nowhere, at any rate.

I saw Martha's hand tighten suddenly on Freddie's arm.

"Freddie, listen to me," she said tensely, "you've got to go in there and *handle* this; what on earth is Kirby thinking about? Say we've got to get to La Fayette; say anything, only get them out of here—"

She almost pushed him across the room. I clutched onto her arm myself.

"What's the *matter*?"

She glanced at me, then at Joe Rigney, who was peering interestedly over my shoulder into the room.

[78]

"We've got a schedule to make, that's all," she said shortly. "We're wasting time."

"Kelly hasn't been wasting his," Rigney observed. "Listen, Marty, what I was saying to you last night—you want to make a little bet?"

Martha looked straight at him. "You're an awfully nice guy, aren't you, Rigney? I can't understand why I've never liked you."

I watched Freddie talking earnestly and impressively to the group at the central table; they were all getting up now, beginning a straggling line of march toward the door. Martha walked up to Kirby.

"*You've* managed things beautifully, haven't you?" she challenged him.

"How the hell could I help it?" He looked hot and guilty, defending himself against her accusing eyes. "Did you ever try to stop him from doing something he wanted to do? Besides, he's all right."

"You tell that to Harvey Whiteley and Mrs. Conway and that crowd of blue bloods Tyler Dewarr'll have waiting for him up in La Fayette."

"All right, I'll tell them. And if they want my job they can have it—see if any damn one of them can do any better—"

They went out the door together behind the others. Nobody was paying any attention to me; I felt all at once like a civilian who has accidentally wandered into the front lines in a battle zone. Only a tall, hopeful-looking Negro waiter in somebody else's white jacket looked at me expectantly, as if he thought I might be someone important too.

I pulled myself together and went out to the lobby. Through the screen door I could see Ivor standing on the steps, just outside; he seemed to be making a little speech to the crowd, thanking them for their hospitality and regretting that he hadn't the time to say more than these few words to them. I couldn't see what Martha was so excited about; he sounded perfectly all right, and a lot more interested in what he was saying than he'd been back in Dannelstown, at the luncheon.

When he had finished there was a burst of applause, and he went on down the steps and got into the car, the crowd standing back admiringly to let him pass. I opened the screen door and ran down to the waiting automobiles myself. Martha was standing at the door of our car, looking indecisive; after a moment she said abruptly, "I'm going to ride up ahead," and went over to Kirby and said something to him. Kirby came back to our car.

[79]

"All right, Ken, let's go," he said.

"What's Marty up to—trying what a good woman's influence will do?" Rigney asked him.

Kirby didn't look as if he thought it was funny.

"I've got enough troubles without trying to figure Marty out," he said shortly. "Come on, Ken; let's get out of here."

We started off down the main street. Nobody was very talkative; I decided to keep my questions for later. Up ahead I could see the lead car proceeding steadily onward at its fixed distance, as if it were drawing us on behind it by an invisible thread. We must have gone on that way for about ten miles, and then all at once, as it passed a rambling eighteenth-century house set close to the road, the car ahead slowed and almost stopped.

"My God, what now—?" Kirby said.

Ken pulled in behind the other car, just as Ivor looked back at us and called something that I lost in a flurry of spraying gravel when the car he was in suddenly started up again.

"What was that?" Freddie asked.

Ken shrugged his shoulders. "Search me. Sounded like something about a battle."

Freddie looked blank. "A *battle*—?"

"Try 'bottle,'" Rigney suggested.

I reached for a vague memory. "There was a battle around here in 1862 or 1863—at least I think—"

"That's the advantage of having a college girl along on a campaign trip," Kirby said. "She knows all the answers; it's just as good as a guided tour."

I let that go. He and I weren't seeing eye to eye about things these days; I'd tried being polite and firm and sisterly, but we seemed to end up arguing about me anyway whenever we were together. Now I pretended to take an interest in the landscape, but that didn't work either; I could feel him still looking at me, and after a moment he remarked abruptly: "If you ask me, you oughtn't to have come on this trip at all. It's no place for—"

"You sound exactly like Father," I began. But it was too hot to quarrel; I slid wearily down again from the sudden pinnacle of my irritation. "Oh, please, Kirby—I don't want to talk about anything but cold showers and iced drinks now. When do we get to La Fayette?"

"We'll be lucky if we make it by five-thirty. It's all right for you;

the amateurs can retire to their cold showers then, but we've got to go to that damn barbecue—"

I looked straight at him. "I love barbecues," I said. "I wouldn't miss this one for the world."

That settled that, and for the next ten minutes there was peace in the car—till we got to the outskirts of a little town named Butlerville, where the car ahead began again to make eccentric maneuvers. As we watched, it slowed down till we were just behind it and could see the people inside discussing something with either animation or dismay; once it made a tentative half-turn down a side road, but it straightened out again immediately as a hand waved out the window at us and a voice we couldn't identify called something unintelligible back to us.

"Pull up alongside of them," Kirby said irritably, to Ken. "I want to find out what this is all about."

We were driving along the main street of the town then—a dozing row of frame houses enlivened, under the hot late-afternoon sun, by nothing more animated than a yellow hound dog looking for a shadier spot to sleep—and Ken swerved the car out to follow Kirby's directions. The other car stopped and we stopped too. Kirby put his head out the window.

"What's going on?" he called. "Trouble with the car?"

Several voices spoke at once; then they had all stopped, in deference to one another, Martha said crisply: "Ivor has an idea that we'd all like to see the Butlerville Battlefield. He says it's only a few miles out of town—if we can find the right road—"

"The Butlerville Battlefield?" It wasn't all just in the family, so Kirby held on to himself, but I could see that it was a strain. "Do you people know what time it is?"

"*I* know what time it is," Martha emphasized.

I looked at Ivor; he was talking to one of the politicians we had picked up in Dannelstown, explaining something to him as pleasantly as if they had been sitting together in a cool, comfortable room instead of in a broiling car in the middle of a deserted street in a town forty miles from where they were supposed to be. The man looked a little dazed; he kept nodding his head and darting occasional glances out of the corner of his eye at the others, as if he were appealing to them to rescue him.

Kirby said to Martha, with intensity: "You know as well as I do

[81]

we haven't time to go sight-seeing this afternoon; that barbecue's going on right now."

"*You* tell him that," Martha said.

"Ivor—"

Ivor glanced around, lifting his brows in slight surprise. "I think we ought to get started," he suggested. "We haven't too much time—"

"We haven't any time," Kirby said. "We're going to be late as it is."

"Oh, no," Ivor said; "it won't take half an hour. It's an amazing thing, Kirby; I've found out that not one of us in this car has ever taken the trouble to see the place where one of the most important battles—"

"All right," Kirby said. "We'll come down tomorrow. Will that satisfy you?"

"But we're here now," Ivor insisted pleasantly. He spoke to the man who was driving the car. "Why don't you go on? We're losing time—"

The driver looked helplessly at Kirby, threw the car into gear, and started off down the street again.

"I've had enough of this," Kirby announced suddenly. "We're going to La Fayette."

We all looked at one another uncertainly; then Freddie shook his head unhappily.

"I really think we'd better stay with the others."

"Oh, brother," Ken groaned. "A hundred and four in the shade, and he wants to see a battlefield—"

He started the car, and we followed the others down the street. Nobody said anything else; I think everybody was a little afraid to, as if a careless word might be as destructive now as a lighted match tossed into a gasoline tank. I tried to decide what had happened to Ivor, but it was hard to know where to begin—it wasn't likely that it was anything as simple as too much to drink when he seemed calmer than anyone else in the party, only completely determined to go off on a tangent of his own.

I can't give a very clear account of the rest of that trip. We found the battlefield—it was only a few miles out of town, as Ivor had said—and the two cars stopped, and Kirby and Freddie got out and went over to talk to Ivor. I sat there listening to the hot breeze in the trees, and thinking about the people who had died here seventy years before. It all seemed very improbable and sad, with the sun shining and the fluty call of a bird coming somewhere through the branches

[82]

and nobody around but us, and I felt all at once that I wanted to cry. From where I sat I could see Kirby and Freddie talking to Ivor, who was standing beside the car in the hot sunlight, the wind blowing his hair as he pointed something out to them across the road. Ken sighed, waiting with me in the car.

"If that battle was in July, a lot of the people who got killed must have been glad of it," he said, "as long as they buried them deep enough that it was cool down where they were."

"It would be just as hot up in La Fayette, if you were at that barbecue."

He shook his head. "Anyway somebody might offer me a Coke up there. There aren't even any concessions in a place like this."

He looked over, brightening, as Freddie and Kirby started back to the car.

"Are we going?" he called to them.

"We're going."

They came up to the car again, Kirby looking grim and Freddie rather hot and blown; the latter, as he got in, finally succumbed to the heat and took his coat off with a violent gesture. A few moments later we were on the road again, driving fast to make up for lost time, and the only thing I remember clearly about the hour after that was Ken's suddenly asking, twenty minutes after we had left Butlerville behind—"Say, who won that battle, anyway?"—as if he had been seriously thinking of nothing else all that time.

Kirby glanced at me. "Ask Betsy," he said shortly. "She knows all the answers."

"I think it was a draw."

"I'd settle for a draw for this one today," Ken said.

Nobody else said anything. It was past six now, but in the long July afternoon the sun was still high. Time seemed to stand still while we raced along the road and wondered if the day would ever come to an end.

In La Fayette we dropped Ivor at the Dewarr house on Charleston Street and then went on into town to a hotel. The speeches were scheduled to begin at seven-thirty, so all Martha and I had time for was to snatch a sandwich and get into some clothes that looked a little fresher than those we'd been wearing all day. I managed to ask a few questions too, but Martha wasn't in a communicative mood. She suggested that I stay behind at the hotel and have a decent dinner there and go to bed early, and when I said I'd rather go to the barbecue with the others she slammed out of the room and went downstairs, leaving me with a dress that buttoned all the way up the back and nobody to manage the buttons for me. I was afraid they would go on without me, and finally went downstairs with some conspicuous gaps that Martha attended to openly in the lobby, like an exasperated mother with a fractious little girl. Then we all got into the car again and drove out to the race track, where the barbecue was being held.

There was a mob of people out there when we arrived, but we found Ivor right away, over near the bunting-draped stand where the speeches were just about to begin. He was with Harvey Whiteley and Polly Conway, who I knew were also staying at Tyler Dewarr's that night, and it needed only a single glance for me to take in the fact that everything was decidedly not as it should be. Tyler Dewarr —a tall, fortyish man, immaculate in white linen, and bearing the burden of his distinguished appearance with the solemnity of a wealthy man who has decided to devote his nonexistent talents to public service—was hovering nervously over a group of equally dedicated and immaculate gentlemen who seemed to be having difficulty in finding something to talk about: I imagined that his chief function was to prevent them from noticing that Ivor was paying no attention to them at all. On Ivor's other side, Harvey Whiteley was doing the same thing for a group of less distinguished but apparently equally important people who looked like professional politicians. And Polly Conway, in a thin green-and-white dress and a wide-brimmed hat that made her look like a *Vogue* cover for July, had engaged a group of women with an intensity that surprised me; somehow I had imagined that it would make no difference to her whether Ivor won the election or not.

Ivor, for his part, was devoting himself exclusively to a seedy-looking but attractive Irishman of about sixty, who was talking to him happily about Parnell. Ivor introduced him to Ken and Freddie as they came up: "This is Martin Flaherty—Mr. Baggott, Mr. Devanter. Kirby, you know Martin—haven't seen old Martin for twenty years —wonderful piece of luck running into him here—"

He talked a little more carefully than usual, in sudden grave, disconnected phrases that seemed to surprise and please him with their coherency—though, looking at him, I could see no change in his appearance from the way it had been a few hours ago. My heart went down. Kirby greeted Martin Flaherty curtly and then drew Harvey Whiteley aside. They stood near me, under the shadow of the platform; I heard their urgent, angry voices.

"Can he make that speech?"

"Why didn't you warn me? He seemed all right; none of us realized—"

"I'm not his keeper. I delivered him to you; he was all right then—I mean as far as making that speech—"

"You should have seen to it that nothing like this—What kind of position do you suppose this puts me in?"

"All right. All right. *You* brought him out here. It's too late for excuses now, unless a merciful God lets lightning strike where it'll do the most good."

"I didn't realize till we were on the way—"

"Well, as long as he can stand up, he can read. I know the bastard that well—"

A cheerful blast of "Dixie" from the band on the platform above cut short their conference. Harvey Whiteley hurried to join the other dignitaries on the speakers' stand, and I went over to sit with Martha. She didn't even see me as I sat down; she had her eyes fastened on the platform, where Ivor was standing near the edge, saying a few last words to Martin Flaherty below.

"Martha—" I said.

"Don't talk," she said tersely. "Pray."

It sounded like good advice, so while the introductory speakers spread their platitudes under the darkening sky and harangued the bonfires that lit the hot dusk with red smoke, I put in some urgent requests to Providence. From where I sat I could see Polly Conway with Mrs. Tyler Dewarr, who looked as if she had got into the wrong church by mistake, and was trying her best to act as if she weren't horrified by the strange ritual. Mrs. Conway herself seemed as cool as ever, but she was biting the corner of her lip—most people have some sort of mannerism when they're angry or upset. I thought that the crowd had noticed nothing yet. There wasn't anything to notice, really, except that Ivor, sitting on the platform in a fresh linen suit that put him practically in uniform with everybody else up there, seemed more interested in a whispered conversation he was having with one of the local politicians than in the speeches that were being made. The politician was a serious young man, and he had to speak in a few minutes himself; I could see that he was doing his best to put

[85]

an end to the conversation so he could concentrate on what he was going to say. Now and then, in spite of himself, he smiled, and then immediately looked sternly serious again. Finally he shifted his chair a little farther away and pretended to be engaged in a frowning contemplation of the speaker's back.

His own speech, when he came to make it, was full of the impassioned incoherence of party politics—or maybe I was getting a little lightheaded by that time, between the heat and the strain of waiting, and wouldn't have been able to follow him even if he had been making sense. When he sat down I applauded automatically, but I was watching Ivor. At the front of the platform a tall, enthusiastically red-faced man was introducing him to the crowd, and I saw Kirby, who was sitting directly behind Ivor, lean forward and say something emphatically in his ear. I glanced anxiously at Martha.

"What will happen if—?"

"Don't say it. Don't even think it."

She was following every move Ivor made as he got up and came to the speaker's stand, as if she were trying to control his actions by her own concentration. We sat there listening to the first words—"Mr. Chairman, ladies and gentlemen"—there was going to be nothing to worry about, then? The crowd had quieted expectantly; this was the feature presentation, and they wanted to hear it from the beginning. I tried to imagine what it would be like to stand there facing all those dim blurs of upturned faces, to be the pinpoint of attention on which the whole night was hung: it was a rather frightening thought. But Ivor looked perfectly serene, standing there before the speaker's lectern with his hands spread flat upon it, leaning a little forward as if he were about to take the audience into his confidence about something.

"Holding on," Martha muttered cynically, beside me.

I turned to her, shocked. "Oh, no. He's all right—isn't he?"

"You're one of the most optimistic—"

She broke off to listen as he launched into his speech. I listened too, but for the first five minutes I doubt if I understood what I heard; at any rate, it took me fully that long to realize that what I was listening to wasn't even remotely connected with the speech I had worked on with Ivor the night before. By the time I did realize it, though, there didn't seem to be anything to worry about, because in the exchange the audience had certainly got the better of the bargain. Instead of a discussion of the lamentable results Ed Dodd's declared fiscal policy would have on the economy of the state, they were getting a brilliantly humorous résumé of the difficulties of political campaigning—something like a capsule presentation of what I had learned during the past weeks, only with all the grief removed, so that it sounded as outrageously amusing as something out of *Alice in Wonderland*. The audience loved it, but I could see that it was being received a little less kindly on the platform, where there were covert frowns and whisperings, and finally signals of outright alarm. I glanced at Martha again for guidance, but she merely looked grim and shook her head without taking her eyes from the platform.

I suppose that went on for a quarter of an hour. I had a queer feeling that everything had suddenly stopped and that I was going to sit there forever, hearing Ivor's voice punctuated by the sudden waves of laughter that swept over the crowd like a gay wind, watching his brilliant, amused glance as it ranged from one to the other of them, as if he were presenting each of them personally with his best gifts—

And then, all at once, it was over. He simply picked up his copy of the speech, the original one that I had typed, and began to read it, like a bored child who is tired of performing and is going through his part as fast as he can so that he can escape again into his own more interesting world.

Of course it didn't go down. People who would have sat there obediently listening to that speech if he had begun reading it to them with the proper gravity at the outset, now obviously felt they were being cheated. You could almost see their expectation turning into astonishment, and their astonishment into resentment—a sort of "nobody-talks-to-*me*-that-way" attitude. He wasn't even bothering to look up from the manuscript, or to wait for the applause that might have come—people are polite down there—if he had acted as if he really wanted it. I turned to Martha rather desperately.

"Does this *have* to go on? Can't anyone stop it?—say he's sick?"

She looked at me without saying anything; she didn't have to say it, because I could say it myself: "If you came for the whole ride, you came for the whole ride. And this is what it's like—" I watched Ivor up there under the lights; there was no pretense now that he wasn't clinging to the lectern for support, or that he even understood or cared what he was reading. From the back of the crowd a few shrill whistles began to come; somebody high in the grandstand said, "Louder, please," in a subdued voice, and then, encouraged by the ripple of laughter that followed it, repeated it more audibly, "Hey,

Kelly—a little louder." I saw Ivor glance up briefly from his manuscript, scan the audience with an air of slight surprise, as if he had just discovered its presence there, and then go on indifferently with the speech again. On the platform Tyler Dewarr and Mr. Whiteley were conferring excitedly. Obviously something was going to happen; they couldn't just sit there while the attention of the audience, held by nothing more tangible now than the thread of its curiosity as to what was the matter with Ivor, crashed and exploded before their eyes.

It was Kirby, though, who finally put an end to it. Watching the platform, I saw him get up and move unobtrusively to a hurried conversation with the band-leader; a minute later, when Ivor came to the end of a paragraph and paused to turn a page, the band broke loudly into "The Star-Spangled Banner," everybody stood up, and in the confusion Ivor was faced with the *fait accompli* that his speech had come to an end.

Almost before the last notes had died away, Martha and I were on our way to the platform. We pushed through the crowd, which was puzzling excitedly over the abrupt end of the program; a brief flurry of additional excitement immediately ensued when, from the platform, a voice suddenly inquired over a megaphone if there was a doctor present.

"Window dressing," Martha flung it back to me succinctly, over her shoulder. "Heat prostration will sound fine in the papers tomorrow."

We got around somehow to the rear of the platform. Back there a car was cutting recklessly across the grass from the parking lot, scattering curious onlookers right and left. It drew up with a sudden squeal of brakes beside a tight knot of white-linen backs and shoulders gathered at the foot of the steps that led up to the platform, and, as Martha and I watched, the door of the car was opened, the white-linen barrier fell apart, and we had an abrupt glimpse of Ivor being helped into the back seat of the car. We pushed nearer to the automobile; Kirby was getting in, and Tyler Dewarr. We heard the voices, puzzled or angry, all around us.

"Chrissakes, wha's a matter with him?"

"Here's a doctor—is this a doctor?"

"Tell him we don't need—"

"—damn near fell off the platform—didn't he?"

"—said he had heart trouble—"

"I just get him out of here—*get him out of here!*"

The car slued desperately, trying to turn in the crowd; frustrated, the driver leaned furiously on the horn. I found myself all at once almost under the wheels. The door of the back seat, still hanging open, was snatched from inside and slammed to, and through the open window I had a brief vision of Kirby's flushed, intent face. At the same moment Ivor sat up suddenly beside him.

"When you say 'campaign,'" he announced clearly, to nobody in particular, "I've seen campaigns compared which this—sensible as a dictionary."

The car started forward with a jerk, and as it bore him away he collapsed again peacefully; with his head leaning against the back of the seat, he immediately and gravely fell asleep. It was only after he had disappeared from sight that I realized that in his right hand, as tenderly and possessively as a child clinging to a favorite toy, he was clutching a small American flag.

Martha and I didn't go straight back to the hotel. The Dewarrs had planned a small party at their home on Charleston Street after the barbecue, and in a few minutes' discussion we managed to convince each other that, in spite of what had happened, it was our duty to show up there for a while.

What was going on when we got to Charleston Street, though, looked more like a wake than a party. Everybody was sitting around gloomily staring at the family portraits on the walls, and the Negro servants who were carrying around cocktails and sherry for the guests stepped apologetically, as if out of deference to a body laid out in the next room. Martha and I sat down and listened to murmurs of ". . . unfortunate," ". . . unreliable," ". . . terribly bad effect," till I wanted to scream. Finally, in desperation, I cornered Freddie and engaged him in what was meant to be a gay conversation; in that room it was at least a conspicuous one. It made Freddie uncomfortable, but I was satisfied with it when I caught some doubtful murmurs of—"*Pat* Donlon's daughter?" behind me; if they disapproved of me too, it seemed to bring me a little closer to Ivor.

Kirby wasn't there when we came in, and neither was Polly Conway, but after a few minutes they both came downstairs—Kirby still looking flushed and angry, and Polly merely enigmatic. The others gave them the sort of welcome that is usually reserved for the members of a conspiracy who have drawn the short straws and the task of disposing of the body.

[89]

"Everything all right?" Tyler Dewarr asked them doubtfully.

"Just fine and dandy." Polly located the nearest tray and said, looking critically at it: "I'd like a Martini—preferably a double Martini. I have a feeling I ought to rise to the occasion."

"My dear, you've been splendid," Mrs. Dewarr observed helpfully. "Hasn't she, Tyler?"

"We've all been splendid," Polly said. "I'm going to see about medals—what is it?—for conduct above and beyond the call of duty— Applications will be taken at nine tomorrow morning."

Harvey Whiteley interrupted her with violent dignity: "This is no laughing matter, Polly. God knows what those people out there thought of that—that exhibition tonight."

"Let's be optimistic and hope they blamed it on the heat," she suggested. "By the way, who was the genius who had the brilliant idea of calling for a doctor—?"

A small, dark-haired man whom I recognized suddenly as Mr. Anonymous put himself forward modestly, if a little confusedly.

"But I thought he really needed—I mean, I didn't know—"

Polly smiled. "I think that's lovely. You see, Daddy, you needn't have worried, after all. Ivor keeps a really splendid façade till the very last moment."

"If I'd known that *before* we went out there tonight—" Mr. Whiteley stared around defiantly at all of us, as if we had suddenly accused him of something. "After all, I had no way of knowing what went on earlier—what the rest of you people—"

"We could keep a log," Martha offered acidly. "Itemize all the pertinent facts and then ask for a receipt on delivery."

"I *really* think—" Tyler Dewarr began offendedly. Everybody looked at him respectfully. "It's my opinion," he said stiffly, "that incidents of this sort *must* be avoided in the future."

As that was about as obvious a statement as if he had informed us that it was a hot day, it didn't do much for the conversation, which immediately lapsed into its former state of hushed gloom. I went over to Kirby, who was sitting by himself at the end of a long sofa, as if he suspected he had some sort of plague that he didn't want to communicate to the rest of the company.

"How is Ivor?" I asked him.

He looked up at me morosely. "How do you think he is? He's sleeping it off."

I sat down. "He really isn't very well, you know. A day like this—"

"A day like this is what he knew he was letting himself in for before he took this business on. I'd like to wring his damn neck."

"All you people—"

I started to say it and then decided against it; it was about as useless trying to put forward any defense of Ivor in that room as it would have been trying to make out a case for Benedict Arnold. Kirby must have seen something in my face, though, because he said to me all at once, in the tone of violent accusation that seemed to be in the air that night: "Anyway, what business is it of yours? What's your interest in all this? A girl like you—"

"I like him," I said. "Does that surprise you?"

"No, it doesn't surprise me. If you think I haven't noticed—" He broke off suddenly. "Pat phoned me this evening—did you know that?" he demanded.

"No." I looked at him, a little puzzled by the abrupt change of subject. "How is he? Is anything the matter at home?"

"Not at home—at least he didn't say—But something's bothering him, all right," Kirby said darkly. "I thought maybe it was something about you and Ivor—"

"About—?" I stared at him; I was too astonished to be angry. "Why, he hardly knows I'm alive!"

"Oh yes, he does." Kirby nodded sagely. "I've seen him looking at you—And what was that business last night, about your having to work on that speech with him instead of Martha?"

"But that's what I came on this trip for," I said. "Somebody had to do it, and Martha'd already gone to bed." All at once I *was* angry. "Do you mean you think we weren't working—?"

"I don't think anything at all," he said stubbornly. "All I'm saying is, Pat hinted I ought to keep an eye on you. He's worried sick about something; he asked me to stop in at the house to see him before I do anything else when I get back tomorrow."

I stood up. "I think Father must be out of his mind," I said distinctly. "I'm going back to the hotel; Martha doesn't seem to be enjoying this party either."

I walked over to where Martha was sitting, but my presence seemed to have an unsettling effect on people that night; all at once, as I reached her, a quarrel that had been smoldering for the past ten minutes in long silences and brief acid comments between her and Harvey Whiteley burst into open flame.

"All I'm saying is—"

[91]

"All right. I've heard it."

"All I'm saying is, his responsibility to us—"

"I'll tell you about his responsibility to you. You expect him to act like Little Lord Fauntleroy eighteen hours a day, and teach you how to run a political campaign at the same time—"

"Martha—" I said.

She looked up; fifteen years of never saying the wrong thing to the right people came winging back just in time.

"I thought we might go back to the hotel," I said. "I'm afraid I'm terribly tired."

Polly Conway came up.

"You're not going?" she asked me. "Just when I was thinking I ought to be better acquainted with you. I suppose you know that the only thing Ivor woke up enough to say after we got him back here tonight was—'I hope Betsy didn't see that'—"

I tried to smile. "He thinks I'm not quite grown up yet, you know."

"I can see his point. You look as if you'd be at home in a Brownie uniform even now. Maybe it's something about the way you wear your hair."

This time it was Martha who managed to keep the peace by dragging me off to say good night to Mrs. Dewarr. A few minutes later, though, in a taxi on our way to the hotel, I finally had the chance to say it: "She is one of the rudest people—"

"You oughtn't to mind it," Martha said. "She's just jealous."

"Of me?" I couldn't believe it. "Why on earth should she be?"

Martha shrugged. "I'm too tired to explain, but I'll give you a start. No woman likes to see the man she's interested in making protective gestures toward another woman—even when she isn't looking for any protection herself. Ivor'd better watch himself."

She was the third person in the space of fifteen minutes who had hinted to me that I was attracting more of Ivor's attention than I realized. I sat back in the taxi, wondering who was mistaken. It was an odd feeling—like the feeling in a dream in which you have been standing for a long time outside a locked door, and suddenly it begins to swing open before you. . . .

V

NEXT DAY, early in the afternoon, we drove out to Charleston Street to pick Ivor up for the drive back to Queensport. It was Sunday—after a morning thundershower a different world from the blurred one of yesterday, full of heat and irritation and fatigue. This one sparkled and swung under a fresh breeze and a sky of sudden blue; I wore a new linen dress, crossed with a little cape that covered my shoulders, and waited expectantly for something to happen.

"Something" was ten minutes alone with Ivor while the others went with the Dewarrs to inspect the famous L'Enfant garden behind the house. It was an unexpected reward of virtue, because I had stayed behind in the house only to pick up the last-minute papers that had to be taken to Queensport for further attention—some mail, newspaper clippings, ideas for political strategy left behind by last night's guests. While I was putting them into a brief case, the library door opened and Ivor walked in. I was going to smile and say "Hello" and let that be that, as far as the night before was concerned, but when he saw me he stopped and shrugged up his shoulders in a little gesture of apology or deprecation.

"You see," he said, "you *have* been disillusioned. I'm sorry; I hoped till this morning that you hadn't been there."

I didn't know what to say; finally I simply remarked: "I know all about things like that, you know. Father's not exactly an angel."

"Pat's a careful man, compared to me. There's a right time and a wrong time for making a fool of yourself. My particular talent is for picking the most conspicuously wrong time—"

He sounded so pleasant and regretful about it that I guessed suddenly at how accustomed he was to scenes like this: after so many times it became nothing more than a matter of words, a game you played, using counters that you only pretended represented something real. I was glad there was something I had learned from living with Father—that you didn't try to change people you cared about. You took them as they were or you hadn't anything at all.

"I'd like to forget about yesterday," I said. "On a day like that everybody does things they'd never think of doing on any other day. We all quarreled so much—it felt like my first morning at school: by ten o'clock nobody was speaking to anybody else, and six little girls were in tears—"

"Not you, though."

"How do you know?"

"You'd have been too busy making peace. I wonder where you learned that wonderful tact?"

"All the Irish are tactful—except when they're being *un*tactful on purpose," I said. "Isn't that true?"

"I suppose it is." He looked at me seriously for a moment. "You oughtn't to cultivate it, though, you know," he said. "It's a terrible mistake to want to please people; after a while they get so they expect it of you, and you end up without any principles or without any friends."

"I wasn't really—"

I wanted to tell him that nothing I had said to him had anything to do with tact, but I didn't know how to put it into words. He understood me, though; he said to me suddenly: "Do you realize I don't even know how to talk to you properly in your own language? What do people in your generation say when they want to tell somebody they're very grateful—?"

"We're not in different generations. We're just at opposite ends of the same one."

"It's nice of you to say that, but it isn't even remotely true. I wish it were." He moved over to the window and stood there looking out at the fresh summer landscape. "What's it like, I wonder, to have a fine new life ahead of you with nothing to regret and everything to look forward to?"

I didn't say anything; I was listening in my mind to that *I wish it were*, wondering what things might be like if he were twenty-two now to my twenty. He might really have fallen in love with me then, because there wouldn't have been any Stella Blair or even any Polly Conway, and everything might have been different from the way it was now. I was so absorbed in that thought that I didn't notice he had turned away from the window again and was standing across the room, smiling at me.

"What were you thinking about?" he asked me.

I came back to earth abruptly; I could feel myself coloring up.

"About the election," I lied. "It will seem queer when you're governor—"

"*If* I'm governor," he corrected me gently.

"Oh, no. You will be. You'll live down in Fidelia, and we'll never see you—"

"You and Pat could come down and visit."

"Could we? That would be lovely. Father loves being with important people."

"Don't you?"

I considered. "No, I don't think so. So many important people got to be important—didn't they? simply because they knew how to walk over other people better than anyone else." I looked at him, smiling. "I don't mean you."

"Not important enough or not ruthless enough?"

"You aren't ruthless at all. You like people too much."

He shook his head. "I used to, but not any more. Don't you know about people like me? We got into the bad habit of wanting people to like us when we were young, and now we go through all the same old motions because we haven't enough energy to change the pattern."

It seemed to me that the conversation was getting complicated; wondering if he was trying to tell me that I was only one of those people on whom he had expended that automatic effort, I lost the happiness of being with him and found myself all at once standing in a strange room with a stranger.

"What's the matter?" he asked me.

"Nothing's the matter."

He stood there a moment in silence; suddenly he said, in a kind of exasperation: "You build up some kind of idea of what I'm like—"

"I haven't built up anything at all. You've always been wonderful to me; if you aren't the way I think you are, you've never done anything to make me believe it—"

My brief case was on the table. I picked it up; I wanted this to be over now.

"Wait a minute," he said.

"I ought to go back to the others. I told them I'd only be a minute."

"I've hurt your feelings. All I seem to be able to say to you today is—'I'm sorry.'"

He sounded different, not so much kind as unhappy. Our eyes met, and all at once things slipped back into focus again; we both smiled.

"All right?" he said.

"All right."

That was the moment that Polly Conway chose to come down the hall and into the room. She stood in the doorway looking at the two of us, and if she didn't like what she saw she didn't show it; she seemed as cool as she ever had.

"*You* look rocky, darling," she said to Ivor, and, to me: "How's the Girl Scouting business today? I suppose you've done your good turn and convinced Ivor that that slight social error of his last night really didn't bother you at all—"

"I thought it was the Brownies," I said. "I'm glad I've graduated."

Ivor looked from one to the other of us.

"What's this all about?"

"It's a private joke," Polly said. "We had a short conversation about you last night—about your touching desire to shield Betsy from finding out about the seamier side of political candidates' lives. Don't you remember worrying about that when we brought you back here?"

"I'm worrying about it right now," Ivor said pleasantly. "If you want to quarrel with me, why bring Betsy into it?" He glanced over at me. "Why don't you go on now and join the others? They're not very exciting people, but you ought to find their conversation a good deal more interesting than this."

"You really ought to let her stay," Polly said. She walked over to the window and stood with her back to it, facing us both, her hands jammed into the pockets of the green linen suit she was wearing; I saw all at once that she wasn't quite so cool as she seemed. "She might find it educational," she said. "She looks like the kind of girl who could use a little education along that line. Or are you trying to keep her altogether naïve, so she'll be more useful to you on occasions like this?—to build you up when you've done such a marvelous job of knocking yourself down—"

"That doesn't come under the category of a joke, Polly," Ivor said. He was not being pleasant any more.

"Doesn't it? I'm sorry. I know you don't like dull conversation—or at least you didn't use to, before you began taking an interest in the kindergarten. I don't really try to be too amusing any more, darling, because I know you may be out of prac—"

"I think I'd better go on," I said.

I started toward the door, but Ivor stopped me.

"Wait a minute," he said. He looked at me, then at Polly. "I realize you're still upset about last night," he said to her, "but that's no excuse for taking it out on Betsy. I think you owe her some sort of apology—"

"It's really all right," I said.

I wanted to get away; I didn't want things to get any worse. Ivor shook his head. "It's not all right at all—"

"You're so terribly polite yourself," Polly said to Ivor. "I understand that, of course; you've practically made a career out of it—but you can't expect everybody else to be as careful as you are to cover up the truth. There's a point where people lose interest in pretending things are the way they aren't."

I made up my mind, said, "I *really* have to go," and walked out of the room. In the hall I came across Ken, who'd been sent in to look for Ivor; there was a newspaper photographer outside, he said, who wanted to get a picture of him with the Dewarrs in the garden. I told him Ivor was in the library and went out to join the others. It's hard to know how you feel at a time like that; you're too busy trying to remember everything that happened and see if it fits any of the interpretations other people have given you.

I wasn't in the same car with Ivor during the drive up to Queensport that afternoon. Kirby managed it that he was the one who drove Martha and me, while Ivor went in the lead car with the others; and the two cars lost each other altogether long before we got near Fort Paris. It wasn't a very cheerful drive, because nobody seemed to feel like talking, but I didn't mind; I had a lot of things to think about myself.

When we finally got to Fort Paris, about four-thirty that afternoon, Kirby let me off in front of the house and then left at once to drive Martha up to Queensport. I went on up the walk to the house. Aunt Bridgie met me at the door, but before she had time to say more than two words to me Father came rushing downstairs, half-shaved, with lather still all over one side of his face.

"Where's Kirby?" he demanded. "Didn't he come in with you? Holy Mother of God, can't he get anything straight? I told him I wanted to see him—"

"He'll be back right away; he had to drive Martha up to Queensport." I went over and kissed him on the cheek that was free of lather. "What's the matter with you?" I asked him. "Aren't you glad to see me? You haven't even said 'Hello' to me."

"I've got something on my mind." He wiped his face distractedly with the towel hanging over his shoulder. "Now you be a good girl, Betsy, and run along—don't bother me. I've got something to talk over with Kirby. Are you sure he said he was coming back?"

"Of course he is."

I wanted to ask him what it was that it was so important he talk over with Kirby, but it didn't seem likely, from the way he was acting, that it had anything to do with Ivor and me, as Kirby had suspected, so I let it go. I took off my hat and went into the living room with Aunt Bridgie.

"What on earth's the matter with Father?" I asked her. "He acts as if he were expecting the Last Judgment any minute now."

"I haven't the slightest idea." Aunt Bridgie closed the living-room door and came over to face me solemnly. "*I* think he's going out of his mind," she said. "I wanted to call Dr. Weaver, but he wouldn't hear of it—said he'd throw him out of the house if he set foot inside the front door—"

I stared at her; Father was always excited about something, but he'd never managed before to work Aunt Bridgie up to the same state too.

"But what *is* it?" I asked her. "You must have some idea—"

"All I know is that it has something to do with the election." Aunt Bridgie confided it to me impressively; I was a little relieved to see that she was rather enjoying the dramatic effect she was creating. "He came in here a few days ago looking like a wild man; he said we were all ruined—said he'd have to give up his business, this house, the furniture, everything, and that you'd have to leave college and get a job. Of course I didn't take him seriously at first—you know how your father is; he exaggerates everything—but when he said he was going to sell the cars, and then went out to the kitchen and gave Ester her notice—"

"He really let Ester go?"

"Well, not exactly. He told her the next morning she could stay, and he hasn't sold the cars either—said we might as well go to the poorhouse in style. But he acted so peculiarly about it all; really, I didn't know what to think. And he hasn't been sleeping—he prowls around here at all hours of the night—and he simply doesn't *see* me when I talk to him—"

Aunt Bridgie was beginning to sound a little incoherent herself; I could see that she wouldn't have been the most satisfactory confidante in the world for Father if he really was worried about something.

"I'll go upstairs and talk to him," I suggested. "Maybe I can get something out of him."

I went upstairs, but I wasn't too optimistic; Father still had a way of treating me as if I were about nine years old when there was anything important in the wind. He had finished shaving when I got up there, and I went on into his room with him and sat on the bed while he put on a tie and brushed his hair.

"You don't seem very glad to see me," I said. "Maybe I should have stayed away a little longer."

Father turned round from the mirror. "I should never have let you go in the first place," he said vehemently. "God knows what might have happened to you. You know a man all your life, and you think you know what sort he is, and then all of a sudden you find an innocent young girl—"

"What *are* you talking about?" I asked. This was beginning to sound suspiciously like the kind of thing Kirby had been hinting at, but I couldn't imagine what either Ivor or I had done that could have sent Father into a state like this. "Kirby said you were upset about something, but I thought—"

"I've got a right to be upset."

"About me?"

He stared at me suddenly. "You? No—what gave you that idea? My God, *you*'re not in any trouble?"

"I'm not in any trouble at all. But you are—and I can't seem to find out why—"

He sat down miserably in a chair opposite me.

"Oh, it's that damn Kelly," he said. "If Kirby doesn't come here pretty soon so I can get it off my chest, I *am* going off my rocker. I told Kirby it wouldn't do to trust him."

"But what's he done—?"

I knew it couldn't be what had happened the night before down in La Fayette that was bothering him; he had phoned Kirby before he could possibly have heard about that. But, whatever it was, it looked as if I wasn't going to find out about it now, because Father realized all at once that he was talking to me and not to himself, and got up and said definitely that it wasn't something he could discuss with me.

"You may as well tell me, you know," I said. "If you don't, Kirby will. Are you afraid Ivor's going to lose the election?"

"I know damn well he's going to lose it." Father checked himself, giving me a harassed glance. "This isn't anything for you to get mixed up in," he said. "Why don't you go downstairs and talk to your Aunt Bridgie?"

"If it's about the election, I'm already mixed up in it," I said. "Don't you remember?—I work for Ivor."

"Well, you're not going to work for him any more," Father said positively. "You're through with him as of this minute, and that's final."

He walked out of the room without waiting to hear my reaction to that. I followed him downstairs and into the living room, but before I could pick up the conversation again the doorbell rang, and Father jumped for the door. It was Kirby; I heard Father berating him in the hall: "It's about time you got here. Didn't you understand what I told you over the phone? This can't wait—"

The two of them came into the living room together and Father shut the door; I think he had forgotten I was in the room till he turned around and saw me there. I forestalled what he was going to say.

"I won't say a word," I offered. "I'll just sit here in the corner. Otherwise—I've never made a practice of listening at keyholes, but I *am* going to find out what this is all about."

Father made a gesture of despair. "All right," he said. "I can't stop you; anyway, maybe this will be a lesson to you. A man can't watch over his daughter all hours of the day and night."

Kirby looked at me as if he had walked in at the middle of a complicated movie and was waiting for somebody to tell him the plot.

"Father thinks Ivor is going to lose the election," I explained. "That's as far as I've been able to get."

"You mean because of last night?"

"Last night?" Father took it up. "Holy God, if all I had to worry about was what happened last night!"

"You'd better begin at the beginning," Kirby suggested, and

Father said resignedly: "All right. At the beginning. First place, you know a fellow named Judson—Ike Judson—works for me?"

"Judson? I don't think—"

"No reason you should. He isn't anybody—just a hillbilly with a worn-out wife and a raft of kids and Jehovah on the brain—nothing you could use for collateral in a bank. He came up here looking for work and I gave him a job, and now I'm his friend, or his father-confessor, or his favorite sinner that he's going to convert to glory— I don't know. That's how I happened to hear about this in the first place—"

Kirby looked impatient, but I was remembering something, searching for a name—fitting it finally to the tall man with the Ancient Mariner eyes who had stopped Father outside his office on the day before I'd left on the campaign trip.

"But what's this Judson got to do with the election—?" Kirby was saying.

"He's got everything to do with it; will you just wait a minute and let me tell you?" Father mopped his forehead desperately with his handkerchief. "A few days ago—sometime last week—he buttonholed me and said there was something he wanted to talk to me about. I didn't think anything of it; he's always coming to me with some kind of problem or other—once it was a teacher sending one of his kids home from school with a note saying he ought to wear glasses—things like that. Anyway, this time it turned out to be something a damn sight more serious. Somebody had gotten his oldest girl in trouble—to make it worse, she's only fourteen—and he told me he had good reason to believe it was Ivor Kelly—"

Kirby shook his head incredulously. "And you fell for that? My God, Pat, that's one of the oldest—"

"Now wait a minute, wait a minute. Sure it sounded fishy to me— first thing I thought was, 'Who's behind this, and how much is there going to be in it for Judson?' But I didn't think that very long. First place, I know Judson; he'd rather see that girl dead than mixed up in something like this—"

"But if she is mixed up in it, he hasn't any objection to picking up a little cash out of it on the side," Kirby said cynically. "And somebody just happened to suggest to him that the pickings would be a lot fatter if he named Ivor as the father of that kid, instead of some John Doe that nobody ever heard of—"

"Will you shut up and listen to me?" Father interrupted him, exasperatedly. "I tell you this is on the level; the only way Judson found out it had anything to do with Ivor at all was when his wife came across a picture of him the girl had cut out of a newspaper. That's what set them on the track; the girl'd been scared enough to tell her mother she was pregnant, but she wouldn't tell her the name of the man. Then they found this picture, and after they'd badgered her with it for a while she admitted the whole thing—"

"That still doesn't prove anything," Kirby objected. "Even if Judson is on the level, the girl could be lying."

"She could be, but she isn't. I've talked to her; she knows Ivor, all right—he picked her up one night last April in a diner on Jessup Street. I've checked it all out: the counter man there remembers seeing her with him; he recognized Ivor, and thought they made a damn funny pair. He says he saw her go out of the place with Ivor and get in his car."

Kirby began to look a little worried.

"Is he sure of that?"

"Sure enough to swear to it, in court or anywhere else." Father looked at him, excited and earnest. "I tell you, Kirby, we've got to do something about this before it's too late. When this gets around—"

"Hold your horses," Kirby said. "It doesn't have to get around. How many people know about it now? Judson, his wife—?"

Father shook his head in despair. "If you think you're going to buy him off—You don't seem to realize—the man's a fanatic; his idea of settling all this is to go out and find Ivor and put a couple of bullets through him. I had all I could do to call him off that."

"What good would that do him?" Kirby suddenly looked skeptical again. "This whole thing sounds pretty crazy to me. First place, it isn't like Ivor. He may not be any plaster saint, but a kid like that—"

"That's just it," Father insisted; "she *is* a kid. Do you realize she's under the age of consent in this state? You know enough law to figure it out that, with a girl that age, Judson wouldn't have just a paternity suit if he took it to court, he'd have a case of statutory rape—and if *that* word ever hits the front page of a newspaper—"

I had kept out of it all that time, but there seemed to be something obvious that needed to be said, and as nobody else had said it, I put it in now myself.

"Why don't you call Ivor and ask him what this is all about?" I said. "There's probably some very simple explanation, and I can't think of anybody who'd be more likely to know it."

I suppose they had both forgotten I was there; Father especially looked as if a piece of furniture had suddenly made a suggestion to him.

"'Out of the mouths of babes—'" Kirby said. He got up. "She's right; do you mind if I use your telephone?"

"Wait a minute—wait—Before you get him over here—" Father looked from one to the other of us, as if he didn't know which one to deal with first. He finally settled on Kirby. "Look," he said hastily, "we've got to play our cards right in this thing, you know. If he can't explain it—and I don't see how on God's earth he can—we've got to make some arrangements—"

"Arrangements?" Kirby said. "What about? Hushing it up?"

"I tell you it can't be hushed up!" Father said frantically. "What do you think I've been trying to do ever since I heard about this? Do you think I'm some kind of God-damn amateur that doesn't know what strings to pull? You can take my solemn word for it that outside of committing murder there's no way to keep that fellow quiet."

Kirby looked at him rather queerly. "Just what are you getting at, Pat?" he asked.

"What I'm getting at is that we have to protect ourselves." Father went over to him; he was so agitated that for a moment I thought he was going to take hold of the lapels of Kirby's coat and hold him there to make sure he didn't get away. "Listen," he said urgently, "we didn't know what we were getting into when we went into this campaign, did we?—and if there was a chance something like this would come up, we had a right to know—" He began again: "What I'm saying is that if Kelly let us walk into this blindfolded, our responsibility to him—I've got a family, a business; I can't just sit down and see them ruined because I was led into something—"

"To put it in words of one syllable," Kirby helped him out, "you want to take a walk."

"All right. All right. Put it that way if you want to. All I'm saying is that I'm going to get out while the getting's good. And you can't say I'm not being one hundred per cent on the level with you. With what I know, I could go over to Ed Dodd and write my own ticket —but I'm giving you your chance too—"

I don't think I had ever liked Father less. For a minute I didn't even believe it; you know how it is—you try to tell yourself you didn't actually hear what you know you heard. I suppose it was the way Kirby looked that really convinced me.

"Not let me get this straight," he was saying to Father. "You mean you want us—the two of us—to go over to Ed Dodd and throw all this in his lap, make a deal with him and sell Ivor out—"

"We're not selling anybody out," Father insisted. "I tell you, this thing can't be kept quiet; it's going to come out one way or another, whether we do anything about it or not."

Kirby just stood there shaking his head.

"So help me God," Father kept on solemnly, "I wouldn't walk out on Ivor if there was one chance in a million we could win now with him. You know me, Kirby; you know what I stand for—but Saint Michael the Archangel couldn't win an election in this state with this sort of thing hanging over him. And I told you before, if I don't get a winner this time, I'm through. I'm in up to my neck—"

"We're all in up to our necks," Kirby said grimly. "I can start chasing ambulances for a living if Ed Dodd wins control of this state— and there are damn few ambulances to chase these days. But, my God, Pat, we can't just sit down and give up without even trying what we can do. This Judson, for instance—there must be some way we can get to him—"

"I can fire him, if that's what you mean," Father said, "and a hell of a lot of good that will do us. He doesn't need money to take this to court; all he needs is to open his mouth. And if you think he's not going to open it, you're making the biggest mistake of your life. You know those hillbillies and their women; he's going to get Ivor if it's the last thing he does. You can thank me that you haven't got a dead candidate on your hands right now."

"Well, that would have solved our problems all right," Kirby said wryly.

I couldn't keep quiet any longer.

"You both seem to have forgotten one thing," I said, "that this story can't possibly be true. And if it isn't true, you can prove it—"

Kirby shrugged. "'Can't possibly'—?" he repeated. "You sound pretty sure of that. Where do you get your information?"

"You said yourself it wasn't the sort of thing Ivor would do."

"People are always doing the sort of thing they wouldn't do. If you haven't found that out yet—"

Father said to me suddenly: "You haven't any business being in here in the first place. What kind of a thing is this for a young girl—?"

He walked over to the hall door and opened it, as if he expected me to take myself out of the room at once. I sat where I was.

[104]

"I think it's a good thing I am here. I seem to be the only person in this room who has any sense left—"

"That's no way to talk to your father. Are you going to get out of this now, or will Kirby and I have to go somewhere else to talk where we can be alone?"

He was so upset and excited by this time that I saw I had better go. I got up and looked at Kirby.

"You *are* going to call Ivor before you do anything?"

"Right away."

He followed me out to the hall; I heard him on the phone as I went upstairs. Aunt Bridgie was up there too, and she wanted to know what was going on, but I told her it was something about the election and to please leave me alone. I couldn't talk about it; now that I was out of it, I felt as if the whole world had suddenly come to an end.

I went into my own room, and in fifteen or twenty minutes I saw Ivor's car pull up in front of the house. He came up the walk and went inside; I heard him talking to Father in the hall downstairs.

"What's this all about?"

"You'd better come in here . . . something serious—"

The living-room door closed behind them. I waited upstairs for a quarter of an hour; then I threw pride and ethics to the winds and went out and sat on the stairs in the hall, listening to find if I could hear what was going on. It wasn't much good; Ivor and Kirby both talked too low for me to be able to do more than identify their voices, and all I got was an occasional phrase of Father's when he raised his voice excitedly: ". . . damn well have to prove it"—". . . says he saw you"—". . . you admit that, but you expect us to believe—" Even that, though, was enough to make me realize that what I had been praying for—that Ivor would be able to explain the whole thing away as some terrible mistake—was no longer in the realm of possibility. He knew the girl, or had seen her, or been with her, under circumstances that could do nothing to allay Father's worst suspicions.

It was over an hour before the living-room door opened and the three of them came out. None of them was looking at the others; Father in particular had the miserable expression of a man who has just come from a funeral and is afraid he will go to pieces and burst into tears if he meets anyone's sympathetic eyes. I looked at Ivor; he was pale and grave, not so much angry, I thought, as serious and incredulous. He was the first of the three to see me, as I stood up, and he flashed a sudden glance round at Father.

"What does Betsy know about this?"

"She knows too much about it." Father came over to me. "I thought I told you to stay out of this now," he appealed to me, almost tearfully. "Haven't I enough trouble as it is, without having to worry about you too?"

"There's no reason for you to worry about me." I spoke to Ivor. "I didn't hear what you told them, but I wanted you to know I don't believe that story."

He looked at me; for a moment I had a confused impression that he thought I was merely being polite.

"You seem to be in the minority," he said, "but I'm glad it's a split decision, anyway. It isn't true, if that's any consolation to you."

I could tell, from the way he avoided looking at Kirby and Father, how deeply he had been hurt by their refusal to believe him, and I suddenly remembered Martha's words: "He's always cared so terribly what people think of him; you might not believe it, but even now—" I don't think he quite understood yet what had happened, in terms of his political future; he was still too involved in his personal adjustment to this new picture of what people were willing to believe of him.

Kirby, to give him credit, did interrupt uncomfortably: "Now wait a minute; I didn't say—" but his voice didn't carry much conviction. I turned to him; all at once I was so angry I didn't care what I said.

"You're even worse than Father," I accused him. "You don't believe him, but you're not even willing to say you don't, because you haven't quite made up your mind yet whether you'll be perfectly safe with Ed Dodd." I looked at Ivor again. "I suppose they've told you their little plan? I'll have to give Father credit for that; it was entirely his idea—"

From the blank expression on all three of their faces I saw that I had opened a door that wasn't intended to be opened; apparently nothing had been said in there about the "arrangements" Father had planned for himself and Kirby, to insure their being on the winning side. Ivor turned to Father.

"What's this about, Pat?"

"Damn it, Betsy!" Father exploded. But he couldn't keep it up; the fact of his betrayal was there, hideously, for us to see, and all the bluster in the world couldn't hide it. "Well, what else can I do?" he cried suddenly, appealing to us all. "It isn't as if we could keep it quiet—" He shook his head desperately, turning to Ivor. "You know how it is with me; I'll go under if you can't beat this thing. And you said yourself, you can't prove—It's not a personal thing; you understand that, Ivor—but I've got to protect—"

He went on, stumbling through excuses, justifications; finally as if he felt our shame for him even if he felt none for himself, he stopped, breathing hard, looking at us like a cornered bull. Ivor was the first to break the silence.

"I think I'll go on," he said carefully. "Good-by, Betsy."

"I'll be down at headquarters the first thing in the morning," I said.

He looked at me. There was the oddest expression on his face for a moment; the only way I can describe it is to say that he looked as if he were seeing something he didn't quite believe in, like a ghost or a mirage. He didn't say anything; he only stood there looking at me, and then he started toward the door. Before he reached it, though, Kirby, who hadn't said a word since I had dragged out that plan for a deal with Ed Dodd, all at once came to life and called: "Wait a minute—" Ivor stopped and turned around. Kirby stood there awkwardly, as if he hadn't really meant to say that; then, suddenly— "Ah, the hell with it," he said. "I'm going along with you. Pat can do what he damn pleases."

I wanted to stand there and cheer. They went out together, leaving Father and me alone with everything that had happened there between us like a dead body that we either had to pretend to ignore for the rest of our lives or decide to dispose of then and there. The first course was the one we seemed to have been following about unpleasant situations up to now, but I made up my mind that this time it was going to be different. If Father went ahead with what he planned to do, he was going to do it with the full knowledge of how I felt; this was too important for me to be able to be tactful about it.

As it turned out, though, I needn't have worried about being tactful, because the moment the door had closed behind Ivor and Kirby, Father turned on me as if I had been his worst enemy.

"You—" he cried excitedly, "you, my own daughter, turning against me—It's bad enough for Kirby, but my own daughter—Well, let me tell you this: what I'm doing, I'm doing for you—"

"If that's true, you needn't do anything at all," I said. "I don't care if we haven't a cent; I'd rather starve than get money this way."

"You'd rather starve—" Father slammed his hand down on the newel. "What the hell do you know about what it's like to go hungry?

Your grandfather knew what it was to go to bed with an empty belly—many's the time I heard him tell it—but you stand there with your fine clothes and the fine education I've bought for you—"

He was so upset that I couldn't help feeling sorry for him; maybe I'd been sorry for him before, but it isn't easy to take that final step from being the one who is weaker and less wise to being the one who has to try to be wise for both.

"I'm sorry, Father," I said. "Really I am. But it doesn't change things. Ivor hasn't done anything; you can't go to Ed Dodd with that story—"

"Hasn't done anything?" Father repeated it furiously. "How do you know what in hell he's done? He admits he picked that girl up on Jessup Street and drove her home; do you think that was all there was to it? Well, I'm telling you this, and you'd better get it through your head here and now: I'm not having my daughter mixed up in a thing like this. You're through with that campaign of his as of now."

I shook my head. "I can't do that. You can walk out yourself—I can't stop you from doing that—but you can't stop me either from going back—"

Aunt Bridgie, who had come downstairs at the sound of Father's raised voice, walked into the discussion at this point with what was meant to be a soothing word.

"Now, Pat—Betsy—" she said, "what on earth is this all about? It sounds dreadful upstairs; people will hear you, you know, Pat, even if you don't shout."

"I'll shout if I feel like shouting," Father said, "and who has a better right, with what I've got to put up with around here? My own daughter telling me what to do, like she was Moses on the mountain, with a direct line to God—"

"I'm sure Betsy didn't mean—"

"I don't care what she meant. But I'll tell you one thing I mean. She's going to stay clear of Ivor Kelly and that damn campaign of his, if I have to send her all the way to California to see that she does it. I'm not going to have it said that my daughter's associated with a man like that. It's one thing for a man without a wife to want some kind of normal companionship, and another for him to go around seducing children—"

I wasn't going to listen to any more of that; by this time I was almost as angry as he was.

"Yes," I said, "we know all about your moral principles. They're broad enough to cover Lucille Hurley—I suppose that comes under the heading of 'normal companionship'—but not—"

I didn't even finish it; it was one of those things that you're sorry all your life afterward for saying, and that you'd take back the instant after you've said it if you could. I wanted to take it back the moment I saw Father's face. Maybe there are families in which it's coolly taken for granted that a daughter is acquainted with the existence of her father's mistress, but ours hadn't got anywhere near that far yet; I'm sure that Father, with his convenient ability to overlook even his most obvious faults, was perfectly convinced that I had been completely in the dark about Lucille Hurley all those years. I know it isn't sensible, but that's the way it was: if you didn't talk about it, to Father, it wasn't there.

He didn't say anything now; he just stood there looking shocked and guilty, with the anger all draining out of his face. Aunt Bridgie started to say something—I don't know what it was: a kind of incoherent remonstrance to me, or Father, or Fate, or all three—but Father didn't wait to hear it. He picked up his hat and walked out of the house, not neglecting to slam the door behind him, though, as a final defiant notice that I hadn't beaten him, even with that.

I stood on the stairs, looking at Aunt Bridgie. There didn't seem to be anything to say; after a moment I turned around and went up to my room and closed the door. I don't think I had ever felt lower in my life.

V I

WE didn't hear from Father again till he called from Queensport sometime around two in the morning, long after we'd gone to bed. I wasn't asleep, so I got to the phone first and answered it, but all he would say to me was that he was staying in Queensport overnight; he simply hung up when I tried to talk to him. I knew we couldn't have done anything but quarrel, because neither of us was going to give an inch, but I wanted at least to try once more to stop him from going through with his plan about Ed Dodd. Afterward I found out that by that time it was already too late; he had gone straight from the house to Ed Dodd, or somebody connected with his organization, so that even if he had wanted to, he couldn't have stopped the whole Judson business from spilling out into the open then.

It was dawn before I finally got to sleep, and when I went downstairs, a little late, Aunt Bridgie said Father had come in shortly before, shaved and had breakfast, and had already gone out again. As far as I could gather from her account of the conversation she'd had with him, he hadn't said anything about my not going up to Queensport to Ivor's campaign headquarters; in fact, he hadn't said anything at all, except that he had a lot of things to attend to, and that he wouldn't be home till late. I thought that was a little peculiar, in view of our last conversation, but then nothing seemed to be happening any more the way I expected it to happen.

Aunt Bridgie, to whom I'd given the bare outline of what was the matter between Father and me, did say something rather hopefully on her own about my staying home that morning—"You didn't sleep well, and you're just back from that trip"—but I told her I felt fine and went out to the garage to get the car. I couldn't imagine what I was going to find at headquarters, but whatever it was, I was going to be there.

As it turned out, what I found was a good deal more than I had even thought of imagining. When I came in there were half a dozen reporters and photographers in the outer office, whom Freddie Devanter, minus his presidential poise for once, was vainly trying to get rid of: "There's no use you fellows hanging around here; we haven't got a story—" Even I, looking at him, would have known better than to believe that.

Besides the reporters, there were a dozen or two other people standing around like sinners who had just heard the Last Judgment announced; they looked, at the moment, as if they were trying to make up their minds whether it was only a false alarm or whether they had better try to beat the crowd and see if, by making themselves agreeable to Satan, they couldn't get a little cooler accommodations in hell. When I walked in the door, there was a universal hopeful turning of heads, followed by an almost equally universal drop to disappointment. I say "almost," because one reporter recognized me and yelled: "Hey, it's Pat Donlon's daughter—how about that?"—as happily as if he had been mining for gold and had at least struck silver. In three seconds I had the whole crowd of them around me—"How about it, Miss Donlon—is your father going over to Dodd?"—"What's Pat got on Kelly?"—"Is he sending you up here to keep a foot in both camps?"

Freddie pushed his way over in alarm.

"Betsy's one of our regular workers here. Now look, fellows, I told you there was nothing to it; doesn't this prove—?" he began anxiously.

From the way he looked at me, I knew that the less I said, the better he would like it, so I tried to seem surprised at all the attention I was getting. I don't know how successful I was, but it didn't make much difference, because Martha rescued me almost at once. She simply marched up, announced that I didn't have anything to say, brought me into the inner office, and closed the door.

She stood there then, in the middle of the room, looking at me.

"Well," she said, "I didn't expect to see *you* here today."

"Didn't you?" I felt a little uncertain; I wondered if she thought I was condoning what Father had done. "I told Ivor I'd be in."

"He mentioned it. But I thought Pat might have other ideas."

"I don't care about Father's ideas. I want to help, if I can."

"The best way you can help is to get out of here and stay out." Martha went over to the desk and straightened some papers, looking at them as if she would have been happier if they had been death warrants. "You're a bright girl, Betsy, but you know all kinds of things you shouldn't know, and if you stay around here you're going to say something you shouldn't to one of those happy ghouls out there."

"But how do they know anything at all about this?" I asked. "I mean—I haven't even seen Father since yesterday afternoon; has he—?"

"He hasn't held any press conferences, if that's what you mean, but he left a fine, broad trail last night; even a second-rate hound dog could have followed it to Ed Dodd's headquarters and figured he had something treed when he heard the howls of joy that were coming out from behind the door. They've got a pretty good idea out there of what it's all about; all they want to know is whether it's true, and what we're going to do about it."

"But it *isn't* true, Martha," I protested. "Can't Ivor talk to this Judson—make him understand—?"

"Any conversation Ivor has with Mr. Judson," Martha said grimly, "is likely to take place in a courtroom, with a judge and a jury and as many other people for an audience as can crowd in without knocking down the walls. I'm reliably informed that Mr. Ike Judson was too busy last night entertaining a few helpful and sympathetic friends of Ed Dodd's to have time for any other social calls, and this morning it seems he has a pressing engagement in town to swear out a warrant for the arrest of a certain Ivor Kelly—"

I stood there looking at her; I suppose that somehow I'd never believed till that moment that it could actually happen.

"Martha—" I said finally.

"Yes?"

"Where is Ivor now?"

"In La Fayette; he and Kirby went down late last night. Harvey Whiteley's still down there."

"Then what will happen? What will Mr. Whiteley do?"

"What Mr. Whiteley will or will not do," Martha said, "will depend entirely on what Mr. Whiteley thinks will be the most profitable course of action for Mr. Whiteley to take. That's all there is to it. Simple, isn't it? I'll bet you could have thought of it yourself if you'd really tried."

"Martha, don't joke—"

"I'm not joking. I never felt less like joking in my life."

She was only bitter and tired—I realized suddenly that she had probably been up most of the night—and it surprised me when I discovered that, in spite of her brusqueness with me, she wanted to talk. Leaning against the desk, she launched into a sudden angry monologue that disposed of Father and Harvey Whiteley and all the others who, in one way or another, were using Ivor in their own desperate scramble for money or self-importance or power.

"They never gave him a chance," she said. "They walked in on him when he was still in the middle of the shambles he and Stella had made of their world, when he didn't care whether he ever saw the hands of a clock go around another circle, and said, 'Boy, we need you, we're your friends, just come along with us and you can't lose.' He should have laughed in their faces—"

She told me the rest of the story that morning, the one she had begun for me in this same office—told it to me as if what had happened had destroyed some need for reticence, some loyalty that seemed more misguided than friendly now. It began again with Stella Kelly; you had to go that far back, it seemed, to pick up the threads of the situation we held now in our hands. It wasn't so much that she and Ivor were in love with each other, Martha told me, as that they were convinced they deserved each other; they were the prince and princess of a fairy tale—the brilliant young lawyer who was going to win all the golden prizes the world had to offer, and the beautiful girl whom everybody was going to admire and love—so of course they had to fall in love with each other and marry and live happily ever afterward. And if living happily ever afterward seemed a rather old-fashioned thing to be doing in the twenties, they were willing to add all the modern improvements—sudden trips and parties and expensive hotels, and friends whose tangible riches they could match with the bright intangible coin of their own wit and charm.

"I don't think Ivor ever in his life wanted seriously to be rich," Martha said. "What he wanted was simply that the world should do unto him as he was willing to do unto it—give him its best gifts as he was willing to give it his. Of course that's an extraordinarily naïve attitude to take; most of us seem to be born knowing that it's not worth while even to try to be kinder or braver or more generous or intelligent than the rest of the world, because that isn't the kind of merchandise the world is willing to pay high prices for. But then you have to remember that the world had cheated Ivor at the outset by promising him extravagantly that that was just what it was going to do. There was the war, to begin with, where being braver and more efficient than other people made him a captain and won him the kind of citations the best success-stories feature; there was Hollywood, where a famous director's beautiful daughter walked down the aisle with him because he was handsome and brilliant and 'most likely to succeed'; and there was politics, where a combination of all those things simply catapulted him into a position of sudden importance and unlimited prospects. Maybe if he'd had more experience before all that began, he might have accepted it as a freak of chance instead of a divine dispensation, but the point was that it wasn't a freak of chance to him; by the time he came back to Queensport he was as involved in what he took to be the inevitable fulfillment of his dream as a five-year-old with his nose pressed against a candy-store window and a whole dollar in his pocket.

"I can tell you the exact day," Martha said, "when the first big crack appeared in that dream. Oh, there'd been smaller cracks before that time, but they were the kind that don't require major repairs—parties that ended in a binge instead of a celebration, friendships that faded into a mutual dislike, small betrayals by people he trusted, and unimportant quarrels with people he loved. Maybe he'd begun to realize by that time that people who are cowards don't particularly care for courage, except in the few special instances where it will benefit them, any more than dishonest people care for honor, or dull people for wit, or cold people for love; maybe he'd even found out that, no matter how rich and important people are, there are an awful lot of cowardly and dishonest and dull and cold people among them. But I don't suppose he had much time to think about things like that during those early days, so he went on automatically believing in the splendid sort of dream world he'd built up in his mind during all the years when he'd been trying so desperately to get into it."

At any rate, the day she was telling me about, the day the first big crack appeared in the dream, was a January day in 1927. There was an obscure bill under consideration in the House then that Ivor intended to vote against on party lines—no great national or moral issues involved, except that if it passed it stood to benefit a certain Charleville company rather substantially. Martha remembered his coming into the office that morning and telling her rather puzzledly that Stella had at last begun to take an interest in politics; she'd been after him half the night, he said, to change his vote on that bill, on the grounds that she'd been at school with the girl whose hus-

[114]

band's company was going to be on the receiving end of the bonanza if that bill passed: "She was my best friend at school, and they've been having a terribly hard time—lost their first child last year, and now this thing's hit them. She says Bill will have a breakdown if this doesn't go through." Everyone knows that sort of story; Ivor must have heard it a hundred times before he'd been in Washington a year, but, coming from Stella, it was different.

It ended in his changing his vote, and as a result the bill squeaked through. Three days later Stella impressed a cocktail party with a new mink wrap; she told Ivor she'd paid for it with "some old Liberty Bonds I didn't even remember I had; Daddy bought them for me at a rally in Hollywood in 1918, and I found them in a trunk with some old dance programs when I was going through things for the charity bazaar—" She was so circumstantial about it that he never thought of not believing her; it wasn't till three months later that he found out by accident that the coat had been paid for by her "friends" in Charleville, for value received.

"Of course anybody who knew her could have told Ivor that was exactly the sort of thing he could have expected Stella to do when she found herself wanting something she hadn't any legitimate means of getting," Martha said; "she'd always imagined she could be a law unto herself simply because she was prettier and more unpredictably interesting than any other girl around. But it hit Ivor like one of God's own revelations; all at once he saw his marriage, that he'd been used to thinking of as one of the great love affairs of all time, as a sort of shabby game in which Stella was using him and in which he was playing the part of the second-rate Prince Charming who couldn't even support his princess in the manner to which she had been accustomed. They finally patched it up, after a complicated quarrel in which the coat went back to Charleville and Stella very nearly went with it, and when people saw them together a week later they looked the same handsome, successful young couple as ever— maybe they even believed themselves that they were. The façade was still there, and you can forget the cracks in the foundation and the dry rot in the walls for a long time if you concentrate on that.

"I don't want to give you the idea, though," she said, "that this one incident was any more important than it was. It was just one that I happened to see myself, and it brought things out into the open that had all been properly covered up before. Nobody loses things like faith and love and hope and courage overnight; it's a process like carrying sand in a sack with a tiny hole in the bottom—for a long time you don't even feel it trickling away. And maybe if you're careful you can even get through your whole life before the sack is empty, especially if there wasn't much in it to begin with. It's when the sack is full that the weight of it widens that tiny hole in a hurry, and before you know it there's a stream flowing out that nothing can stop. Which is a practical way of saying that the very quality that made Ivor so successful, his ability to believe—in himself, in Stella, in the possibility of a finer, more splendid life than the rest of us even dreamed of—was the quality that made him so vulnerable to all the daily meannesses, the petty betrayals, the personal failures, that the rest of us simply take for granted. It doesn't rock most men off their pins to find out that their wives are small, selfish women who are interested only in their appearance and the admiration it excites, any more than it particularly worries them that their own consciences are capable of being tampered with by their desire for success or for love—'What the hell,' they say, 'that's the way the world goes; I'm no worse than the next fellow, and neither is Stella'—or Mary, or Annie, or whatever her name happens to be. But when Ivor saw the fraud instead of the miracle, he wanted to throw the whole damn mess away.

"Oh, he did a fine job of throwing his success away," Martha said. "I was there, and I saw it happen—not all at once; in fact, it went so slowly at first that only the people on the inside knew anything about it. Stella knew it, and she was the one who was in the position to do the most about it, but she couldn't be bothered; she was too busy trying to convince herself she was still the prettiest girl at the party. And after a while I don't suppose even she could have done anything, because by that time Ivor had begun using a first-class intelligence to observe the human race—including himself without benefit of faith or hope or love or pity, and had come to the logical conclusion (which is one proof that God is Love, and not Reason, or He would have come to that conclusion long ago Himself) that the human race, including himself, had no real reason for existing. Under those circumstances the personal choice that was open to him seemed to lie between a permanent and a temporary oblivion, and while I suppose he would have been happier if he had been the one who was carried out of that auto accident to the morgue instead of the hospital, still he'd managed to do a pretty good job of it up to that time in the way of the temporary oblivion you can get out of a bottle.

"But the point was that he wasn't the one who ended up with that problem in oblivion neatly solved for him, and after the doctors had stopped shaking their heads over him and had decided that he was going to have to go on like the rest of us, earning his daily bread and living with people and making up his mind what was important and what wasn't, he had to try to put things back together again. I don't suppose it was easy. He was like a hopelessly crippled man who has to learn how to walk again; he knows he will never be able to run or move like a normal person, but he can at least manage to the point where he isn't a burden on society.

"That was about the time that Harvey Whiteley heard the voice of God telling him now was his chance to move into the political big time in this state; all he needed was a small matter of a name that would draw more votes than Ed Dodd's would. All right—I know as well as you do that if Ivor had been Sir Galahad he would have told Whiteley to go to hell; he would have told him that anyway ten years ago, even if he'd been only plain Ivor Kelly. But ten years ago was ten years ago, and a lot of water had run over the dam since then, and once you've come to that highly logical conclusion that the human race—including yourself—has no real reason for existing, it's hard to get excited about anything it does. Well, you can say this much, anyway: Ivor's been keeping his feet on the ground even if he hasn't managed to keep his head in the stars, and that's some kind of accomplishment, if you're handing out medals, when you remember where he was going a couple of years ago. But what happens now, if this thing sticks, and Whiteley and the whole crowd walk out on him—?"

That was all of it; that was the story—and Martha came back from the past with the same question with which she'd started out. We were there in the present again, in that hot empty room, with reporters and scared politicians milling around outside the door, but it was still the same question that we had to answer. So I had to be the hopeful one; I had to be the one who said: "But what if he doesn't walk out? Father did, but he had something to gain, not just something to lose. What will Mr. Whiteley have to gain—?"

"Not the undying gratitude of Ed Dodd, anyway," Martha said. "You're right about that; Pat's already got all of that there is on the market sewed up tight. I suppose what you're really trying to tell me is that if Whiteley doesn't win with Ivor he can't win at all. But even he—as much as he wants to win—won't risk backing a candidate in this state with a charge like that hanging over him, unless he thinks he has at least an outside chance—"

"And he hasn't got that?—that outside chance?"

"Maybe he has. He has if he's smart enough and wants to win bad enough. You can fight fire with fire, even in politics, and sometimes it works—"

"With fire?"

She looked at me; it was almost as if she hadn't been talking to me all that time, but had been reasoning something out for herself, remembering out loud and then trying to reason out what would happen next.

"Oh, for God's sake, will you go on home?" she said. "Go home, and stay there, and keep out of this."

"But you'll let me know—?"

"You can read it in the papers. You won't even have to go past the first page; just look at whatever's under the biggest headline."

The telephone rang on the desk and she picked it up.

"Who?" she said. "No, he's not here. No. No, you can't. I can put Freddie on if you like, but he can't—All right, hold on a minute."

She put the phone down.

"Another one of them," she said. "I thought I told you to go on home."

"I'm going." I went to the door. "Shall I send Freddie in?"

"Tell him it's Alec Bates, in Charleville."

I went out. I didn't think she was angry with me, personally, but she might as well have been. It occurred to me that Father had done a good job, after all; it was no wonder that he hadn't bothered to press his point about my not coming up here any more.

I didn't go straight home when I left the Sadler Building. I suppose I put in as much as a couple of hours driving around on back roads in the hot summer-morning quiet—the sort of thing you do when you haven't any place to go because somebody has suddenly closed the door on the place you thought you were supposed to be. When I finally got home Aunt Bridgie was waiting for me at the door.

"Where have you *been?*" she asked. "I called you an hour ago in Queensport, and they said you'd gone home."

"I drove around for a while." From the way she looked, I couldn't tell whether she was furious or just upset. "What's the matter? Has Father—?"

"It isn't your father at all—or it is, in a way—but he hasn't been near here. It's that woman—"

"Mrs. Hurley?"

"She had the boldness to call here and ask for you. She wouldn't give her name, of course, but I'm sure that's who it was—said you were to call her at some Corioli number—"

"What number?"

"You're not going to call her? Betsy, you can't—I won't—"

"Please, Aunt Bridgie. She must have had some reason for calling; it may be important."

"I told her I wasn't sure I could reach you."

"All right. You thought you could tell me, and I wouldn't call, but you still took the number—"

She gave in suddenly. "I wrote it down on the pad on the telephone stand. But you're not going to—"

I went back, looked at the number on the pad, and picked up the phone. It was a woman's voice that answered the long ring at the other end of the wire.

"This is Betsy Donlon," I said.

Then the pause—the moment she must have foreseen and been ready for, only when it came she didn't know how to say it any more than she would have if we had met by accident on the street. The voice tried to be formal for a moment, shifted to confidential appeal, gave up finally in despair: "Miss Donlon—I suppose you don't know who this is. My name is Lucille Hurley; I wonder if I could—I mean, I'd like to talk to you—"

It was a warm, frightened voice, not quite uneducated—the kind of voice that goes with little frame houses and matinees at neighborhood movies and a best set of dishes with roses on them and a permanent twice a year at the La Mode Beauty Shoppe on the corner. You know what to expect from voices like that, or at least I did, because I'd grown up with them till I was fourteen—and all at once, listening to it, I knew what Father, with his stubborn insistence on Bryn Mawr and the Old Southern Mansion on the La Fayette Pike and the country-club set in Fort Paris, had been looking for and had found. You can get to the top all right, if you're willing to fight the odds with every weapon in the book, but it's likely to be pretty cold up there.

"I'm at home," I said, over the wire. "Do you want to come out, or shall I—?"

"Oh, no," the voice said, in quick alarm. "I wouldn't—I mean, I didn't—Couldn't I meet you someplace—?"

"The Briarley?" I suggested. It was a restaurant in Corioli. "I can be there in half an hour. If that's what you were thinking of—"

"Yes." The voice appealed to me suddenly again. "I wouldn't have called you, but you see I didn't know—"

"I'm sure you had a good reason. In half an hour, then?"

I couldn't talk there, with Aunt Bridgie hearing every word I said. She came forward as I hung up the phone.

"What does she want?" she asked.

"I don't know. To talk to me about something—"

"About Pat?"

"I suppose so. What else could she talk to me about?"

I started toward the door; I hadn't even taken off my hat, so there was nothing to do but get past Aunt Bridgie and out of the house.

"Betsy—" she said to me.

"I'm going, Aunt Bridgie. How could I possibly not—"

"Your father will be furious."

She threw that at me as a last forlorn hope, trying to bring the weight of Father's authority into it even in his absence, but she must have known herself that it wouldn't work.

"I'm sorry," I said. "I can't help that. I'll have to go now—"

I walked past her and opened the door and went outside. The car was still in the driveway where I had left it. I could feel Aunt Bridgie watching me from the house, and then I had started the car and was beyond the driveway, out on the Pike again, alone in the hot midday sunlight with the sound of the smooth-running engine and the breeze blowing past and another problem to think about. Only I didn't even think about this one. This one was going to have to wait till it actually walked up and spoke to me.

That was a little under a half-hour later, in the Briarley. When I walked in, the first person I saw was Lucille Hurley; she was sitting at a table near the door, wearing a brown printed voile dress and a white hat and gloves—even then I realized that she had got herself up for me and was worrying that the effect might not be right. I went over.

"You're Mrs. Hurley, aren't you? I'm Betsy Donlon."

"Yes, I know. I've seen you before. But I didn't think you—"

She stopped. We were both embarrassed, but something came to our aid in time—maybe the thought that, however bad the moment was, it was there only because we were both doing something we had to do. A waitress came up and I said: "I haven't had lunch—"

"Yes. You go ahead and order something. I'll just sit here and have a cup of tea."

The fact of the waitress's presence settled us both; it gave us a surface of everyday matters on which we could walk for a little while. When she had gone, Mrs. Hurley said: "I suppose you're wondering why I asked you to come here. I didn't know whether you *would* come—"

"Of course I'd come. It's about Father, isn't it?"

"Yes." From the way she looked, I guessed that she was trying to think how to say it to me. "You see, I didn't know any other way to find out—"

"To find out—?"

She made a distracted little gesture. "Whether it was true what he told me this morning. I suppose I may as well tell you—he wants us to stop seeing each other—for good; he said it was on account of you. So you were the one—"

She didn't finish it; she just sat there, waiting for my reaction to her words. But I didn't say anything, and after a minute she went on more tentatively: "He said you'd get yourself in some trouble and he couldn't stop you, not with you knowing about me and putting him in the position where he—So he said it was the way now he'd always told me it would have to be, if the time ever came when it would hurt you—He even wants me to go away; I've got a sister in Chicago, and he said I could go up there for a while—"

She stopped again and waited for me to say something, but I still wasn't ready yet; I was remembering what Martha had said that morning: "You can fight fire with fire, even in politics, and sometimes it works—" Somehow there seemed to be a connection, but I couldn't find it yet; there was too much that I still didn't know.

"Go on," I said. "What else did he tell you?"

She shook her head. "Oh, I can't tell you all of it. He was excited, and then I was too—he said a lot of things—"

"About politics?"

"Yes, that too—about some trouble he was in over the election. He didn't explain; I just knew he was worried—It didn't seem to have anything to do with this." She looked at me suddenly. "Do you think it did?"

"I don't know. I don't know enough about anything yet. I haven't even seen Father since yesterday afternoon, and people talk around things in front of me—"

"He said you'd had a quarrel—"

"Yes. That much is true, all right."

The waitress came back with iced tea and a salad, and I realized all at once that we had been talking to each other like a pair of conspirators, people with too much at stake between them to care about or even notice the peculiarities of their relationship to each other. Now, engaged with teaspoons and napkins, we had to go back to the ordinary world again, and with the ordinary world the embarrassment came too. I saw her sitting there, waiting. You try to guess about people's feelings, but it's only a guess; all I could see was a kind of awkwardly wistful envy, the sort of expression you see on the faces of the women who make up the crowds in newsreels, watching somebody a great deal more fortunate than they are themselves.

"You know," she said to me, in a sudden burst of frankness, "It's not the way you think, about Pat and me. I always thought it was just like we were married; Pat always said we would be married if Frank— my husband—was ever to die. And for a long time, you know, we were just good friends; it wasn't the way you think—"

"I don't think anything at all," I said. "Please don't think you have to explain—"

"Only I'd like you to know how it really was." She kept sliding into situations like a desperate amateur on skates for the first time, then extricating herself and starting out all over again to fall into another one. "At first he'd just come to the house for a glass of beer," she said, "and we'd sit around and talk, or play a game of honeymoon bridge— things like that. He was always talking about you—what a fine girl you were, just like your mother—and how he didn't ever want to do anything to hurt you. I used to feel like I knew all about you; I even cut your picture out of the paper once, when you were in a high-school play. Afterwards—after things got serious between us—he used to worry that somebody might find out about it and tell you. He always said you didn't know anything about us, but I thought that was just one of his ideas—you know how he never sees anything he doesn't want to see—and I guess I was right—"

"Yes," I said. "Please, don't—"

"I just wanted you to know. You see, at first it didn't seem to matter so much, because Frank—my husband—he was out in Arizona; he got t.b. three or four years after he left me, and I found out through a friend of mine that he wasn't expected to live. I wrote to him, but we never did get along, you know, and he didn't even answer the letter; there for a while I thought maybe he was dead. But then I got a postcard from him, from Phoenix—said he was giving up his religion and getting a divorce and going to marry a girl out there. They've got two children now; I hear about him every once in a while from a friend of mine who went out there to live—"

I wanted to stop her; it was like sitting in a confessional without being a priest. But she kept on with her awful, commonplace, vaguely comic, genuinely tragic revelations: "We talked a lot about getting married, but both being Catholics—well, unless Frank died —Pat always did say he had to think about you, what kind of an example it would be for you if he gave up his religion. And of course it would have hurt him in business—"

"Of course," I said. "And that was important, wasn't it?" She looked at me, a little taken aback by my tone. "I'm sorry," I said. "I suppose I'm not feeling very friendly toward Father just now. You see, he walked out on somebody yesterday because it happened to be good for 'business,' and now I'd say it looks as if he'd done the same to you—"

She sat there looking at me; you can have some dignity left even if you are a perfectly ordinary, not very important or interesting person, who has just had to say the sort of things she had said to me.

"You told me you didn't know—" she began.

"I don't. I'm just trying to put two and two together. But 'business' and 'Betsy' seem to have been his reasons once before, and maybe they're both in it this time too. Maybe this time he even mentioned the wrong one by mistake."

She shook her head unbelievingly, and I realized suddenly what I should have known all along—that she had convinced herself it really was because of me that Father had wanted to break off with her; otherwise she would never have brought me into this at all. So she had given me her story, counting on me—or at least gambling on my pity, understanding, whatever you wanted to call it—to give her in return another chance. All I would have to do, she had told herself, was to say a word to Father. Only it wasn't that simple. She sat there saying to me: "No. I don't believe it. Pat wouldn't do that"—and I had to try to explain to her why it wasn't that simple.

"That's what I'd like to think too," I said. "But I'm afraid I don't know how to think it any more—not since yesterday. I was supposed to

[123]

be the reason for what he did yesterday too—and maybe I even was, a little—but I wasn't the real reason. The real reason is that Father thinks he has to be successful."

"But I'd never do anything to hurt him; he knows that," she protested. "Why, it's been six years—it was six years ago last month that I met him; we always called it our anniversary—"

She looked at me as if she expected me to tell her I had been mistaken.

"I'm sorry," I said. "I'm just telling you how it looks to me."

"But Pat and I—" She flushed suddenly, the blood rising patchily in her soft, fading face. "You don't understand," she plunged on. "Pat and I—we're in love with each other; why, he *cried* when he told me—"

I looked down at my plate; I hadn't eaten a bite. All at once I wished I were a thousand miles away.

"That's why I can't believe—" she said. She was pleading with me now, clutching the white gloves and the bag nervously as she leaned across the table toward me. "I can't believe it had anything to do with politics, or business, or things like that. He was just worried about you—he always did say there wasn't anybody except you that he'd ever think of before me—and if you could talk to him now, tell him it wouldn't make any difference to you if things kept on just the way they were—" The unhoping envy was there in her eyes again. "You've got such a lot of things—a pretty girl like you: plenty of beaux now, and good times, and then in a few years a husband and kids of your own—and I haven't got anything but him."

"I know." There wasn't anything else to say; I wanted to get it over now. "All right, I'll talk to him, if that's what you want. It might be better if I didn't, but if that's what you want—"

"Just tell him it won't make any difference to you. You can tell him that, can't you?"

"Yes. I can tell him that."

The waitress was passing the table; I stopped her and asked her for the check.

"Oh, no," Mrs. Hurley said. She fumbled with the catch of her purse. "I asked you to come."

"You better let me get it. If you're going to have a score to add up against the Donlons, I can at least make sure it doesn't include paying for a meal for one of them that she didn't even eat."

We walked together toward the door. I thought she was consider-

[124]

ing how to thank me; neither of us knew quite what to say to the other, now that the exigency that had brought us together had been settled. At the door she broke the silence anxiously.

"Pat always said you were such a fine girl, and he was right. I didn't want to call you, but you don't know what this means to me." She stood there hesitating outside the door, the afternoon sunlight cruel on the dulled blonde of her hair, the careful pink of her make-up, the comfortable figure uncomfortable now in the tightly fitting brown dress. "I don't know how to thank you."

"You haven't anything to thank me for. I told you, I don't think it really makes any difference to Father how I feel about this."

"Oh yes, it does." She shook her head, a little shocked by my having said that, and secure in her own conviction, or at least clinging to it because there was nothing else for her to cling to. "I'm sure it'll be all right if you talk to him."

I wished I could be as certain of that as she was, but, at any rate, she couldn't say I hadn't tried to warn her. I said good-by to her and left her standing there, looking hopefully after me, as I went off down the street. It wasn't till I was half a block away that it occurred to me what a really extraordinary position I had put myself in; Father and Aunt Bridgie were going to think I had at least lost my mind, if not my sense of all the proprieties. But I didn't care; I rather liked Lucille Hurley, and I was certainly sorry for her, and if Father was cutting her adrift because she might be an embarrassment to him when the fighting got rough in what was left of the campaign, he wasn't going to be able to blame it on me. I didn't seem to be able to do much for the people I wanted to help, but at least I could keep the record straight.

The afternoon papers were out when I left the Briarley, and I picked them up on the way home. If I'd had any lingering hopes that Martha was being too pessimistic in her predictions of what was going to happen that day, one glance at the front pages was enough to change my mind: there was the whole ugly story in three-inch head-lines and huge photographs and columns of print. I couldn't read it; I wanted to stop people on the street and tell them it wasn't true. But all I did was to drive home and cope with Aunt Bridgie, who was waiting to hear everything that Lucille Hurley had said to me, and then go upstairs to my room and lie there staring at the ceiling. I didn't even try to think what was going to happen next; there didn't seem to be anything I could do but wait.

Father didn't come in for dinner, and Aunt Bridgie and I ate alone. I'd given her the outlines of Father's present position in regard to Lucille Hurley, so she was feeling rather guilty and exalted, like most good people when it seems to them that heaven is at last about to visit retribution on one of their favorite sinners. I was glad when a friend of hers, who was as innocent as a babe unborn about what was going on in our house, dropped in and gave her the chance to spend the evening happily discussing plans for the next luncheon-meeting of the Women's Improvement League. She went to bed about ten-thirty, after her friend had gone home, and I sat down in the kitchen with a cup of coffee to wait for Father.

I didn't have long to wait; it wasn't eleven when I heard him come in. I went out to the hall.

"Betsy?" he said.

He looked at me as if he weren't quite sure whether he ought to act like a culprit or a stern parent, but I don't think he would have had enough energy left for a convincing performance of either role, even if he could have decided which of them to concentrate on.

"I'm having some coffee in the kitchen," I said. "Do you want some?"

"No; the damn stuff'll keep me awake all night." He seemed relieved when I spoke to him, as if he hadn't been sure I would. "I'll come back with you, though; I want to talk to you."

"That makes it mutual."

I went on back. I suppose he thought I was cool enough, but I wasn't; I was ashamed for him and almost for myself when I looked at him. Somehow it seemed that there must be something terribly wrong with me too, if my own father could do the sort of things he had done.

In the kitchen I opened the refrigerator door.

"Would you like a glass of milk?"

"All right. What?—milk—? No." He woke up suddenly to what he was saying. "Look here, I want to talk to you—"

"You said that before. But maybe there are a few things I ought to say to you first. One is, that you needn't worry any longer about my being 'mixed up' in Ivor's campaign; they don't want me up there any more than you do. And the second is, that I had lunch with Lucille Hurley today—"

If I had told him I had had lunch with Beelzebub he couldn't have looked more shocked. For a minute he couldn't even say anything; he just stood there as if he expected me to tell him that I really meant something entirely different from what I had just said. Then he exploded: "Lucille—! How the devil did you—? What did she—?"

"She phoned me," I said. "She wanted to talk to me. It seems she had the idea that I might have some influence with you."

Father sat down; he really seemed incapable of standing up any longer.

"Holy Mother of God," he moaned incredulously, "will you tell me what gets into people these days? That damn woman—"

"You needn't take it out on her," I said. "She was awfully upset, and she thought this whole business of her having to go away was on account of me. If anyone's to blame for her coming to me about it, it's you; you certainly gave her the idea—"

"*I* gave her the idea! I told her to stay away from you; I told her I didn't even want you to know—" He leaned his elbows miserably on the table. "I know I've made mistakes, Betsy, but as God is my witness, I never wanted them to hurt you; I tried to keep you out of them altogether."

I wished I could have believed that was the whole story, but I had gone a long way past that by this time. I stood there beside the refrigerator, watching him.

"We'll take that part of it for granted," I said. "Only now I'm not out of them; I'm in a lot of things—and one of them is that I promised Mrs. Hurley I'd tell you I didn't want her to have to go away on my account. I told her I didn't think it would do any good, but anyway I promised—"

Father didn't look at me; he was still holding his head in his hands.

"She had no business bringing you into this," he said. "This is something absolutely—She must be out of her mind."

"She's not out of her mind at all; she's just worried and upset. What I don't like about all this is that she thinks I'm responsible for it—"

"And isn't that the truth? Isn't it—?"

"I don't think so." I cut him off before he could go any farther; things were bad enough without his lying to me too. "Or maybe it's part of the truth," I said, "but the other part—and the most important part, isn't it?—is that you're afraid of what may happen now in the campaign. If Harvey Whiteley decides you've started a game that two can play—"

He started up. "Who told you that? Who told you that? Kirby—or that little bitch of a Martha Madden—?"

"Nobody told me anything; I *can* figure out a few things for myself, you know. After all, you started this; you must have known when you began throwing mud that some of it might land on you too."

He shook his head unbelievingly; the burst of anger died down as quickly as it had flared up. I wondered if he had been drinking; he was in the kind of mood of depressed self-pity that only that would seem to account for.

"My own daughter—" he said. "My own daughter to talk to me like this, when all I want in the world, everything I do, is for her—"

"Oh, stop it, *please!*" I couldn't keep it up; I'd thought I could have it out with him calmly, but I couldn't. "I'm tired of being your conscience," I said; "I'm tired of being the excuse you have for doing all the things that'll benefit you—because they'll benefit me too. You make me feel as if I have to be part of the whole rotten mess, whether I want to or not—"

I stopped; all at once he had put his head down on the table and started to sob. I wanted to feel sorry for him, but I couldn't. It was too easy—to make a shambles of other people's lives for your own profit, and then think you could expiate it all with a few tears. I couldn't keep the tears out of my own eyes, but they weren't tears of sympathy; they were tears of shame and anger and frustration.

"I know I oughtn't to be the one to say these things to you," I said, "but somebody has to—I've got to make you see somehow that I won't be a part of this. I don't care what you do about Mrs. Hurley —that's between you and her—but I never can forgive you for what you've done to Ivor—"

"Ivor—Ivor—" Father jumped up, staring at me furiously. "What's so sacred about Ivor Kelly, then, that I can't even tell the plain truth about what he's done? You sound like you were in love with the man."

"What if I am?"

For a moment Father stood there, breathing hard; then all at once he slammed his fist down on the table so the dishes jumped.

"By hell—by hell," he said thickly, "if he's been playing any games with you—"

"He hasn't done anything; he hasn't said anything. He doesn't even know how I feel about him—"

"Ah, that's the story, is it? And I'm to believe that—?"

"If you think I'd lie to you about it, I'll walk straight out of this house tonight and never come back. I'm not a child, you know; I can get a job and take care of myself."

He collapsed suddenly, weeping, into his chair again.

"Ah, Betsy, baby, you wouldn't do that. The whole world's against me, but you wouldn't go along with them—"

I didn't know what to say or do; the whole day seemed to be piling up around me in a sort of intolerable chaos. In the silence the living-room clock struck eleven, the strokes loud and hurried in the quiet house. After a little Father raised his head, took out his handkerchief, and dried his eyes wretchedly.

"All right," he said. "All right. I've made some mistakes. But we all make mistakes; you're making one yourself, a bigger one than you know, when you let yourself in for a schoolgirl infatuation with a man who—"

"I don't want to talk about that. I wouldn't have told you if—" I stopped and drew a long breath to steady my voice. "Anyway, we're out in the open now," I said; "you know how I feel and I know how you feel. And now that that's settled, I'm going to bed."

I picked up my cup and brought it over to the sink. Father sat there looking at me.

"You're young, Betsy," he said to me after a moment, miserably. "You're young and you judge people; you think they ought to act like they had the Ten Commandments pasted up someplace inside them like a set of hotel rules. Well, that's all right; maybe I deserve it—but if you knew the kind of pressure I've been under—"

"Can we *please* not talk about it any more?"

I went over to the door; I had had enough for one day. Going upstairs in the dark I started to cry too—for Father, for Ivor, for myself, even for Lucille Hurley; I didn't know which. It was like the kind of bad dream from which it doesn't do any good to wake up, because what you are dreaming is real; you know when you wake up it will still be there.

V I I

THE next day dragged by. I didn't want to see people, so I spent the morning at home with Aunt Bridgie, and then drove her into town after lunch so she could do some shopping. She wanted me to go with her, but instead I picked up the afternoon papers and read them sitting in the car where I had parked it on Monroe Street. Nothing like this had hit the state since a governor-elect had been assassinated down at the capital almost forty years before, and the papers were full of politicians' statements, reporters' speculations, and angry demands that Ivor withdraw from the campaign.

But what was actually happening behind all this was something I could only guess at. And I had to know; I had to see Ivor too, if I could—if only to explain to him why I had apparently walked out on him along with the others. Finally I made up my mind and went into a drugstore on the corner and called the Sadler Building. Martha answered the phone.

"Martha," I said, "this is Betsy. I'm in town and I'm coming up—" I heard her exasperated sigh over the wire.

"Listen, child, I'm busy—and I'm trying to keep this line open. You go on home and play with your little friends; go and marry one of them, if you feel you've got to have some excitement—"

"I want to see Ivor."

"He's not here. Don't you read the papers? He has a pressing engagement with Judge Reese."

"But I thought that would be over by now—Don't you expect him?"

"I don't expect anything but bad luck." She relented suddenly. "All right. You can come up later and I'll tell you all about it. But not till five-thirty—wait a minute, six o'clock will be better." She paused a moment. "How's Pat making out?"

"I think he feels terrible about all this—"

"He ought to."

"—but of course it's too late to do anything now—isn't it?"

"It is. You can tell him from me that I hope he'll be very happy with his thirty pieces of silver."

She hung up, and I went back to the car. It was only a little after two; I had more than three hours to wait. I went into a movie theater and sat through a double-feature about two assorted love affairs, one in the South Seas and the other in Wyoming, both of which ended happily: I couldn't concentrate enough on either of them to know exactly what was going on, but the final scene in both of them showed a man and a girl walking off hand in hand into the sunset, so I could only presume everything had turned out all right. It seemed very simple in the movies; it was always the right people who got shot or involved in the clutches of the law, and if anybody made any false accusations, they were all cleared up within the next three reels.

When I came out of the theater I was in the clutches of the law myself, to the extent that a policeman was giving me a ticket for parking overtime. He gave me a short official lecture when I came up, and then embarked on an enthusiastic appreciation of the fine points of my car; I had to cut it short to be sure I'd have time to park the car somewhere else before I went up to the Sadler Building to see Martha.

It had clouded over during the afternoon, and the office was dim and quiet and deserted when I came in; the black-lettered posters and the pictures of Ivor looked down silently and a little inappropriately from the walls, like billboards for a circus that had already left town. Martha and Kirby were in the inner office; they both looked at me, when I walked in, with the complete lack of interest of people who are so tired and defeated they can't even manage to summon up the energy for the ordinary social greetings.

"Come on in and join the wake," Martha said. "It looks as if we've about run out of mourners."

I stood in the doorway, looking at them.

"What's the matter?" I asked. "Hello, Kirby; you look terrible."

"I feel terrible. I haven't had any sleep in two nights. If I had any sense I'd go home and go to bed."

"Why don't you?"

"I just told you—not enough sense. If I'd had any, I'd never have got into this mess in the first place; I'd have pinned a 'Dodd for

Governor' button on my coat and trotted right along with Pat, holding out my little tin cup for the nickels and pennies—"

I turned to Martha. "What *is* it?" I asked. "Has Mr. Whiteley—?"

"Mr. Whiteley," Kirby said, "has taken himself home to Ashbourne, where he will spend the next couple of years making bricks and cursing the name of Kelly. I'm not sure I wouldn't like to join him."

Martha shrugged. "You'll make out all right. Who knows?—maybe in a few years there'll be another candidate for governor or senator in this state who won't mind at all having a campaign manager who was fool enough to stick to his man, win, lose, or draw."

"But what *hap*pened?" I appealed to Martha. "I thought you said there was an outside chance—"

"There was. The only trouble is that at this stage of the game Ivor decided we were going to use Marquess of Queensbury rules, and it so happens that that outside chance goes only with a strictly bare-knuckles fight. Mr. Whiteley has politely asked to be excused from holding the towel while his man gets his brains kicked out trying to defeat the other fellow on points."

I sat down on the edge of the desk, looking at her puzzledly; I didn't know what she was trying to tell me.

"I'm afraid you'll have to put it in words of one syllable," I said. "What is Ivor going to do?"

"It isn't what he's going to do; it's what he isn't going to do. For instance, he isn't going to take that precious father of yours for the kind of ride he deserves to be taken on—"

She stopped, as if she thought she might have said too much. I realized suddenly what she was driving at.

"If you mean Lucille Hurley, you can say it," I said; "I know all about that. But what good would that really do—?"

"Only as much good as it ever does to point out that the fellow who's throwing the stones lives in a pretty fancy glass house himself," Martha said grimly. "But it wouldn't stop there. I'll say this for Harvey Whiteley—he's got an inventive mind when it comes to the finest high-grade type of gutter-politics. If he had his way, Pat would be trying to explain to an eager public just what his personal interest in the Judsons was—whether there wasn't at least a possibility, for example, that he knew about the Judson girl's trouble before anybody but God and the father of that child she's carrying could have known about it, and whether Judson just decided Kelly

[132]

was as good a name as Donlon for that kid, as long as there was a job that went along with it—"

I looked from her to Kirby and back again; I felt a little sick. "Oh, Martha," I said, "you don't think—"

"No," she said, "I don't. But there's no telling what other people might think if Harvey Whiteley put some money and effort behind spreading that story around. They might even believe another one of his bright ideas, which is that you didn't come up here on your own at all to help in Ivor's campaign; you came because Pat thought he might be sitting on at least one arm of the governor's chair come November if he threw his pretty daughter at Ivor's head and it ended in wedding bells. Unfortunately—this is the way it runs in *Whiteley's Fairy Tales*—you fell down on your assignment, so Pat had to resort to sterner methods and another candidate—"

I just sat there; I couldn't look at either of them. Kirby said angrily: "You didn't have to tell her that, did you, Marty? It's no use taking it out on her because you want to get back at Pat."

"I'm doing her a favor," Martha said. "She's been trying for a long time to find something about Ivor to be proud of. Now she's got it: there aren't many men who'd throw away even an outside chance of a governorship—are there, Betsy?—to save a couple of women, and a s.o.b. who happens to be the father of one of them, from some highly embarrassing publicity."

I didn't know how she felt about it; the way she sounded, she would have been happier if Ivor had decided to go along with Harvey Whiteley. Kirby broke in again: "You're in a hell of a mood. If that's the way you're going to put it up to her, you'd better get out of here and let me talk to her."

"You'd like nothing better, would you, sonny? Only it won't work; she came up here to see Ivor; she wants to tell him she'll be faithful unto death. It might have done a little more good if she'd managed to talk her father out of laying into what's left of Ivor's life with a sledge hammer, but she was too busy being romantic to be bothered with that."

She jumped up abruptly and walked into the outer office and slammed the door. Kirby stood up, put his hands in his pockets, and looked at me uncomfortably.

"She's just upset," he said. "She and Ivor have been together pretty long; she's bound to take this hard. There wasn't anything you could have done, Betsy."

"I tried, Kirby—really I tried."

"Sure you did. I saw you myself. Pat's been all tied up in knots for months; the Angel Gabriel couldn't have reasoned with him. Marty knows that too; she isn't really sore at you."

"I know; it's Father. Kirby, how could he do it—?"

He shrugged. "Maybe he believes that story's true. Maybe I even believe it myself—"

"You don't."

"All right. I guess I don't. But you've got to admit it could look pretty damn plausible to a lot of other people."

"To Harvey Whiteley? Does he believe it?"

"Lock, stock, and barrel. Only it wouldn't make any difference to him, as long as he could still make Ivor governor of this state. He'd just advise him to be a little more careful in the future about what he did with his spare time."

"And Polly?"

He lifted his shoulders again. "What do you think? Polly takes all the chances—except the really big ones. She went up to Canada this morning—last seen heading for Lake Louise, with no thirty-day return ticket clutched in her hot little hand, either."

I didn't say anything. Kirby stood over by the window, looking at me. All at once his face changed.

"Listen," he said, "if you think—"

"Shut up, Kirby."

"You've been all ready to make a damn fool of yourself for months now, haven't you? Ever since that night on the train—"

"I said, shut up." I stood up, facing him. "What do you want me to do? Be my father's daughter and play it safe—look out for Number One—?"

But he went on, explaining it to me harshly: "Look, have you any idea what this really means? Ivor's been bound over to the grand jury on a charge of rape with consent; even if it never goes any farther than that—and it'll go a damn sight farther if Judson has his way—he's as dead as a mackerel in this state as far as his political career is concerned. And there's more to it than that: if he can't clear that charge up a lot better than he's got even a prayer of doing now, he'll be disbarred too—and where do you think that's going to leave him?"

"I don't know. But it'll make it so much easier for him—won't it? —if his friends walk out on him."

[134]

"I'm not talking about 'friends.'"

He was at the point where weariness and frayed nerves might have made him say anything; I was glad when Martha suddenly walked in again.

"I thought you were going to talk to her nicely," she said to Kirby. "I could hear you outside—You're a walking wreck; why don't you go home and go to bed?"

She went over, took his hat from the desk, and handed it to him. Kirby looked at it, glowering.

"I told Ivor I'd see him here when he was through with Pardee."

"I'll tell him you'll get in touch with him tomorrow morning—tonight if there's anything urgent. He needs some rest himself, you know."

Kirby gave in. "All right," he said. He turned to me. "Can I drop you someplace?"

"I've got my car."

He started to say something else, changed his mind, and went on out. Martha stood there looking at me.

"I suppose you think you're going to stay here and wait for Ivor—"

"I just want to talk to him for five minutes, Martha."

"All right. But remember he won't be any more responsible than Kirby was for what he says." She went out to the outer office again and I followed her. "He ought to be just in the mood to have somebody tell him he's a great man," she said. "He might even believe it—"

"What would you like me to do? Tell him that naturally, since he's not going to be successful, I don't want any more to do with him?"

"I suppose he'd survive. You wouldn't be the first one; that's been pretty much all he's been hearing for two days now." She stopped; the outer door opened and Ivor walked in. "Speak of the devil—" she said.

Ivor looked at me. He looked even worse than Kirby, his face gray in the soft cloudy late-afternoon light that came in through the open windows with the sound of traffic below. He smiled at me slightly.

"Oh, no," he said. "I hope Betsy doesn't think that badly of me."

"She doesn't think badly of you at all. She thinks you're a knight in shining armor—Samson among the Philistines—William S. Hart without a horse. Did you see Kirby?"

Ivor glanced over at her, a little startled by the sudden transition. "No. Should I have?"

"He just went out of here; you must have missed him on the elevator. I told him to go home and go to bed; he was asleep on his feet. You don't have to see him right away, do you?"

"Any time."

Martha opened a desk drawer and took out her purse.

"What did Pardee say?" she asked.

"Just what we've all been saying: the chances are it won't stand up in court. The girl's scared; she'll say just what she thinks she's supposed to say, but sooner or later she'll let something out."

"And by that time it will be too late to do any good," Martha said. "That will be just fine." She put on her hat. "Well, I'm going home; if you want to write any interesting letters to anybody, get Betsy to do them. She's very anxious to make herself useful."

She picked up her bag and walked out the door. Ivor turned to me.

"That was a rather remarkable conversation," he said. "Is there something going on that I don't know about?"

"Everybody's upset." I was standing near the window; the quiet building and the traffic-sounds from below made us seem very much alone up there—almost lonely. I glanced down at the street below. "I just wanted to tell you how sorry I am—about Father—about everything—"

"What Pat did had nothing to do with you. Everybody realizes that—or wait a minute—has anybody been saying anything to you?"

I shook my head. "Not really. Martha told me to stay away from here, but it wasn't because of that. I suppose she's afraid I'll be in an embarrassing position—or put somebody else in one—"

He looked at me kindly. "She's right. It'll be much better if you stay out of this from now on. That's not a very grateful thing to say, but you know how it's meant. I wouldn't want you to be mixed up in anything like this."

"I'd like to be mixed up in it, if it would do any good." I couldn't tell what he was thinking; he stood there in the fading gray light as if he were saying good-by to me. "I wanted so to help," I said. "And all I seem to have done is to get in people's way."

"That's a bad way to put it. You've helped a good deal; you're helping now."

"Am I?"

"More than you realize."

He was different now—tired and kind and full of regret; all at once it seemed possible to imagine that saying good-by was as hard for him as it was for me.

"Then let me stay on," I begged. "If I promise not to embarrass anybody—"

He shook his head definitely. "I couldn't put you in a position like that."

"I wouldn't care about that. I wouldn't care about anything as long as I could *do* something instead of just waiting—" In the still, gray, empty room, with his eyes not simply kind now, but reflecting my own sad feelings as if in a sudden mirror, I found all at once it was natural to say it, more natural than anything had ever been in my whole life. "Because I'm in love with you—" I said. "Didn't you know?"

The silence slowly engulfed the words, left them suspended somewhere in the quiet air, as if no one had spoken them, as if we had both simply thought of them at exactly the same time. After a moment he said, gently and unbelievingly: "You're not real. To tell me that now—as simply as that—"

"Don't you want it to be real? You can tell me—I never expected you to love me; I just wanted you to know—"

There was that awful moment, the worst of all—the moment before he moved and lifted my chin gently and kissed me, then again, his arms going around me then and the world stopping and our hearts beating and finally his voice different and amazed, only the words something I might have expected five minutes before, as if they were merely remembered and repeated, though no longer valid to this moment: "This won't do. It won't do at all." And not even convincing himself with them, because then again, though more troubledly, his hand turning my face to read what was in it, and this time I was smiling—I could feel how faintly because when you are too happy it always stays deep inside and only the shadow of it there for anyone else to see—and we kissed again with a little gasp. Then it was over and he was standing beside me at the window, and the world came back in a far-below rush of wheels and blare of horns and shriek of brakes.

"Betsy—" he said, "Betsy—Betsy—" shaking his head, trying to be wise and sensible, the troubled look there more strongly in his eyes.

"Don't say anything. You don't have to say anything. You weren't just being kind; that's all that matters."

"I wasn't just being kind. I suppose I'm in love with you, in a way —but it won't do; I shouldn't even have told you that—"

He was going away from me again, drawing himself down somewhere behind the stubborn, worried eyes. Like a book in a foreign language I had only begun to learn, he was all new for me to read; I had to try to imagine what it would be like to know really what was going on behind the dark eyes and the sudden frown dividing the black Irish brows.

"Why shouldn't you tell me?" I said. "Polly? Or because things are the way they are just now? They won't always be this way."

"Polly doesn't enter into it; that's all over. But there are some things that won't ever change, even if matters were arranged entirely differently than they are now. In the first place, I'm twenty years older than you are; we don't even live in the same world—"

"You could teach me things; I learn awfully fast."

I had made him smile, and for a moment it was all right—then the shadow once more, like the mild gray shadow of the overcast day, darkening slowly to evening around us.

"I couldn't take your fine new life and make it into something bitter."

"You wouldn't do that. People are only bitter—aren't they?—about something they want and can't have."

"Or about something they have and find out too late they don't want at all. You've never thought of that—"

"I don't have to. I know what I want."

He shook his head over my certainty. "The way you say that makes me realize more than ever how wrong all this is. What I should have done was send you home with a few wise words, but I'm too tired to be wise this afternoon." I saw him drawing himself together, retreating into gentleness as he tried to repair the damage of what he had already done. "What I'm trying to say is that the best thing you can do is go home and make up your mind that all this never happened. It couldn't have happened; there are too many reasons why it shouldn't have."

"But it did happen." I faced him in desperation, frightened by his growing decision; it couldn't end now, before it had fairly begun. "You said you were in love with me; nothing can ever change that. And it's all that matters—"

"It's the one thing that matters least of all." He explained it for me: "I wouldn't have anything to give you—none of the things you'd have a right to expect—"

"I don't expect anything at all." All at once I was crying in a chair by the window, looking blindly in my bag for a handkerchief. "I only want us to be together. I love you—you can't make me say that isn't true—and if you love me—"

"We're not speaking the same language even there." He came over, upset and unhappy, and sat down beside me. "You don't understand," he said; "I'm all finished with what you think of when you talk about love, and I wouldn't know how to go back to it any more than I'd know how to go back to being as young and as happy and as hopeful as you are. It's a luxury for me to have somebody believe in me, because I can't really believe in myself any more—but it would be sheer self-indulgence for me to ask you to devote yourself to a lost cause like that; you'd end up losing the best part of your life without even having anything real to remember."

"Then what about Polly—?"

"Polly's different; she's as bankrupt as I am when it comes to having any feelings she can take out in the cold light of day and still believe in. That wasn't a bad bargain, as bargains go—but I couldn't make bargains with all your fine hopes and your nice young feelings—"

He was comforting and wise and harshly frank; there was even an arm around my shoulders after a little, as if he could trust us both not to be foolish now with so many rough truths between us.

"You're going to find somebody your own age some day," he said, "and have a fine life with him—"

I shook my head. "I've found you. I don't want anybody else, ever—" I dried my eyes, looking up at him desperately. "It was real when you kissed me—wasn't it? What happened to us both then was perfectly real—?"

"Nothing seems more real than a dream, when you're in the middle of it." He turned to the window and stood looking out, his back to me now. "Some day, when you're all awake again and can see this for what it really is, you'll understand how much cause you have to be thankful that it is only a dream—"

There was nothing I could say; if he persisted in speaking to me from his vantage ground of twenty added years of living, there was no way for me to prove to him that what I felt at that moment was valid for more than the moment itself. I stood up, trying to be calm;

I even took out my compact and repaired rather forlornly the damage done by my tears—as if that would have made any difference then.

"Then you don't even want to see me again?" I asked him. If we were going to have it out, at least I wanted to know all of it, the very worst.

"It would be better that way—wouldn't it? There are going to be so many wonderful things in your life, Betsy; you won't even miss one that would only have turned out to be sad."

"It's better to be sad than not to be alive. I'm old enough to know that; I've never really *been* alive till these last few months—till I met you—" I stopped; he was too tired and unhappy, standing there watching me and trying to be wise for both of us, for me to burden him with any more problems. "All right," I said. "I've finished now; I'm not going to say any more. But what are you going to say to me when it's a month, or six months, or a year from now, and I tell you that nothing has changed—?"

"It will change. When people are in love they always think it won't, but there are so many ways to lose love—and one of the easiest ways of all is to find out that the person you thought you were in love with never really existed."

He walked across the room with me; at the doorway I stopped, grasping at moments.

"Aren't you coming too? I've got my car; I can drop you—"

He shook his head. "You go on. I have things to do here."

"You haven't."

"All right. I haven't. But you go on anyway." He looked at me in an odd way. "Would you think it was strange if I were to thank you—?"

"I've never heard of thanking anybody for falling in love with you. It isn't something a person does because she *wants* to."

"Then I'll just say good-by."

He opened the door for me and I went out. I suppose I should have felt that the world had come to an end, but I didn't. I knew it wasn't over, it couldn't be, and I went down in the elevator holding on to that, down to the ordinary world, to all the ordinary people who didn't matter and to all the ordinary places where he wouldn't be. It wasn't till I was outside in the thin warm dusk, with rain falling quietly now and the lights beginning to come on, that I realized I must have known that all along, because I remembered then that I hadn't said good-by.

VIII

THE next day Father said something to me about my going to Colorado for the rest of the summer, but I wasn't having any of that; if I couldn't do anything about Ivor's campaign, at least I was going to stay where I had some chance of finding out how it was going. There wasn't much argument on the subject, anyway, because Father and I were strictly on a "business only" basis during the days that followed the Judson explosion. He went his way and I went mine, and when we sat down together in the same room, which wasn't often, we stayed in neutral territory as far as the conversation was concerned. He hadn't even mentioned Lucille Hurley's name to me again, for instance, and I didn't ask about her; I was pretty sure, though, that what I had said to him hadn't changed matters, and that Mrs. Hurley was safely in Chicago by this time, out of reach of embarrassing questions and what—if I knew her—might have been equally embarrassing replies.

I had lunch a couple of times with Martha up in Queensport, and from her—and from the newspapers—I learned that Ivor was having almost no success in trying to pick up the pieces of his campaign. The first time I talked to Martha, she wasn't so much discouraged as furious; there had been cancellations—tactful or not so tactful—of speaking engagements all over the state, and that, coupled with the fact that the defection of all his major backers had left him almost without funds, made it practically impossible for Ivor to get his side of the matter before the public. He was leaving on a trip into the eastern part of the state the day I saw her, where he would have to depend almost entirely on impromptu street-corner meetings and speeches made from courthouse steps or in town squares—"so that if the weather's bad, he may as well stay home," she said to me. She added, "I hate people, don't you?"—as if that was going to make anybody feel any better, and then got up and walked out of the drug-

[141]

store where we had been eating, leaving me with the checks for two cups of coffee and two hamburgers, and a hollow feeling in the pit of my stomach.

I don't know anything at first hand about the trip Ivor left on that day, or about any of the others that he made before the primaries, but I heard a good deal about them later, from Martha and from Kirby, so I have a pretty fair idea of what they were like. But there wouldn't be any point in my trying to cover the whole itinerary here. Campaign trips, as I'd found out for myself during the one I went on, have a way of repeating the same incidents, with local variations, over and over again, and a kaleidoscope of the events of any given day, if it were shaken often enough, would eventually give you a reasonably accurate picture of the events of any other day. So I've chosen one particular day to illustrate all the rest—a day that began in a hotel room in Zane's Mill, and ended a hundred and eighty miles and fifteen hours and eight speeches later in a hotel room in La Fayette. This happens to be a day that came about midway in the period between the Judson exposure and the primaries, but except for one incident it could have been any one at the beginning or the end; as a matter of fact, that incident too was repeated more than once, so it isn't unique, though it isn't exactly typical either.

At any rate, this is that day, as accurately as I can piece it together, from the beginning in Zane's Mill to the end in La Fayette.

At seven-thirty in the morning Kirby came down to the lobby of the Congress Hotel, walked through a door labeled *Dining Room,* and headed for the single occupied table in the small desert of silent furniture and gummy napery inside.

"You're up early," he said, pulling out a chair beside Ivor.

"I couldn't sleep. That damn storm—Where's Ken?"

"Nothing keeps *him* awake. I finally managed to convince him it wasn't still the middle of the night just before I came downstairs."

Kirby looked out the window at the small-town street; the river was somewhere off below, but all he could see of it was a glint of brighter sunlight between the hardware store and the dentist's office across the way. It was late July, and the nights were a little longer than they had been a month before, but at seven-thirty in the morning it had already been full day for some time, and he saw a milk-wagon horse take a few more steps forward on the still-wet bricks of the street to halt in the shade instead of the sun.

"What about Maysboro?" Ivor said. "Did you get a hall?"

"You'll sound just as good from the courthouse steps."

Ivor looked at him. "All right," he said. "If that's the way it is. But if it rains—"

"If it rains, they won't come anyway."

The waiter came up to take their order. He was a tall friendly Negro boy, and very obliging, and it was a relief to talk to him after the clerk at the desk, who looked at them suspiciously whenever they went past and then ostentatiously turned his back so he would not have to say good morning or good evening to them.

At Maysboro there were the usual dozen overalled figures squatting on their heels on the courthouse lawn. The local politican who brought them over was a little nervous: two or three people on whom he had relied had not appeared, and the small group that was converging now on the courthouse steps was too silent to be reassuring. One of them—a bulky, dark-haired man, with a holster official and conspicuous on one hip—paused to pass the time of day with the squatting figures on the lawn and then strolled up to the local politician.

"How you makin' it, Mike?" he said.

"Fine. Just fine." The local politician watched the bulky man's eyes going over the three strangers. "This is our sheriff, Mr. Kelly," he said to Ivor: his confidence was leaking out of him so fast that you could almost measure the difference in its interior level between the beginning of the sentence and the end. He spoke to the bulky man. "Like you to meet Mr. Kelly, Cappie—Mr. Hays, Mr. Daggett—"

"Baggott," Ken said.

He shook hands heartily; every day he started off without suspicion, and every day he took the whole ride from discomfort through incredulity to heartbroken anger. Apparently the human race was going to present itself to him as an entirely unclassified set of phenomena as long as he lived—as if he were a retarded child confronted with the unintelligible symbols that to anyone else eventually become the alphabet.

The bulky man looked at Ivor and meditatively spat.

"I had you figured wrong," he remarked. "I never figured you'd show up. I figured anybody that was smart enough to get himself elected to Congress three or four times was smart enough to know when he wasn't wanted."

[143]

The local politician, trapped and sweating, bleated feebly: "Now, look here, Cappie—"

"All right," Kirby said. "We don't want any arguments." He looked at the bulky man. "The way I learned it, in this country a man's innocent till a jury says he's guilty, and if there's any law that says he hasn't got a right to tell people he's innocent if he wants to, they must have passed it right here in Maysboro some day when they decided the Constitution of the United States wasn't good enough for them, and they were going to write one of their own."

They had an audience now, the crowd clustering around, silent and curious, under the brassy glare of the sky that was darkening again to storm. Ivor said pleasantly: "All I want is a few minutes' conversation with you good people. With you, for instance"—he let his eyes fall on a ruddy-cheeked, respectable-looking, gray-haired farmer standing in the front ranks of the gathering crowd. "You have the advantage of me, I'm afraid," he said; "you know my name, but I don't know your—"

"John Carpenter." The man, reddening, drawled the name out emphatically, as if to show he had no objection to anyone's knowing who he was—then, like the bulky man before him, meditatively spat.

"Thank you." Ivor might have been talking with a new acquaintance in a chance, friendly meeting, but his voice carried in the silence to the small crowd about him; in speaking to one of them, he was speaking to them all. "I'm glad to know you, Mr. Carpenter," he said, "and I hope the next time I come back here we'll meet under pleasanter circumstances. Because the next time I come here, the misunderstanding that's giving you reason to distrust me now—and it must seem good reason to you, since you don't know me and you do know that an accusation has been made against me—will have been cleared up—"

"Now, look here—" the bulky man said. "Look here—You're not makin' a speech here; this is county property, and you're not makin' a speech—"

"No," Ivor said. He looked equably at the bulky man. "I'm not making a speech. I'm talking to a few friends of mine who want to know the truth about something that vitally concerns them, about a man who has asked them to make him governor of their state. Some of you, I'm sure, had your minds made up a couple of weeks ago to vote for me"—he turned to John Carpenter again; "maybe you even did yourself—"

Somebody snickered, the sound underlined by a low mutter of thunder from the west.

"Maybe I did," Carpenter acknowledged reluctantly, "but if I'd-a known then what I know now—"

"All right," Ivor agreed. "Let's look at that. What did you know then? Either you knew enough about me to think I'd make a pretty good governor of this state, or—it might have been this too—you knew enough about Ed Dodd to be sure he wouldn't. So you decided to pick an apple out of the barrel that at least didn't seem to be rotten, rather than take one that you knew for certain was—"

Another snicker, a slight movement forward on the part of those standing nearest, as if they were involved now as participants in an argument, rather then standing apart as spectators to a speech.

"Now what happens?" Ivor pressed on. "You picked your apple, and it looks as if this one has turned out to be rotten too. At least there are people who are telling you it's rotten—telling you that the man you picked for governor not only isn't fit to be governor, he isn't fit even to walk the streets as a free citizen of this state. But how do *you* know that—you yourself?" He paused a moment to look over the crowd before him, putting the question to each of them in turn, meeting each pair of eyes as directly as if he were standing in conversation with them alone. "How do you judge any man?" he asked them. "By his past actions, by his record, by what you see of him with your own eyes and what you hear of him from people you trust and people you know are sure of their facts—isn't that the way any honest man judges his neighbor? You don't listen to that neighbor's enemies when you want to form a fair opinion about him, any more than you'd want him to listen to your enemies when he makes up his mind what kind of man you are—"

The wind stirred the heavy tops of the sycamore trees; overhead the brassy glare dimmed as blue clouds massed darker in the west. Ivor went on, a little more quickly: "I said I wasn't going to make a speech to you, and I'm not. All I want to do is to ask you to judge me as you'd judge any one of your neighbors—to look at my record, to look at me standing here talking to you this minute—and then to ask yourselves whether anything I've ever done or said would justify you in thinking I was the kind of man who would do what Ed Dodd says I've done, and then stand up in front of you and lie to you about it—"

[145]

"It's your skin, mister," a voice came out of the crowd. "A lot of lyin' gets done to save people's skins."

"All right," Ivor said. He waited for the stir of the crowd to die away. "All right. It *is* my skin. And if I had any regard for it I'd stay right at home where Ed Dodd wants me to stay, and get out of this campaign, and after the election was over and you had Ed Dodd sitting in the governor's mansion down in Fidelia, those charges against me would be quietly dropped and you'd never hear any more of them and neither would I. Maybe if I even went to him nicely right now and said I was sorry I'd ever thought of running against him, he'd keep that in mind, and in a couple of years, when he needed a judge, or a highway commissioner, he'd remember how obliging I'd been and give me the job. But I'm not going to get out of this campaign, and I'll tell you why I'm not going to." The rain was beginning now; he spoke against a rising wind and the long sough of trees against the sky. "I've done a lot of things in my life that I'm not proud of," he said—"you probably know about most of them yourselves because I never tried to make any secret of them—but I always thought of myself as an ordinary decent human being, and I thought that was what other people thought of me too. Now it looks as if there are some people with other ideas about that—people who are trying to tell you they can prove before a court of law that they know something different about me. And if I let them say that, don't I admit they're right in at least one respect?—because what ordinary decent human being would listen to a charge like that being made against him without standing up and telling everybody it was in his power to reach that it wasn't true, that—?"

A crash of thunder rocked the trees. The rain suddenly became a deluge, washing the reluctant crowd off the courthouse lawn; there was a hurried scramble for the shelter of doorways and parked cars. Kirby grabbed Ivor's arm.

"Let's get out of this." He shouted to Ken, who was running across the square toward the car: "Get that over here in a hurry—"

By the time they had reached the walk, the car was already swerving across the street on three wheels. They got in; the local politician, panting with the effort of his sudden sprint across the lawn, his coat collar turned up against the rain, stuck his head beseechingly in the door of the car, regardless of what was happening to the rest of his anatomy outside.

"You won't forget me, Mr. Kelly?" he said. "Mike Findlay, Harl

[146]

Green's cousin—you remember Harl Green, over at the courthouse in New Vernon? Now if we could-a just got you that hall today—we done our best, you know that, Mr. Kelly—"

"I know that," Ivor said. "You did splendidly, Mike, and I'm very grateful—"

The politician nodded, satisfied but still anxious; a moment later his head vanished abruptly and they saw him scampering nimbly across the street to the shelter of the barber shop.

"There's a real optimist," Kirby commented dryly. "He actually thinks you have a chance."

Ken shook his head. "You almost had them that time," he said to Ivor. He looked discouragedly out the window. "This lousy rain— Well, what do we do now? Get out of here?"

"Toss a coin," Kirby said. "That's the practical way to decide an important matter like that."

"I don't think there's any use in waiting around," Ivor said. "We'll go on to Albemarle."

Ken put the car into gear and it started off down the street in the rain. Kirby looked at Ivor.

"You want to know something?" he said. "Sometimes you almost have me believing those speeches you make."

Ivor looked out the window at the empty courthouse lawn. It was hot in the car with the windows up against the rain. Nobody said anything for quite a while.

When they got to Albemarle the rain had stopped; the sun came out as they drove down the main street, and the steamy air rose in damp waves from the asphalt. Here the local politician who met them was even less encouraging than the one in Maysboro had been. The man who should have taken charge of the arrangements, he vaguely explained, had been called out of town by the illness of one of his wife's relatives, and in his absence "things got kind of snarled up"—in other words, as it turned out there had been no arrangements made at all. Their informant himself—he was the local undertaker and furniture dealer, a man by the name of Finnyberry—professed to be too busy to introduce Ivor around town for more informal talks with any of the leading citizens; one of those same leading citizens, he said, had died a few days before and was scheduled for an impressive funeral that afternoon, and he, as the undertaker in charge, was bound to give the entire matter his closest supervision.

"Matter of fact," he suggested hopefully—they were in the office of the funeral parlor at the moment, with mournful steel engravings on the walls and the leading citizen himself, though entirely invisible, presumably lying in state somewhere across the hall or over their heads—"matter of fact, it might be better if you didn't stop here today at all. Harry'd be glad to run a little item in the paper Thursday, that out of respect to Mr. Thompson—"

"Was Mr. Thompson a Democrat?" Kirby demanded.

Mr. Finnyberry looked startled.

"Why, no," he said, "I don't think—that is, he didn't take much interest in politics—"

"Then we don't take much interest in Mr. Thompson," Kirby said firmly. "I don't want to be unsympathetic, Mr. Finnyberry, but there's an election coming up, and the people in this town are going to vote in it whether Mr. Thompson is laid to rest today or not. What we'd like to do is get the facts to them so they know how to vote—"

Mr. Finnyberry looked at Ivor—he seemed to be torn between the impression that it was an honor to have him sitting in his office and the nervous idea that he would be disgraced for life if anyone else saw him there—and suggested indistinctly that perhaps the people had already made up their minds how they were going to vote.

"If they have," Kirby said bluntly, "they've made them up the wrong way, and we're going to do our best to change them. Come to think of it, Mr. Finnyberry," he remarked suddenly, "maybe you've made your mind up, too; you don't seem too happy about this whole business."

Mr. Finnyberry, who was apparently wavering more and more toward the view that a gubernatorial candidate, even one who might be so unfortunate as to end up behind bars, was still too important a person to be treated cavalierly, protested that he was entirely happy.

"Naturally I want to do everything I can for you," he said, "but in my position—"

"All right," Kirby agreed. "We'll put it down to your professional manner; I can see where it wouldn't exactly pay to cultivate a cheerful expression in your business. But you might happen to have a fine gregarious young fellow around who spends his time selling furniture instead of greeting mourners, so he can afford to smile when he shakes a few hands and introduces the next governor of this state—"

Mr. Finnyberry thought there might be such a young man; in

[148]

fact, he grasped eagerly at the idea of delegating his responsibility to someone who would be in no position to excuse himself from accepting it. For a few minutes he left them alone; when he returned triumphantly he had with him a tall frightened young man who seemed all eyes and Adam's apple, and who was apparently being pushed—morally, if not physically—as unwillingly into their presence as a reluctant child is pushed on-stage by a determined parent.

"This is Will Watkins," Mr. Finnyberry said. "He'll take charge of things, Mr. Hays. Now, Will, I want you to meet these gentlemen—"

When they left the funeral parlor five minutes later, though, it was Kirby who had to "take charge of things"; Will, whose entire conversation had so far consisted of "How d'y' do," "Yes, sir," and "No, sir," seemed incapable of making any suggestions of his own, and went along with them more as a resigned and dedicated victim than a guide. As a matter of fact, when they started their tour of the town in the drugstore across the street, it looked for a few moments as if he wasn't even going to serve his primary purpose of mentioning names in the right places, but he recovered himself in time to make some rudimentary introductions, eventually arriving at a formula that served him throughout the hour that followed: "'ster Smith—'ster Jones—'ster Brown—want you meet 'ster Kelly—'ster Hays—'ster uh—" Then he would drop modestly into the background, while Ken helpfully supplied his missing name and Kirby or Ivor took it from there.

The town had the ordinary number of stores, selling dry goods and hardware and groceries and drugs and feed and grain and automobile accessories, and they covered them all, going up one side of the main street and down the other. After the first ten minutes they had attracted a gallery of onlookers, consisting mainly of little boys and whispering women, who remained across the street watching their progress from one store to the other. Two of the boys, more enterprising than the rest, made it their business to go up and down the street alerting the occupants of each store to what was happening, with the result that the visiting party faced a stonily prepared audience after the first few stops. In one place, the dry-goods store, the proprietor even took the drastic step of hastily locking his door and hanging a *Closed* sign on it, behind which he stood glaring defiantly at them, as if he expected them to try to make an entry by force.

"Goin' out to lunch, I reckon," Will explained it to them nervously.

"It *is* gittin' on for lunchtime; maybe if you folks have some other engagements—"

"We've got some engagements right here," Kirby said firmly. "What's next—the barber shop? Maybe the barber doesn't have these peculiar ideas about closing hours."

They went up the two steps beside the striped pole; Ken pushed open the screen door, and they went inside. Here all business had been suspended, though there were half a dozen people inside, including the barber, a pale, efficient-looking man in a white jacket who stared at them with a pair of cold, light-blue eyes.

"'ster Friend—'ster Isham—" Will began his unconvincing litany, "want you meet 'ster Kelly—"

Mr. Friend, the barber, looked at Ivor, then back at Will.

"This isn't a public meeting place, Will," he snapped; "this is a place of business. If your friends want a haircut or a shave, they've come to the right place; if they don't, they're wasting their time and mine."

"We've got plenty of time," Kirby said. He looked around, a polite dangerous Irish glint in his eyes. "And if you don't mind my saying so," he went on, "you seem to have too; none of these gentlemen here seems to be in any more of a hurry for a haircut or a shave than we are. Maybe you're just holding a little public meeting of your own—"

"If I am, it's my affair." The man moved forward a little, glancing around briefly at the others behind him. "But I don't recollect that you and your friends were asked to join it."

"Ah, let 'em stay, Harry," a stout man in a blue shirt remarked. "I always did want to know what a son-of-a-bitch that ran for governor in this state looked like; none of 'em ever bothered to come here before."

Ivor regarded him pleasantly. "Well, you see one now," he said, "and I reckon it hasn't done you any permanent damage. As a matter of fact, it might even do you a little good if you'd listen to what I have to say; you might change your mind about calling a man names before you know a few facts about him—"

"We know all the facts about you that we want to know around here, Mr. Kelly," the barber interrupted. "If you want to get up on a soap box somewhere and try to talk people into believing facts aren't facts, I can't stop you, but you won't do it in my shop—"

"Maybe we can all step outside then," Ivor suggested. "Or are you afraid to hear what I have to say?"

He was talking to them all now, the familiar routine of drawing them all into it, attaching their interest, almost their participation, in spite of their resistance. In the background Kirby relaxed again, wondering if it was conviction, Irish charm, or merely the long weary practice of politics that was responsible for the unfailing setting up of that personal relationship. "If he could only talk to enough of them," he thought, "he might even have a chance—that is, if he could get them to the polls within five minutes of the time he walked away from them, before they could start wondering what the hell had come over them, that they were thinking of voting for him—"

This time, though, at least one member of the audience remained convinced and impregnable behind his barrier of stern morality; in the middle of a sentence the barber suddenly walked across the shop, flung open the screen door, and called sharply to one of the small boys who stood loitering hopefully outside.

"Eddie—I want you to get the marshal. Tell him to come up here right away."

"Now look here—" Ken began. He walked over, astounded, to Mr. Friend. "What do you think you're doing? Who needs the marshal—?"

"I want you people out of this shop," Mr. Friend said. He looked at Ken out of his pale eyes, his lips working with anger. "If you won't go of your own accord, there's law in this town—"

"All *right*." Kirby turned around, spreading his hands peaceably, in resignation. "If that's the way you want it, we'll go; just keep your shirt on."

Ivor, undisturbed, suggested to the others that they could continue their conversation outside—a suggestion that, under the spur of Mr. Friend's sudden action, was received without much enthusiasm. When he and Kirby walked out the door, though, they found another audience already gathering for them there; the news that the marshal had been called had spread up and down the street with the speed of light, and people were clustered in every doorway, waiting to see what was going to happen.

The marshal himself, a tall, slow-moving, gray-haired man who probably owed his position more to the fact that he had an extraordinarily large number of voting kinfolk than to any natural affinity for enforcing law and order, was walking up the street in the wake of an excited escort of small boys.

[151]

"Now then—" he said, when he reached the barber shop, in the immemorial voice of authority trying to sound as if it believed in itself, "Now then, what's going on here?"

The barber appeared suddenly in his doorway.

"These people refused to leave my shop, Marshal," he said shrilly. "Now you've come, they've decided to think better of it."

"Well, that seems to solve that problem," Kirby remarked. He looked around for Will, but Will had disappeared. "My name is Hays," he made his own introduction resignedly, to the marshal, "and this is Mr. Baggott, and Mr. Kelly, the next governor of this state—"

Somebody laughed, and the barber called angrily, from the rostrum of his doorstep: "These people are trying to make a speech here on a public thoroughfare, Marshal; that's not allowed. They're obstructing traffic—"

Ivor murmured quietly: "There may be some dispute about *who* is trying to make a speech"—and the laughter rippled up again. The barber went on, his voice rising angrily: "People come in here—no better than criminals—and try to browbeat decent people into voting for them—"

"I'm afraid what is actually happening," Ivor said, "is that you are trying to browbeat decent people into giving up their right to hear both sides of a disputed question and make up their own minds, Mr. Friend. Surely you're not denying that I—"

"Nobody asked you to come here," the barber cried. "We know all about you; we don't need anybody coming in here and telling us how to vote."

At the other side of the gathering crowd the owner of the dry-goods store, having emerged from behind his barricade, was beginning an indignant harangue of his own; the situation was rapidly getting out of hand. The marshal said uneasily, to Ivor and Kirby: "Now look here—you people *are* obstructing traffic. Why don't you just move along now before you start some real trouble? We don't want any trouble—"

Kirby glanced quickly around at the crowd, appraising the situation.

"He's right," he said to Ivor. "Come on; we might as well get out of here."

Ivor shrugged stubbornly. "I think I'll just—"

"You want to be a hero? In a pint-sized comic opera? That'll look just fine in the newspapers tomorrow."

[152]

Ivor looked at him, still resistant; after a moment he suddenly shrugged again.

"All right then, if you're afraid—"

He moved forward through the crowd toward the place where the car stood parked across the street. Kirby followed him; at the car he exploded: "If I'm afraid—Who the hell do you think you are? You couldn't go two rounds with a high-school flyweight, the shape you're in."

Ken came up. "Brother, what a day. What a town. How're you going to tell people if they won't even listen—?"

"They've got a fine lot of open-minded, hospitable people here, all right," Kirby agreed. He opened the door of the car. "What happened to our friend Will?"

"The last I saw of him, he was still in that barber shop."

"Probably still there," Kirby said. "Probably hiding behind the barber chair and won't come out again till it's good and dark, when nobody can see him." He looked at Ivor. "What are we doing this for?" he said. "You tell me. What are you doing it for? You know as well as I do how far this is going to get you."

"We'd better get out of here," Ken said. He got into the car, behind the wheel.

"I'd feel better about it if I just knew what you expect to get out of it," Kirby said. "Or do you happen to like days like this?"

"Come *on*," Ken said anxiously. "You can talk in the car."

They got into the car; the crowd, not yet dispersed, stood watching them go, and a few little boys cheered ironically as they drove out of town. Kirby thought of continuing the conversation, but it didn't seem worth while; if there was anything to say, it had been said before. He looked out of the car window and watched the last houses of the town go by. It looked as if there was a good chance that it was going to rain again.

I can shake the kaleidoscope faster now, because even in one day things repeat themselves, and there isn't much use in telling about them when the people all look as if they were the same "supers," only in a little different costumes, that you've already seen twice before in a play, and the towns like a stock company's one set of a village street, with different names painted over the store fronts to fit the exigencies of each drama. There were a few incidents that didn't quite fit the pattern—the one in the hotel dining room in New Vernon, for example, when a woman sitting at the table next to the

[153]

one where Ivor and Kirby and Ken were having lunch suddenly recognized Ivor and got up conspicuously and left the room, remarking indignantly to her embarrassed husband that it was "a disgrace to allow a man like that to come in here." That in itself wasn't anything unusual, except that this time it was Kirby who lost his temper and inquired audibly and ungallantly who the hell she thought she was—the Virgin Mary in a two-piece suit?—and the husband overheard and came back to resent it, and there was some prospect for a few minutes of their all winding up before some local magistrate on a disorderly conduct charge.

That was about one o'clock in the afternoon, and it was after five, and raining again, when they got into La Fayette; you can fill the interval with four or five more towns and four or five more incidents like the ones I've already described, and draw your own conclusions about how they all felt by that time. At La Fayette they checked into a hotel, where a tall, correctly dressed young man, who looked more like a minor member of an embassy staff than an aspiring politician, was waiting to present them with one more in an unending series of crises. There had been a slip-up, he said, about their using the high-school auditorium for a meeting that night, and so successful arrangements had not yet been made about getting them another hall. Kirby, resigned, took charge and went out with him to see what he could do; three quarters of an hour later, when they came back together and went up to Ivor's room at the hotel, they had at least the minimum appearance of success.

"Well, we got you a hall," Kirby said, "didn't we, Jack? It's no Grand Opera House, but it's a hall."

"You're a pair of enterprising young men," Ivor said.

He was sitting in a chair near the bed with a whisky and soda on the table beside him. Now that he had had time to let down for a while, he looked worse than he had all day; his face was drawn with fatigue. Kirby looked at him sharply.

"Are you all right?" he asked.

Ivor raised his brows. "I've had one whisky and soda, if that's what you mean."

"It's not what I mean. You look like hell."

"I feel like hell," Ivor admitted. "But since you two have gone to the trouble of lining up a hall, I imagine I've got one more speech left in me." He said to the correct young man: "How's it going here?"

"Well—" The young man hesitated, embarrassed. "You know how it is—"

"I know just how it is," Ivor said. His manner changed suddenly, as if he had turned on some sort of inner light that transformed the occasion from a sad and embarrassing meeting at the gray end of a rainy day into something promising and amusing and even hopeful. "I suppose you think I'm slightly eccentric to be going through with this," he said. "You're probably right, too—but think of the awful gaps in history and the front pages of the newspapers if everyone was as sane as Ed Dodd. Three or four of our better historians would probably have shot themselves for lack of material if Napoleon had never come back from Elba, and a whole generation of editorial writers would have gone out of business if Robert E. Lee had decided God was on the side with the heaviest battalions—"

The young man glanced at Kirby; he owed Kirby a political debt, which he was paying with his reluctant participation in this campaign, but he had no more intention of enjoying it than he would have had of enjoying his own funeral.

"Well—it's your decision, of course," he said unhappily, to Ivor. And, to Kirby: "You haven't had dinner yet, have you? You'd better get started."

They all ate together in the hotel coffee shop, and afterwards, in the rain, started out for the hall—a former lodge hall that was in the discouraged process of being turned into a movie theater. The hurried transference of the meeting meant a small crowd, but at least there were people there, a good many of them merely curious, some reluctantly loyal, a few even grimly enthusiastic for old times' sake.

"Best chance you've had all day," Kirby commented. "A few people on your side can carry the whole crowd with them if you get this thing off the ground."

He listened impatiently to the local politician who had been prevailed on to introduce Ivor; too much oratory now could be worse than none at all. The hall smelled of damp umbrellas and damp plaster, and was as stifling as the hold of a ship sailing a tropical sea; you couldn't expect people to give you their undivided attention for very long in an atmosphere like that.

There was a small, determined scattering of applause when Ivor stood up to speak. Kirby, on the platform, let his thoughts wander as the speech began; there wasn't anything Ivor could say, at this stage of the campaign, that he hadn't heard before. In the midst of a vague, expert mental run-down of the next day's schedule, he heard Ivor's voice, weary and practiced and persuasive, with its campaigner's hoarseness and its understated Celtic eloquence; twice it was interrupted by applause, the first time when he quoted Iago's lines on reputation, and again, more vigorously, when he spoke of his reasons for continuing the campaign. The voice went on:

"Nobody fights any fight just for today. I'm going to lose this fight" —Kirby suddenly began to listen; this was something he hadn't heard before. "I can tell you that in all frankness, because you know, and I know, that it's true. It's a question of my word against a couple of other people's word and some particularly damning circumstances, and as far as taking a man's word goes, in a case where he has something to gain by it, the age of faith is gone. Probably half of you who are sitting here tonight came here only to see what a man looked like who was foolish enough, or vicious enough, to think he could corrupt a child and still get the people of this state to elect him governor. Well, you can set your minds to rest about that, because I'm telling you now that I don't expect them to elect me governor. But what I do expect them to do is to remember, when the truth finally comes out, that I told them the truth, and that any lies they heard came from somebody else, not from me."

Kirby saw Jack Turlow glance at him a little alarmedly across the platform; he woke up suddenly to the fact that Ivor was leaning against the reading-desk in a way that he had seen before. He whispered angrily to Ken, who was sitting beside him: "What the hell was he doing while I was gone this evening? I told him I wasn't going along on this ride unless he stayed sober."

Ken shook his head. "I think he's sick," he said worriedly. "You want to try to stop this?"

"Because the truth, ladies and gentlemen," Ivor's voice was going on, "is a strange and precious commodity." He was looking out over the half-empty hall now at the audience—a few curious little boys whispering and scuffling in the front seats, the skeptical, half-attentive faces scattered here and there in the gloom, a woman with a baby going defiantly out a door at the rear and letting in a burst of traffic sounds from the street outside. It was a strange confessional for him to have come to, but now that he had begun, he wanted to go on. "You can think for a long time," he said, "that it doesn't matter —and maybe it doesn't matter, as long as you're successful; maybe God made truth just for the defeated. When you're successful the world is a fine place full of people and money and places to go, and truth is something on a bathroom shelf that you take in small doses the morning after; you don't need to bother with it at all as long as your constitution holds up and your money holds out and your friends are still glad to see you when you walk in the door. It's only—"

He gestured suddenly with his left hand and fell against the stand. There was a gasp—of indignation or puzzlement from the hot peopled darkness before him.

"It's only when the glitter is gone and the people have all faded into thin air," he went on, with more difficulty, "that you realize —you realize—" He stopped altogether; for a moment he stood there, swaying slightly against the stand, his brows contracted painfully as if there were something else he had to say to them. Kirby got up quickly, and he half-turned to look at him, then turned immediately back to the audience. "Excuse me, ladies and gentlemen," he said, clearly and politely. "I'm not—I'm afraid I'm not—"

He walked unsteadily across the platform; Kirby and Ken caught him as he collapsed in the small vestibule just out of sight of the audience. Jack Turlow came hurrying out.

"Where can we take him?" Kirby asked.

"There's a room up the stairs. What's the matter with him? My God, it's not that barbecue all over again—?"

"Not this time. At least, I don't think—You'd better get a doctor; I'm going to talk to that crowd out there."

Kirby went out on the platform again. The hall was in an uproar by this time, and he faced a chorus of shrill whistles and angry boos that only diminished while he made his announcement, and rose again in disbelief when he had finished.

"All right," he said under his breath. "All right, you bastards. Have it your own way."

He walked sharply off the platform. A delegation of worried politicians immediately waylaid him.

"What about it, Kirby?"

"Damn it, don't he realize things are bad enough, without him coming in here like this—?"

"Why the hell can't you at least keep him sober—?"

"He's not drunk," Kirby said. "He's sick. God damn it, you try keeping the kind of schedule he's had and then come in a place like this that hasn't had a fresh breath of air in it since McKinley died, and smells like the inside of somebody's coffin—"

[157]

"All right, Kirby, you make it sound good for the newspapers, boy, but don't try to kid us."

"I'm not trying—"

It was no use; after a little he gave up, walked away from them, and went upstairs to see what was happening there. On the stairs he ran into Jack Turlow.

"How is he?"

"He's all right—seems all right, anyway. We got Dr. Miller over; he was having office hours next door. Just a little too much heat, I guess."

"A little too much of everything. He hasn't been in good shape since that auto accident, and a campaign like this is enough to knock out an elephant."

"Why doesn't he quit, then? He said himself he hasn't got a chance."

"You ask him, brother."

Kirby went on up the steps. In a little bare room at the head of the stairs he found Ken and the doctor; Ivor, his coat and tie off, was sitting on a straight chair beside the window. He looked over as Kirby came into the room.

"Well," he said, "I guess that did it."

"It did it, all right," Kirby said. He spoke to the doctor. "What's the matter with him?"

The doctor shrugged. He was a little gray man who didn't seem too happy at having been dragged into this.

"If he wants my advice, he'll have his own physician give him a complete check-up as soon as possible," he said. "In the meantime, he'd better get some rest—"

"I'm sure that's a splendid piece of advice," Ivor said politely. "It was good of you to come, Doctor."

He watched the doctor close his bag and pick it up. Ken went out of the room with him.

"You're damn right it's good advice," Kirby said then. "You're going to cancel that schedule tomorrow and go back to Queensport; I don't want any more nights like tonight."

Ivor got up and went over to put on his tie before the small cracked mirror that hung in one corner of the room, over a stationary washstand.

"That won't be necessary," he said. "I've had a complete check-up; I've got half a dozen things wrong with me, but most of them aren't very interesting and none of them's likely to be fatal—at least just at the present moment. A good night's sleep is all I need now." He glanced around over his shoulder at Kirby. "Was it very bad down there tonight?"

"It wasn't good."

"Things kept fading out on me. I had an idea I wasn't making much sense, but I didn't seem to be able to get any of it clear enough to figure out what was wrong with it."

"You made a lot of sense. You said you didn't have a chance to be elected governor of this state."

Ivor glanced around again, giving a final straightening hitch to his tie.

"Yes, I seem to remember that." He turned back to the mirror, surveying his blurred reflection on its wavering surface—the gray face and the brilliant eyes. "I may have been right; I don't look much like a governor, do I?" he remarked.

Kirby picked up his coat and handed it to him.

"All right," he said. There was no expression on his face. "You said it down there: you haven't got a chance. So why don't you quit?"

"Didn't I answer that one down there too?"

"You said something about God making truth for the defeated. Well, brother, you are defeated, and that's one truth you may as well face right now."

Ivor looked over at him, putting on his coat.

"I didn't ask you to stay, Kirby," he said pleasantly, after a moment. "I'm not asking you now."

"The hell with that," Kirby said angrily. "It isn't that I want to walk out of this; it's just that I don't see what you have to gain—"

"Of course you can't get much for self-respect on the open market," Ivor agreed. "Still, it's a useful thing to have around at three o'clock in the morning, when you can't get to sleep—"

Ken came back into the room.

"You know what that guy wanted for coming over here?" he demanded. "Ten bucks—said he had to leave people in his office, and they'd probably be gone when he got back. How do you like that?" Nobody said anything. He stood there, puzzled. "What's the matter with you fellows?" he asked.

"We've been having an interesting conversation," Kirby said.

"Well, you picked a fine time for it. We ought to get back to the hotel; you heard what that doctor said. Jeez, if we're going to pay him ten bucks for it, the least we can do is take his advice."

He turned to the door; after a moment Ivor and Kirby followed him. It was still raining when they got outside. Nobody had waited around to see them, so they went back at once to the hotel.

I X

ALL this, as I've said before, is something I only learned later, at second or third hand; at the time it was taking place I was in Fort Paris, trying to persuade Martha to give me something to do that would at least furnish me with the illusion that I was helping Ivor. She finally let me have some form letters to type at home—they were mostly polite reminders of campaign pledges that people hadn't sent in, and probably had no intention of sending in—and I borrowed a typewriter from Father's office and got to work. But I think by that time even I realized that I was only going through the motions in a battle that was already decided; anybody who could read and had two cents a day to buy a newspaper couldn't help eventually finding that out.

I brought the letters back to headquarters late one afternoon, about six o'clock, and I hadn't been there two minutes, talking to Martha, when Kirby came in. I hadn't seen him since that last disastrous afternoon there, and I hoped he would just say, "Hello, Betsy," and let it go at that, but he didn't; he sat down on the edge of the desk and looked at me severely.

"I thought you were going to stay away from here," he said.

"I *am* staying away." I brought Martha into it, indignantly, for confirmation. "I haven't been around here at all; I only came today to bring these letters back."

"All right, all *right*." He gestured with both hands, palms down. "Don't get so excited; it's your life. If you find this sort of thing in-teresting—well, a lot of people have peculiar tastes."

"I don't think it's peculiar at all to want to help—to want to know how things are going—"

"Well, I'll tell you how they're going. They couldn't be worse. Now you know all about it, and you can go home happy."

[161]

Martha was opening drawers in the desk, putting things away before she left for the day; he glanced around at her as if to make sure she didn't get away without his seeing her go.

"Is it really going that badly?" I asked. "I thought—I mean I hoped—"

"Well, you can stop hoping, baby. It's plain murder. I'm still trying to find some good reason why I go on with this thing—or why Ivor does, either. We can't both be crazy."

"He's not crazy; he's just stubborn," Martha said. "You tell him he can't do something and he goes right ahead and tries it, just to prove he can—"

"If you could only find out the truth about that Judson girl," I said, "everything would be different." I looked at Kirby. "There must be some way—"

"If there is, you'll have to invent it. We've tried everything; as far as anybody knows, she's a fine upstanding little character who never went farther from her mammy's apron strings than the door of a church till Ivor—or whoever the real villain of the piece is—led her astray." Martha started to put on her hat. "Hey, are you going?" he interrupted himself to say to her. "Wait a minute—I came up here to ask you something. Can you drive Ivor down to Williamsburg this evening? Ken and I are going over early."

Martha turned around. "I wasn't planning on going at all," she said; "I've got work to do tonight. What's the matter with him—has he forgotten how to drive a car?"

"Give the guy a break, Marty; he's on the ropes."

"I know he's on the ropes. And I also know why he's on the ropes. He hasn't any business going on with this campaign—"

"Let me drive him over," I suggested.

They both regarded me disapprovingly. After a moment Kirby said: "I thought you were staying out of this."

"Only as far out as people make me." The disapproving expressions stayed right there on their faces. "Oh, for heaven's sake," I said, "what possible harm can it do for me to drive him there? I'm not going to put signs on the car—"

Kirby still shook his head, but Martha abruptly came over to my side.

"You may as well let her go," she said to Kirby. "If you don't, she'll find some other way of getting herself into trouble; she's really a very ingenious girl." She added: "And if Ivor wants to know why you

[162]

let her do it, you can tell him she presented you with full credentials to join this lunatic asylum—"

Kirby gave in reluctantly. "Against my better judgment," he said. He looked at me. "If I were Pat, I'd send you to Europe," he remarked. "Or South America—that's a nice safe distance."

"I don't know anybody in South America."

"That's what I mean. You oughtn't to be able to get in much trouble there, unless you have the bad luck to run into another train wreck—"

He said I was to pick Ivor up at seven-thirty, so I went home to get something to eat, and then drove back to Queensport again. Ivor was up at headquarters talking to a politician who apparently considered that was the safest place, at that hour of the day, to meet him, and they both looked at me as if I were some sort of apparition when I walked in.

"Didn't Kirby tell you?" I said to Ivor. "I'm going to drive you over to Williamsburg."

"He said *some*body would pick me up—I haven't seen him since this morning."

The politician didn't know me, and Ivor didn't introduce him to me; he simply got rid of him with a few agreeable words. I couldn't guess if he was angry because I was doing this; I stood there watching him say good-by to the politician at the door and feeling afraid that he would be—it seemed an hour before the man went away and we were alone.

He came back across the room then, shaking his head.

"Kirby shouldn't have let you do this," he said.

"Don't you want to see me?"

"Much more than I'm going to tell you. But that doesn't change matters—"

"I wish you would tell me," I said forlornly. "I feel terrible—like a —like a designing woman—"

He smiled and came over and put his hands lightly on my arms for a moment, then shook his head again and went over to get his hat.

"No, I'm not going to make you feel any better about it," he said. "You ought to feel guilty; this isn't fair." But he wasn't feeling the way he sounded; his face was unhappy again, full of all the sad compromises people make for compassion or duty, as he turned to the door. "I shouldn't let you do this at all," he said; "I ought to take a cab and send you home."

"It's twenty *miles*."

"Fifteen." He smiled at me again. "You're such an honest person, Betsy; you couldn't lie convincingly even about something like that." Then he gave in and said: "All right. If you promise you won't stay —that you'll simply turn around and come straight back as soon as you get there—"

We went downstairs together through the empty building. It was a hot, clear night; the street outside had a lazy, summer-evening feeling—the newsboys' cries faint and persistent as crickets', and people strolling along, window-shopping or going to the movies. Somebody spoke to Ivor as he got into the car, but it was no one I knew. I put the car into gear.

"You see," I said, "nobody recognizes me; I'm not as famous as you are. I'm a perfectly anonymous young woman, as far as anyone knows—"

"You wouldn't have been so anonymous if that policeman down the street had been two car lengths nearer. A ten-minute parking zone—that was pretty optimistic, wasn't it?"

"It would have been poetic justice if I'd gotten a ticket; I got my last one because of you, too." I smiled at him across the wheel. "I paid it without telling Father, and he was horrified when he found out about it—said people would think he was through at City Hall if his own daughter had to pay her parking fines—"

I remembered all at once that I oughtn't to be talking to him about Father; I was so happy, being with him, that I had forgotten for a moment how things were. But he only said to me, as if nothing were the matter: "How is Pat?"

"I don't really know. We're hardly on speaking terms these days, but I don't suppose he's very happy. People usually aren't—are they? —when they've done something they're ashamed of."

He looked at me gravely. "You oughtn't to quarrel with him because of me."

"I already have. I told him I was in love with you—at least I didn't tell him I wasn't—"

He shook his head, looking amused and faintly alarmed.

"My God, I can imagine his reaction to that."

"He didn't say much. I think he thought for a minute that you'd ruined me, but I convinced him you hadn't—"

[164]

"I'm not going to ruin you. You're a fine girl, and you're going to have better things to do with your life than starting it off all wrong with the wrong man. I thought we had that all settled."

"All we settled was that I was in love with you and that you were in love with me. *You* said all that other, about your being the wrong person for me; I never agreed to any of it."

We crossed the bridge over the Cherokee River. With the sun going down there were glimpses of the broader river into which it flowed, looking pale blue now under the coming night-blue of the sky, with an even paler mist rising over it in long trailing sheets. The Corioli skyline, on the opposite bank, was a soft, inky-blue silhouette with tall buildings pierced at intervals by sudden lights.

"It's such a lovely evening," I said. "Can't we just pretend we're happy, and that everything's all right? I've waited so long for to-night—"

"Not half so long as I've waited," he acknowledged suddenly. He looked at me, giving up some inner reticence as if he had no way of holding on to it any longer. "You've done something extraordinary to me, you know," he said. "For the past few weeks I've been mixed up with emotions that for years I was firmly convinced were only illusions of my youth, with no foundation in reality."

"I'm glad." I was, but I was sad too, feeling it had all happened before, and I hadn't been there. I didn't say any more, driving automatically for a while, hardly seeing the little business districts with their lights coming on in the dusk, the people sitting outside on galleries or front steps, all looking hot in their hot-weather clothes. "I suppose you were awfully in love with her—with your wife," I said then humbly, "but I don't want—I can't help wanting it not to be the same."

"Nothing's ever the same. After fifteen years you turn into a different person, and you care about different things."

"But you cared about her once." I grieved about it still, in the hot August night. "And she was beautiful, and exciting; everybody says so. I suppose I'm not either of those things. Kirby says I'm beautiful, but he thinks he's in love with me, and even he doesn't pretend there's anything particularly glamorous about an evening with Betsy Donlon."

"Now you're trying to make *me* jealous."

"Am I?" I looked at him, startled. "I didn't realize—but I'd like to, if it wouldn't make you unhappy. You have enough unhappiness now; I wouldn't want you to be unhappy about me till some day when everything is perfectly all right again, and you've just been elected governor, or senator, and everybody is telling you what a wonderful person you are—then I'd like you to be just a little unhappy."

"I'm unhappy now. You've made me want all kinds of things I thought I'd learned how to do without."

I didn't know what he meant; I managed an uncertain glance at him as I turned the car south on the Williamsburg Pike.

"What kind of things?"

He looked straight ahead at the road before us.

"Once upon a time," he said ironically, "I thought there were certain things a man had to have to love and to be loved—not so much money and success as the things that brought them—courage, talent, wisdom, strength. I know better than that now—as a matter of fact, I finally learned, after a good many years, that you need an entirely different set of ingredients if what you want to end up with is money and success—but all the same you've made me wish I had them to give you—"

"You have all those things."

"I *had* them," he corrected me gently. "Or wait a minute—even that comes under the heading of bragging; I liked to think I had them. Now I can't even keep up that illusion any more; there are too many other equally disillusioned people to remind me of the way things really are if I happen to forget it myself."

I didn't know what to say to him; how can you argue with anyone about something like that? I drove on; we passed fields, houses, trees, vague in the fading dusk, then the sudden lights of a screened shanty advertising BEER—CARRY OUT, with a thin old man—bare-torso'd above dark trousers, his body brown and hairless as an Indian's—on the front steps, framed in gaudy advertisements for tobacco and soft drinks.

"I don't think any of that has anything to do with loving someone," I said finally. "But I can be strong enough for both of us if that's what you want; I could learn anything—how to walk a tightrope, or to keep a dozen gilt balls in the air at one time—if that was what you needed—"

He shook his head. "I'm afraid the only thing that makes sense about that statement is the kind of comparisons you've used," he said. "Some day you *are* going to look back at all this the way you would at a day at the circus, and you'll realize then that it was just as un-real, under the spangles and the glitter—that what you took for gold was only tinsel, and that a politician like me isn't even the young man on the flying trapeze, but the clown of the piece, mocking his own shortcomings for other people's amusement. It's not good enough for you, Betsy; after the band has stopped playing and the crowd has gone home, there's only the sweat and the bad air and the money to be counted—"

I couldn't say anything; if it was only an argument between us, which had to be settled logically, I was at a disadvantage; all I had was feelings, not reasons. It was dark now, and I switched on the headlights of the car; the beams went rushing on before us, swallow-ing up trees and road and the sudden sideways apparition of a house.

"I drove down this road once with a boy," I said, "and he stopped the car somewhere around here and kissed me and I cried, because I thought I was never going to be in love. I was eighteen then—"

"You're in such a hurry."

"Yes, I suppose so. But there's something else you don't know about me. I may be in a hurry, but I can wait too."

We were coming near to Williamsburg now; I glanced at my watch —a quarter past eight.

"You'll be there in plenty of time," I said. "What will it be like tonight? Kirby says—"

He smiled. "Nothing's ever quite as bad as Kirby says."

"I suppose not. But I wish it were over."

"It won't be long now."

"And then what? They won't really bring that Judson business to trial, will they? Not after the election—after they've got everything they want out of using it?"

He didn't answer for a moment. "I'm not sure," he said then. "Logically, they won't—but it doesn't look as if logic had much to do with all this. The girl's being used now, but she had her own reason for telling the story she did in the first place, and apparently politics didn't enter into that."

"She *can't* realize what she's doing to you. Nobody only fourteen could be that callous—"

"Well, I don't suppose she's even thought of that," he said. "She probably used all her available imagination to invent that story; now I'm only a convenience to her, like a life preserver to a drowning man."

I drove down Williamsburg's main street—the lights again now, green and red and bright-white in the summer darkness, and the people staring lazily from porch swings or front steps as we passed, a radio's voice lamenting somewhere behind them to a fiddle's persistent whine.

"You can let me off here," Ivor said. "It's just around the corner."

"I don't know a soul in this town. If anyone wants to know who I am, you can tell them I'm Kirby's girl."

"I'm glad you're not Kirby's girl."

I swung the car round the corner.

"That's one of the nicest things you've said all evening." Bringing the car to a stop, I looked at him, putting everything about the way I felt there for him to remember. "If I'm anybody's girl at all, I'm yours; I would be, if you'd let me be."

He shook his head, but for a moment, sitting there in the half-darkness of the car, seeing the serious and unhappy expression in his eyes, I felt that we both wanted exactly what I wanted—to hold on to this special little piece of time and forget there would ever have to be any others. But Ken was already coming up to the car; there wasn't going to be even another moment for us. Ivor opened the car door and got out.

"Good night, Betsy—you'll go straight home?"

"Good night—good luck."

Ken called to him and he turned around; I put the car into gear and drove away. It hadn't been the best kind of evening, but it hadn't been the worst, either; while I drove back to Fort Paris I remembered the good things about it, and for a long time I didn't think at all of the bad.

X

THE primaries came on the following Tuesday. I didn't see Father all that day; he went out early in the morning and at midnight, when I went up to bed, he still hadn't come in again. I'd listened that long to the returns on the radio—not that I'd needed to, because there was never any question about how things were going to turn out. Every precinct in the state was reporting big majorities for Ed Dodd, and Ivor had already conceded by eleven o'clock.

I wasn't in any mood for sleep after I'd got to bed, and I hadn't even dozed off when, about two o'clock, I head a car roar up the drive. A moment later one of the big oleander tubs—or what sounded like it, anyway—on the front gallery rolled down the steps with enough racket to wake the dead. I got out of bed, put on a robe and slippers, and went downstairs. Outside the front door I could hear Father muttering and cursing under his breath as he tried one key after another in the lock. I switched on the hall light and opened the door. Father looked at it triumphantly as it swung open before him.

"A-at's the daisy—a-at's the trick of it—" Then he saw me standing there and blinked at me, surprised, in the sudden light. "Betsy, baby, what're *you* doing here?"

"I live here; don't you remember? And so do you—"

Aunt Bridgie's voice called in alarm from the upper stairs: "Betsy —are you down there? What is it?"

"It's only Father," I said. I reached out and took his hand and pulled him into the house. "You'd better come on in," I said. "This isn't going to look too good to the neighbors."

Aunt Bridgie came down the stairs in a Japanese kimono, with her front hair in curlers, looking like a frustrated owl.

"Patrick Donlon," she said, "aren't you ashamed—?"

[169]

"Never felt better 'n my life, Bridgie. Been having celebration—"
He flung his arm suddenly around my neck—whether out of affection
or because he felt the need of something to hang on to, I couldn't
decide. "You and Betsy ough' celebrate too," he said. "Ever'thing's go'
be all right now—no more troubles, no more cares—"

"I never saw anything like it," Aunt Bridgie scolded. "Men!—if
they're miserable they have to drink to drown their grief, and if
they're happy they have to drink to enjoy their good fortune. The
only *possible* way to live with them is to see to it that nothing ever
happens to them."

"We'll get him upstairs," I said. "Come on now, Father. You can
tell us all about it in the morning."

Father planted himself stubbornly on his heels.

"Wan' tell you 'bout it now," he said. He cocked his eye in the
direction of the dining room. "You all like to join me in l'il drink?
Been drinking with enemies—thing to do is to drink with friends."

"We're not your friends," Aunt Bridgie said; "we simply have the
misfortune to be related to you. Betsy, you take his other arm—" She
said to Father, as if she were about fifteen years old to his ten: "I
don't know what Pa would say if he could see you now."

"Prob'ly 'gratulate me on knowing good whisky—whole case of it
gone tonight—treated everybody in town. Treated all Ed Dodd's l'il"
—he tried it again—"l'il lickspittles."

"Now that's enough, Patrick. You're going up to bed."

"Not till I tell you funny thing happened tonight." Father drew his
arms free and looked at us determinedly. "Funniest thing happened
t' me in twenty years. Fellow din' wan' drink with me—refused my
whisky—"

"That's all right now, Father. You're keeping Aunt Bridgie out of
bed; it's two o'clock in the morning."

"Is it?" He looked with exaggerated concern at his wrist watch.
"Too late for you to be up, Betsy. Young girl like you ough' be in
bed this hour."

"All right, we'll both go up," I said. "You take my arm—"

"I tried bring you up way your mother would have wanted," Father said. All at once his voice broke; he sat down suddenly on the
stairs. "I tried be good father to you, Betsy. Now people look at me
like Judas Iscarrot-cariot—"

"This is ridiculous, Patrick," Aunt Bridgie said. "How you can boast

[170]

to this poor child of being a good father to her, when you come home to her in this condition—"

Father sat there on the stairs, shaking his head and weeping quietly.

"I was a poor boy, Bridgie; I knew what it was to wear patches on my pants. Now I'm successful, and the whole world's against me—"

"Nobody's against you but yourself. And I don't like all this talk about your being so poor, either. Pa was a good, sober, hard-working man, and it's a reflection on him to say he didn't make a decent living for all of us."

"He was a good, sober, hard-working God-damn fool," Father said. Aunt Bridgie said, "Patrick Donlon!"—as shocked as if he had broken three of the Ten Commandments at once, but he went on stubbornly: "God-damn fool—that's what I said. Never thought big—acted big—never took a chance—Charlie Martin made his million feeding moldy beans and rotten beef to the poor devils that built the railroads in this state, and then sat in his fine office on Henrico Street and ran the railroad he'd soured good men's guts to build, but Timmy Donlon was in on that same ground floor and where'd it get him? 'Charlie Martin's errand boy—Charlie Martin's errand boy'—I heard him called that to his face. Well, by God, nobody can say that about me."

Aunt Bridgie looked as if the walls had collapsed on top of her; all at once she leaned against the newel and began to cry.

"Now look here, Father," I said, "this has gone far enough. You're going up to bed."

He stood up, staring guiltily at Aunt Bridgie.

"All right now, Bridgie—all right," he said thickly. "I never meant to hurt your feelings."

"You can ask God to forgive you," Aunt Bridgie said passionately, "ask Him to forgive you, if He can, for slandering the dead. Your own father—"

"Yerrah, the hell with it—my own father!" he said, catching fire again at her tone. "If he'd had the sense of a gosling we'd all be rolling in millions today, and there'd be no need for me to go dodging around corners for fear of meeting an old friend who wouldn't even pass the time of day with me—"

"If you're dodging around corners, it's your own fault then," Aunt Bridgie said, trembling with emotion, "because there never was a

Donlon—never!—before this day who couldn't hold his head up with the best man alive."

Apparently she considered that dramatic bit a fitting exit line, because she gathered her kimono around her and swept up the stairs when she had finished it; if Father ended the night in his own bed, it wasn't going to be by any ministrations of hers. Father stood staring up after her as if she had been a comet in the night sky.

"Damn hypocritical women—" he muttered. "When the old man was alive, they fought each other like Kilkenny cats, but now he's dead, the saints themselves aren't good enough to keep comp'ny with him." He turned to me fiercely. "When I'm dead, Betsy, you tell t' truth about me."

"I'll tell the truth about you now," I said. "You've had too much to drink, and you're going up to bed. Come *on* now."

I got him up the stairs; at the head he stopped and began haranguing me again.

"All my life," he said, "I've been an honest man—"

"I know all about your life, Father. Now you're coming along with me and go to bed."

"Made plenty of money—spent it like a lord—no, like a king—" He nodded at me solemnly. "I'll tell you God's truth, Betsy: the Donlons were kings of Ireland when these Johnny-come-latelies were knocking at back doors for a handout."

"That's fine," I said. "We certainly look like a royal family tonight. Now let's see if we can't get this king of Ireland to bed—"

He went into the bedroom with me. By that time the burst of energy his quarrel with Aunt Bridgie had aroused in him had died down again, and he submitted docilely to having me help him off with his coat and tie.

"You're a fine girl, Betsy," he said to me. "Not like Bridgie—all talk and tears. You go back to that college now—wha's a name?"

"Bryn Mawr," I said. "Only I'm not going back." I folded back the bedspread. "All right, Father; sit down now and take off your shoes—"

"Meet a nice young man—plenty of money—family like wha's name down in La Fayette, got a pedigree long as his horses'—Tyler Dewarr—"

"That's a nice dream," I said. "You go on to sleep now; you've got a good start on it already."

"Give you biggest wedding you ever saw," Father said drowsily.

"Have every big shot in 'a state there, drinking champagne. Plenty of money now—plenty of money—"

I left him still muttering, "Plenty of money," and went back to my own room. A moment later Aunt Bridgie came in. She was still crying.

"I'm sorry, Betsy," she said. "I shouldn't have left you—I couldn't help—"

"It's all right," I said. "Stop crying, Aunt Bridgie; he didn't mean half of what he said. He's living in some damn world of his own, where everybody's to blame except him." I found some cigarettes in the night table and lit one; my hands were shaking. "*He's* sorry for himself—" I said. "I wonder how he thinks Ivor feels tonight."

"Ivor—?" Aunt Bridgie looked at me as if I had introduced a strange new character into the conversation. As far as she was concerned, what had happened downstairs was something that referred back to events and tensions of thirty years before; she was far more absorbed in Father's unfilial references to their father than she could ever have been in any political treacheries he had performed. "What has that—?"

"All right," I said. "Never mind. We don't have to talk about any of this, do we? Why don't you go back to bed?"

She looked distractedly at my cigarette. "You oughtn't to smoke in bed, Betsy."

"I'm not going to smoke in bed. I'm going to sit right here and read a magazine till I get sleepy."

It was a good plan, but it didn't work. I couldn't read; after a little I turned out the light and got back into bed and lay there wondering if things were ever going to be right again. It seemed highly improbable that they would, but even at two o'clock in the morning, when you're only twenty, it isn't hard to be hopeful if you're willing to look a couple of years into the future. I was electing Ivor senator and getting married to him in a big wedding in St. Denis Cathedral up in Queensport when I finally dozed off, and if my dreams weren't quite as good as that after I feel asleep it was only because I didn't dream of Ivor at all but of my grandfather Donlon, who was solemnly dancing an Irish jig with Aunt Bridgie and the presidents of half a dozen railroads.

It was after eight when I got up the next morning. What woke me was the front door closing sharply downstairs; it wasn't Father who had left the house, because his bedroom door was still shut when I got up, so I figured it out that it had been Aunt Bridgie, on her way to church, probably, to pray for Father's sins. I got dressed without much enthusiasm for the task and was just going downstairs to breakfast when the doorbell rang; a moment later Ester came upstairs and said it was Mr. Hays to see Father.

"Kirby?" I said. I couldn't believe my ears. "What on earth—?"

He hadn't been near our house since the afternoon Father had broached the Judson business to him, and eight-thirty in the morning seemed a rather peculiar hour to come calling, anyway. I knocked on Father's door and told him who was downstairs, and then went down myself to see what it was all about.

Kirby was in the living room, with the sort of expression on his face that a man might reasonably be expected to wear who was going to settle something with pistols at twenty paces. It turned a little friendlier, though, when he saw me.

"Hello, Betsy," he said. "Isn't Pat here? I came early so I wouldn't miss him—"

"He isn't up yet. I told him you were here." I wanted to find out why he had come, but there was something else I had to find out first. "How was it last night?" I said. "I heard the returns—"

"Well—" He considered it. "I've been to livelier wakes."

"Was it worse than you expected?"

"Let's just say it wasn't good. I'm not going to get any pleasure out of talking about it, you know."

But there was something else I had to know; I asked him about that next: "And Ivor—?"

He shrugged. "He'll live. You want to know something? I once knew a fellow who ran for the town council down in Caldwell and got exactly one vote—his own. Even he ate his breakfast the next morning."

There were footsteps on the stairs; I saw Kirby stiffen. It was Father, of course; he came to the doorway, in robe and slippers, and stood there looking at Kirby as if he weren't awake enough to be sure he had heard what he had heard from me upstairs or that he was seeing what he saw now.

"It's Kirby, Father," I said helpfully.

"I can see it's Kirby." He looked at Kirby belligerently. "What the hell are you doing here? I'm not running any unemployment agency,

[174]

if that's what you're after. You picked your man; now let him take care of you—"

"Father!" I said. Kirby started to say something, but I stopped him too. "I don't know what this is all about," I said, "but I'm not going to stand here and listen to either of you saying things you'll be sorry for later. Kirby's in your house, Father; the least you can do is to be civil to him."

Father simmered down at once; he was too subdued this morning anyway to be able to keep up that belligerent attitude for very long.

"All right, all right," he said. "Sit down, Kirby; I didn't mean that. I feel like the devil this morning; you picked a bad time—"

Kirby regarded him unsympathetically. "A little too much celebration last night?" he said. "Well, you had something to celebrate, all right; Ed Dodd must have broken every record in the book with that vote, and you're the boy who did it all."

That didn't help matters; Father immediately flared up again.

"You didn't have to go through with it, did you?" he asked. "If Kelly'd had any sense, he'd have got out of the race; nobody wanted to crucify him."

"That's nice to know," Kirby said. "I've been wondering about that; as a matter of fact, that's the reason I'm here this morning. I want to know what Ed Dodd's going to do about that Judson business— whether he's willing to call off the dogs, now that the election's in the bag, or whether he just enjoys kicking a man when he's down—"

Father interrupted him indignantly. "Nobody enjoyed anything about this mess; you ought to know that. *Sure* Ed wanted to win— so does everybody, when they're in a race like that—and he had every right to use the Judson business for what it was worth to him. If Kelly took a beating on account of it, he should have thought of that before he got the Judson kid in trouble."

"For your information," Kirby said, "he didn't get her in trouble, but I'm not going to argue about that with you now. All I want to know is whether Ed Dodd's willing to let Judson drop that charge against Ivor. He's got what he wanted out of it; he's not going to sit in the governor's mansion any longer for letting that case go into court and having the whole thing thrashed out all over again on the front page of every newspaper in the state."

Kirby hadn't sat down, but Father sat down then himself; as a matter of fact, he looked as if he weren't sure of his ability to stand up any longer.

[175]

"All right, I know all that," he agreed. He took his head in his hands. "My God, Kirby, do you have to bother me with this now? I feel like the end of the world—"

"You're getting too old for these kind of tricks," Kirby said. "What were you trying to do, anyway?—show Ed Dodd's little friends you were as good a man as any of them?"

"Ah, the hell with the whole crew of them!" Father said. He looked up at Kirby suddenly, between fury and self-pity. "I tell you, Kirby, there isn't one of them I'd trust beyond the turn of the next corner. A gang of mealymouthed hypocrites, all of them, looking at me like they'd expect me to rob the poor box in a church if they didn't keep a good eye out for me—"

I could see this wasn't what Kirby had expected; for a moment he looked the way the poor but honest farmer in an ancient melodrama might have looked if the mustachio'd villain who had just foreclosed his mortgage had suddenly appealed to him for sympathy. Then he shook his head and sat down and said: "What do you want me to do about it? Give you a certificate saying you're a trustworthy character of the highest moral caliber—as long as you're sure you're on the winning side?"

Father flushed up, and I said quickly: "That's not going to do any good either, Kirby. I thought politicians knew how to get around people; you'll never get anyone if all you're going to do is antagonize them."

Kirby nodded at me; he seemed tired and irritated. "King Solomon," he said. "You're getting mighty wise for your years, aren't you?"

"You leave Betsy out of this," Father said. He glanced at me as if he would have liked to tell me to leave the room, but after last night he was probably pretty doubtful about how much moral authority he could muster. "She's right, too," he said darkly, to Kirby. "If you want to ask a favor of a man, the least you can do is not insult him in his own house."

"I'm not asking a favor of anybody," Kirby said stubbornly. "All I want is some information: is Ed Dodd going to let that Judson business go into court or isn't he?"

"God Almighty, man, it's not up to him!" Father got up again and walked over and picked up a cigarette nervously from a box on a table, but decided against it, with a look of revulsion, before he had so much as struck a match to light it. "As far as he's concerned, the whole thing can be dropped right now," he said, "but I told you when this first came up—Ike Judson's in dead earnest about it. Somebody's fed him the comforting idea that in this state a man can go to the chair for rape—which is true as far as it goes, of course—and nobody ever bothered to explain to him that rape with consent is an altogether different thing, that as a matter of fact he'd be lucky if this business ended with Kelly getting a six months' sentence. And as for calling the whole thing off, withdrawing the charge—"

"Well, he must have cooled down a little by this time," Kirby said. "You haven't talked to him lately, have you?"

"No." Father looked unconvinced. "But I know how he feels."

"A lot of people feel that way when they find out the women they're related to aren't any different from any other women," Kirby said. "But they don't go on feeling like that the rest of their lives. Judson's done a pretty good job of it, singlehanded, in seeing to it that Ivor isn't going to be governor of this state; I should think he'd be set up enough about that right now to be willing to call it quits, if the right person put it to him in the right way."

"Meaning that I'm that right person, I suppose," Father said, belligerent again. "Well, you give me one good reason why I should stick my neck out and get into this mess again."

"I can give you a couple of them," Kirby said, "but the best one is that you seem to have the inside track when it comes to getting your friend Judson to do what you want him to do. The way you tell it, anyway, you're Emily Post and a father-confessor rolled into one, as far as he's concerned."

Father looked as if he were going to resent that too, but I interrupted again to ask Kirby if he had had breakfast; I knew if I could put either him or Father in a little better mood there was less chance of the whole thing's breaking up in a quarrel. I finally persuaded him to have some coffee, and then went back to the kitchen to fix a pick-me-up for Father; after that things got a little less edgy, and before Aunt Bridgie came back from church the two of them were talking to each other with at least as much civility as a pair of opposing lawyers outside a courtroom instead of inside one. I think, at heart, Father was so glad to have a chance to talk to one of his old friends, and so anxious to redeem himself in Kirby's eyes, that he would have ended by promising to reason with Ike Judson even if I hadn't done anything at all. But I liked to think I had helped too, and Kirby did say, "Thanks for the assist, Betsy"—just before he left the house.

I didn't see Father again till dinnertime; he dressed and went out as soon as Kirby had gone. I hoped he was going to see Ike Judson, but I couldn't be sure; as far as I knew, his haste to get out of the house might have been inspired more by a desire to avoid Aunt Bridgie, who was in a moralizing mood, than to see what he could do about Kirby's request. I could understand his point of view; when something happened to open the capacious coffers of Aunt Bridgie's family recollections, every Donlon peccadillo and virtue of the past fifty years was likely to be brought out for review before she closed them up again. I'd been invited out for lunch and tennis myself, and though I felt about as much like playing tennis as I did like climbing Mount Everest, I went, just to have something to take me out of earshot of that depressing catalogue of family history.

It was about five-thirty when I got home. A thunderstorm had interrupted the tennis, so I'd spent half the afternoon trying not to fall asleep while I lisened to a Princeton junior explaining why Notre Dame wasn't going to beat Army next season—or maybe it was the other way around. I hadn't gone up to change yet when Father came in, looking as if he'd had about as bad a day as I'd had; he only grunted when I asked him if he'd seen Ike Judson, and went on upstairs to his room. When he came down for dinner I cornered him, though, and said I wanted to hear all about it.

"There isn't anything to hear," he said irritably. "All right, yes, I talked to him—told him the chances were the thing wouldn't stand up in court, that he'd be sensible to settle for the fact that he'd ruined any chance of Kelly's ever being governor of this state—But he's such a damn queer duck; he stands there looking at you like he was a deaf-and-dumb idiot when you try to argue with him."

He looked so uncomfortable about it that I was sure there was more to it than that.

"But he must have said *some*thing," I said to him. "Are you trying to tell me that he still wants something worse to happen to Ivor?—that he won't drop the charges?"

"He didn't say he would or he wouldn't. I tell you, he didn't say much of anything—just kept standing there looking at me with that dazed look on his face, and then went off muttering something about doing the Lord's work. He acts like he's off his rocker, if you want my opinion; *I* can't help it if I can't pound any sense into that collection of damfool ideas he calls a brain."

He was getting excited about it, and Aunt Bridgie came in just

[178]

then to say dinner was ready, so I dropped the subject for the moment, but only for the moment; the way he had talked about Judson had started me worrying. At the table I slid in between Aunt Bridgie's pointed reminiscences to ask him if he had talked to Kirby about his conversation with Judson, and when he said he hadn't I said: "Don't you think you should?"

"Why?" he asked. "To tell him I didn't get anywhere with Judson, and have him act like he didn't believe I even tried? I'll have another go at it tomorrow; if I keep at it long enough, I may be able to get a few rational ideas into that fool's head."

"But if Judson should do something in the meantime?" I said. "I mean—if he really is irresponsible, and you've made him believe he can't get a conviction in court against Ivor—? You said once that his idea of settling all this was to go out after Ivor with a gun—"

Father shook his head impatiently. "I tell you he's still got that court idea on the brain; he's not going to do anything else right now, except maybe talk the whole thing over with Jehovah." He stopped and regarded me with sudden suspicion. "You're awfully interested in all this," he said. "Is it that damn Kelly still—?"

"It wouldn't make any difference who it was, as long as there was any danger of Judson's getting violent about it," I said. "I think you *ought* to talk to Kirby, Father."

Father looked at me angrily. "I'm not going to talk to anybody. Damn it, Betsy, if I thought you were likely to get mixed up with that fellow—"

"What on earth are you talking about, Pat?" Aunt Bridgie asked. "Betsy and *Kirby*—? Why, she was out all afternoon with one of the Butler boys."

"Well, she'd better stick to the Butler boys, if she knows what's good for her," Father said. He turned a harassed face on Aunt Bridgie. "You ought to be looking out for her, Bridgie; that's *your* job—but you don't even see what goes on under your nose. Betsy and Kirby—!"

"Kirby's a fine young man," Aunt Bridgie said firmly, "but he's too ambitious to make a good husband. That's always been your trouble too, Pat; my goodness, you'd think you had to own the whole world, and then you get involved with all sorts of people, and things happen like last night—"

"What has last night got to do with it?" Father shouted. "I'm talking about Betsy."

"Then you should have thought of her before you came home to her in that condition," Aunt Bridgie said. "I'm sure you didn't mean to do it, Pat, but you really should realize—"

Father gave up; he pushed his chair back violently, got up, and slammed out of the house without another word. Aunt Bridgie looked at me.

"What did I *say?*" she asked.

"It's all right, Aunt Bridgie. We're all upset today." I got up too. "I'm going to call Kirby," I said. "Someone ought to."

I went out to the hall and called his home number, still hearing her uncomprehending, protesting voice behind me in the dining room. It was Mrs. Hays, Kirby's mother, who answered the phone; when I told her who it was on the other end of the wire, we had to go into a long polite Irish catechism about the health of all the members of both our families before I could ask her if Kirby was there, and then I was disappointed, because he wasn't. She hadn't any idea when he would be back, but she promised that she'd have him call me when he came in, and I hung up and went into the living room to wait.

It had begun to rain again outside, and Aunt Bridgie, who came in to join me, was carrying on a conversation that didn't require any more from me than an occasional *yes* or *no*, so I had plenty of time to worry about what Father had said about Ike Judson. By eight o'clock I was so uneasy that I went out to the hall and called the Hays number again and asked Mrs. Hays if she knew where I could get in touch with Ivor, if Kirby still wasn't home. She was a little reluctant to tell me at first—she was a shrewd old woman, who managed to keep herself very well informed about all of Kirby's business —but I told her it might be urgent and she finally said: "Oh, he's out at a house somebody lent him on the Williamsburg Pike, but nobody's supposed to know; they don't want those reporters after him. Mr. Hieronymus it is, or something like that—"

"Mr. *Who?*"

"Hieronymus, if I've got it right. Isn't that the devil of a name? He had something to do with the campaign—a little, dark man— you've probably seen him yourself—"

"Oh—!" I realized all at once whom she meant. "Yes, I know him. I never knew his name; I've been calling him Mr. Anonymous."

I thanked her and hung up and then called the only Hieronymus in the phone book, but it was disappointment this time again; I ended up talking to the operator, who said that that number had been disconnected for the summer. I sat there in the hall trying to think what to do next—feeling like a fool to be so worried, but it seemed I couldn't be sensible about it. I made up my mind to drive out to the Hieronymus house myself.

I got a raincoat out of the hall closet and called to Aunt Bridgie, in the living room, that I was going out for a while. It was pouring rain outside, and she called some astonished question back to me, but I didn't wait to argue about it with her; I wasn't sure enough myself that what I was doing was making sense to be able to convince anybody else that it did. But I had to tell someone what was worrying me, even if I was laughed at afterward for seeing goblins in the dark.

I had a hard time finding the house; it was set back from the road, and I missed it in the rain and the darkness. At the place where I stopped to inquire they told me firmly that Mr. Hieronymus was away for the summer and the house was empty, but I went back anyway and found it by their directions. There was a light somewhere in the rear of the house, and the door was opened almost as soon as I rang: it was Ivor, looking at me in complete astonishment.

"Betsy—! What are you doing here? I heard the car; I thought it was Kirby—"

"I had to see you; I tried to call Kirby, but he was out—"

All at once I was perfectly convinced that I oughtn't to have come, that he would be sure to think this was only another maneuver on my part to see him again; I even started to back away from the door, as if I had no intention of coming in. I saw his puzzled face.

"What's this all about? Come in out of that rain; are you trying to catch pneumonia?"

"I only wanted to tell you—" I came into the hall, where white-shrouded shapes of furniture stood solemnly in the dimness; the house had a closed, deserted feel. "I thought someone ought to know, and I couldn't reach either you or Kirby by phone," I said. "It's about Ike Judson; Father talked to him today, about his dropping the charges against you, and I'm afraid he may have made things worse—"

Ivor looked at me as if I had been speaking to him in Arabic.

"You'd better begin at the beginning," he said; "I'm way behind you. Come on in and sit down; there are a couple of rooms in this house that are a little more cheerful than this."

"I oughtn't to stay. I just came to tell you—"

"Well, we can stand here if you like, but it seems like a pretty uncomfortable thing to do." Then he smiled and I smiled too; everything began to be all right. "Let me take your coat," he said. "We can't have you dripping all over Hieronymus's furniture; I promised him I'd take good care of things."

I followed him back through the hall to a sunroom cheerful with chintz and wicker furniture.

"Are you here alone?" I asked him.

"Hieronymus's cook comes in to get dinner and straighten the place up. She's gone home now." He motioned me to a chair and sat down himself on a chintz-covered couch across the room. "Now what was it you wanted to tell me?" he asked.

"It's about Ike Judson." Now that I had to put it into words, it all seemed rather melodramatic and absurd; I didn't know how to explain it to him. "I suppose it's silly of me, but I was worried," I said. "You know Kirby came to see Father this morning and asked him to persuade Judson to drop the charges against you?"

"No, I didn't know." There was an unreadable expression suddenly on Ivor's face. "What does Kirby think—that I'm a charity case now, and he can go around soliciting contributions?"

"It wasn't like that at all. He simply wanted to know whether Ed Dodd was going to insist on letting the case go to court, and when Father said he wasn't—well, of course Father knows Judson better than anyone else does, and he's the logical one to talk to him."

The expression went away as quickly as it had come; he shook his head, smiling at me a little.

"I don't know how you do it, but you always manage it so that, whatever happens, it isn't *my* pride that's hurt. Don't you ever think I do *any*thing wrong?"

"Of course I do. But I don't see why you've done something wrong because Kirby had a perfectly logical conversation with Father—"

A sneeze interrupted me; I slipped my feet out of my damp shoes and tucked them up under me in the chair.

"You shouldn't have come out in this rain," Ivor said. "What did you think was going to happen to me?"

"I don't know. Father said some things tonight that started me worrying. You know he always did say that Judson's idea of how to settle this whole thing was with a gun."

"I'm not sure I wouldn't agree with him, if it was my daughter,"

[182]

Ivor said. "But why now? He's had plenty of time to do something drastic if he'd wanted to."

"Because Father talked to him today and tried to convince him that he wouldn't gain anything by taking this to court," I explained it. "Of course Ed Dodd's people have been telling him just the opposite all this time; he may not even have believed Father—"

"What does Pat think about it?"

"He doesn't think there's anything to worry about, I suppose. He told me I was being foolish when I said he ought to call Kirby."

"And he doesn't know you're here, of course?"

"No. He was out when I left."

"Then I think we'd better see to it that you're there when he gets back." Ivor stood up decisively, smiling at me. "The next thing you know, *he'll* be coming around here with a gun."

I looked up at him. All at once I realized what was so strange about all this—not being alone with him, but being here with him in this deserted house, with no one else around, or likely to come around; I was so used to seeing him surrounded by admiring crowds and busy followers. I thought that Kirby should have stayed with him; someone should have stayed. . . .

"Do you really want me to go?" I asked.

"What I want you to do isn't important. It's certainly the sensible thing for you to do, from any angle."

"I don't care about being sensible." I stood up; in my stocking feet I was a whole head shorter than he was; I concentrated on the knot of his tie. "If you wanted me to stay, I'd never go away; I told you once how I felt—"

He kissed me once gently, then again, differently—the two of us breathless suddenly in the quiet room.

"My God, you're a wonderful girl," he said. "If I could only believe—"

"What?"

"—that anything I could do would make you happy—"

"I'm happy just being with you."

He shook his head. "You're not like anyone I've ever known. Everyone else wants something from you—strength, or money, or the ability to make them feel important—but you don't want anything."

"There isn't anything else to want when I'm with you."

Then it had to happen again; we were too close together to be apart now—afterward he drew me over to the couch.

"Come here and we'll talk about this."

I sat down in the circle of his arm—frightened now, because something was going to be decided; my whole life suddenly seemed at dead center, with incalculable forces spinning wildly outside it.

"We can't go on this way," he began. "At least I can't; I'm in love with you, and I've got all the normal human reactions that go with it—"

"Then there isn't any problem—is there?"

"There are all the problems there ever were—the biggest one of all is that I'd like to forget the rest of them and marry you, no matter how many regrets either of us might have later."

"You haven't even asked me yet." I sat up, radiant. "I'd like to be asked."

"I'm not going to ask you—not now, anyway. Maybe some day, if I can get my life straightened out to the point where somebody not involved in this might think I had an outside chance of making you happy—" He broke off. "You see what you do to me when you look at me like that; I'm even capable of making optimistic plans for the future."

"There's no reason why you shouldn't make optimistic plans for the future if they have anything to do with me. And even if they haven't—things won't always be this way, you know. Some day the truth will come out about the Judson girl, and you can start all over—"

"I've got to start all over whether the truth comes out or not. That's not a very pretty picture, Betsy; I wonder if you have any idea what it means." He smiled at me a little ruefully. "I'm not young and enthusiastic any more, you know, with a lot of nice illusions; I have to work with what I have—"

"You have everything you need."

"Secondhand hopes and cut-rate ambitions—I'm lucky to have even those. Bringing you into that would be like bringing a diamond into a five-and-dime store."

But we moved together again suddenly; for a while there didn't seem to be the necessity of saying anything at all. I finally said it first: "Ivor—"

"Yes?"

"We *are* in love—aren't we? We can't change that—"

"No, I suppose we can't." I was sitting again in the circle of his arm, perfectly happy, watching the rain slide down the windows;

after a while I heard his voice, sober and thoughtful, over my head: "I told you once I couldn't take your fine new life and turn it into something bitter, but I wonder if it was really you I was thinking of then or myself. It's always easier not to try for the best; when you get older you learn what to tear yourself to pieces for and what isn't worth it, but it's a continuing process and after a while, if you aren't careful, even the best things seem priced too high—"

"You wouldn't have to tear yourself to pieces for me."

"No. I'd only have to try to get back all the things I lost or gave up or destroyed somewhere along the line during the past twenty years. That's what I'm afraid of; it's an even worse problem. And if I failed at it, I wouldn't just be failing for myself; it would be for you too."

"You won't fail. You can do anything you want to do."

"The way I won that election?"

"You didn't even want to win it—really. You were going through the motions—weren't you?—because that was what people expected of you."

"You're such a wise child."

"I can be wise for you. I told you once—I'll be anything you need—"

We were in the future now, not in the past or even in the present, where there were things to worry about and nothing was sure and settled except that we loved each other—for a while so much in the future that it was Ivor who had to try hard to remember the present and say at last, abruptly: "You're going home now. This isn't the wisest thing—"

"Not for just a little. I want to pretend that we really are married—that this is our house and I never have to go away." I got up, looking around happily at the room—the strange walls and furniture, a picture on the table of a younger Mr. Hieronymus smiling in proud parental worry between two small serious children and a young woman with dark flashing eyes. "I didn't know Mr. Hieronymus was married," I said. "Are these his wife and children? Where does he keep them?"

"They all died in a fire seven or eight years ago. He's an unlucky little man—"

"I'm sorry. They look so happy." Something clutched at my own happiness; you could lose things so quickly, then? But I brushed it aside and went over to the window and looked out—at the fireflies rising from the wet grass, the dark trees moving against the sky, the gleam of a metal garden chair. "The rain's almost over," I said. There was a faint flicker of lightning in the west, and the gentle sound of rain on wet leaves. I turned around to Ivor. "What's going to happen to us now?"

"You're going home, like a sensible girl, and wait till we see how I make out."

"I suppose I'll have to go back to college next month. Father wants me to go East again, but I'll go down to State; I want to be where I can see you."

He came over and touched my cheek gently with one hand, chiding me and approving of me with one gesture.

"You're not going to see me till this Judson business is over," he said. "I'm not going to have you dragged into that."

"And then—?"

"Then it's up to me—isn't it?—to prove that I can do at least half as good a job at putting things together as you think I can."

"You could do it for me. It's always easier to do things for someone you love."

I stretched my face up for his kiss; we clung there together for a moment in the quiet room while every difficulty solved itself and questions answered themselves or became unimportant.

"Now you really are going home," he said.

I sighed. "Yes. You always know best about everything."

"I couldn't do anything to hurt you—if things don't work out—"

"Don't say that." I looked up at him. "They're going to work out; I know they are."

"You're too young even to believe in failure." He reached down abruptly and found my shoes, as if he wanted to do something to change the subject. "Here, you're not going without these—"

I slipped them on, and he went out with me to the dark, shrouded hall. My coat was hanging on the rack; he picked it up and held it for me while I put it on.

"Maybe I'd better drive up to Fort Paris with you," he said. "What time is it?"

"It's only around ten. I'd like that, but you'd have to take a cab back, and there might be some trouble with Father. I'll be all right."

"That's the only thing that's important—that you *are* all right." His hands were still on my shoulders; he turned me around slowly so that I was facing him. "I wish you'd remember that, Betsy. I've had all the chances to be happy and successful that anyone has a right to

[186]

expect in one life, but you're just starting on yours, and you want to gamble them all on me—"

"I want *you* to be happy," I insisted. "You're always talking about how important it is for me to be, but it's just as important for you. Couldn't I make you happy?"

"You've made me realize that I'm going to go on living; in a way, that's even more important."

I stared at him, a little frightened. "Did you think you mightn't?"

"It's a very complicated subject—" He realized suddenly what I was thinking and said, smiling: "My God, don't get any ideas in your head; I was talking about something a lot less dramatic than that. It's just—you go through your whole life worrying about what it would be like if you really hit bottom, and when you do—well, you find out that you can still have the most important things left, after all. That's a big discovery for somebody like me to make, Betsy, after spending half a lifetime under the illusion that if a lot of people didn't admire me the world would automatically end."

"A lot of people do admire you. I do, and all those people who voted for you, and Martha, and Kirby—he doesn't really want to, but he does."

"You're going to make me believe I'm a great guy yet, if you keep this up. Don't you know a little humility's good for me?"

The door was open now on the fresh rain-washed night; I went down the steps reluctantly and got into the car. He came with me; when I had gotten in, he closed the car door between us and I put the window down and looked out at him.

"You will take care of yourself?" I said. "It may be foolish of me, but I'll be a lot happier when I know that Judson business is all settled."

"I'll be careful."

"And you'll phone me, or write to me?"

"Wait and see how this comes out, Betsy."

I shook my head. "I can wait. Maybe you don't think I can, but I'll prove it."

I started the motor and put the car into gear; it had already begun to move backward down the drive when he called: "Betsy—"

I stopped the car. "Yes?"

He came up and put his hand on the car door; as I leaned my face to the window he stood there looking at me, bareheaded and serious in the mistlike rain.

"Don't wait too long, Betsy," he said.

"I'll wait as long as I have to."

"No. Don't wait too long."

He didn't say any more, and I didn't know what else to say; after a moment's silence I backed the car on out to the road. As I turned it north toward Fort Paris I looked back and waved, and I saw him raise his hand in a grave salute. He was still standing there in the rain, looking after me—or maybe only into his own uncertain future—as I drove off, it was that picture that I carried away with me. . . .

When I got home and went up the steps to the house somebody was waiting for me at the door. It was Father, with Aunt Bridgie materializing nervously out of the shadows behind him as soon as I was inside the house.

"Betsy—?" he said, immediately and peremptorily. "I want to talk to you—"

"All right, Father—as soon as I hang up this coat."

"I want to know where you've been—"

I turned around, astonished; I had never heard him sound quite so grimly determined before. I looked at Aunt Bridgie, but she didn't meet my eyes; apparently whatever ideas Father had about where I had been were based on a conversation he had had with her, and she was feeling guilty about it now. I tried to remember how much she might have been able to gather from what she had heard of my conversation with Mrs. Hays, and came quickly to the conclusion that she had probably heard enough to make the whole truth not only wise but necessary. At any rate, I wasn't ashamed of it; I was perfectly willing to tell it to everybody, as long as it didn't make any more trouble for Ivor.

"I've been to see Ivor," I said. "I tried to reach him or Kirby by phone, about that Judson business, but I couldn't—I thought somebody ought to know—"

I was trying to sound matter-of-fact about it, but it didn't work; the expression on Father's face didn't change.

"I'll tell you something *you* ought to know," he said violently, "and that is that a decent girl doesn't pay visits to a man like Ivor Kelly alone, at night. I want to know what the hell kind of business is going on here, anyway, and how long it's been going on—"

"Now look here, Father—" I began.

He banged his hand on the newel. "And don't give me any of that,

[188]

either," he said. "I want to know, without any beating around the bush. Have you been seeing that fellow—?"

"Yes, I have—not as often as I'd like to, but as often as he'd let me. This wasn't his idea tonight, you know."

He looked at me incredulously. "And that's what you'd like me to believe?—that you—a girl like you—would go running after a man like that—"

"Nobody's been running after anybody. You may as well know it, Father—I'm in love with him, and he is with me. But it wasn't something either of us planned; it just happened—"

"And I suppose it just happened too that he's made you act like the kind of cheap little bitch that goes sneaking around to hotel rooms—"

"There weren't any hotel rooms." All at once I was so angry that I couldn't even pretend to be taking this calmly. "He's out at Mr. Hieronymus's house, on the Williamsburg Pike; there wasn't anybody else there, but if there had been, I wouldn't have been ashamed of anything that happened. And there's something else you may as well know, too, while we're about it," I went on—"that I'll marry him any time he asks me—"

Father looked at me, breathing hard. "By God, you're not going to marry him. By God, you're not—"

"Now, Pat—" Aunt Bridgie had an alarmed expression on her face. "Betsy—You're both taking all this much too seriously. Of course Betsy isn't going to marry anybody now; she's going back to college next month, and some day, when a suitable young man comes along—"

"I'm not interested in 'suitable' young men," I said. I turned to Aunt Bridgie. "If you and Father have any ideas of getting into the Social Register by marrying me off to some 'suitable' young man, you'd better drop them right now. Because I know what I want—"

"To marry a man any decent woman would be ashamed to be seen walking the streets with?" Father said. He turned furiously to Aunt Bridgie. "Isn't this what I've been telling you?—that you ought to have looked after her better than this? Where did she get ideas like this?—not in this house—"

Aunt Bridgie began to cry.

"This is ridiculous, Father," I said. "I haven't done anything disgraceful, and neither has Aunt Bridgie; you're not going to gain anything by bullying *her*. I have my own life to live; you both have to realize that—"

[189]

"And what kind of life do you think it would be, with a half-reformed drunk twenty years older than you are, a man who'll be lucky if he can make a decent living in a decent job from now on? You'd be better off under the sod with your mother."

"We don't have to be melodramatic about this, Father. People have different ideas about what they want out of life; if I don't care as much as you do about being rich and important, it doesn't mean I'm completely out of my mind."

Father didn't say anything for a moment; then he remarked suddenly: "I'm not even going to discuss this with you. There's somebody else I can talk to about this—"

"You're *not* going to Ivor. Father, if you do, I'll walk out of this house and never come into it again; this time I really mean that. Ivor has enough trouble now without your trying to make any more for him. Besides, there's no earthly use in your quarreling with him; he feels exactly the way you do about this whole thing—that I'm too young and he hasn't any future. But he won't always feel that way—"

"You're damn right he won't—if he feels that way now," Father said excitedly. "Do you think he's such a fool he doesn't realize what a fine berth he'd be falling into if he could get you to marry him? He knows damn well I wouldn't let you want for anything—"

That was the absolute limit of what I was going to listen to; I walked past him up the stairs and went to my room. He shouted something after me—I thought for a few moments that he might even come upstairs after me—but I suppose Aunt Bridgie stopped him; I could hear her talking to him for a long time down in the hall. After a while she came upstairs herself, but I said I didn't want to talk about it. I suppose the whole situation had begun to appeal to her romantic mind by that time, because she was unexpectedly sympathetic as she said good night to me. At any rate, I thought, the worst was over now; Father knew how I felt, and he might storm about it for a while, but eventually he would come around too. That was what I thought at the time; if I had any premonitions that things wouldn't work out quite that easily, they weren't strong enough to survive the fact that I was dead-tired, and in love, and happier than I had ever been before in my life. . . .

X I

FATHER was out when I got up in the morning, and Aunt Bridgie had apparently made up her mind, for once, to let well enough alone. She asked me a few cautious questions about Ivor at breakfast, and when I wasn't very responsive she prudently decided to act as if nothing of importance had happened the night before, and invited me instead to go shopping with her. Father's announcement that our financial troubles were about to be solved had inspired her with the opulent idea of doing over the living room, and, though I couldn't have been less interested in that project just then, I went into town with her anyway and looked at decorators' samples and pondered the relative merits of French Provincial and Early American for hours—or at least I pretended to ponder.

What I really had on my mind, and with more intensity as the day wore on, was Father—whether he had talked to Ike Judson again, or had gone out to the Hieronymus house to see Ivor. I don't really know what I was afraid would happen, but I finally told Aunt Bridgie that I had to make a phone call, and, after being installed behind somebody's impressively French desk with a chaste white-and-gold telephone, I put in a call to Father at his office. He wasn't in, and when I tried to find out where he was and what he had been doing his secretary, Miss Purdon, was apologetic but firmly evasive; her—"I really can't say, Miss Donlon"—finally began to sound so unhappy and alarmed that I took pity on her and hung up.

But I couldn't go back to drapes and upholstery after that; I think from that moment on I knew that something was wrong. I told Aunt Bridgie I had a headache and was going home, and I did go there—for five minutes. After that, alone except for Ester in the quiet house, my uneasiness had mounted to the point where I simply went out to the garage, got the car out again, and drove straight down to the Hieronymus house.

But it might be better to begin at the beginning of that day. . . .

At eleven-thirty that morning Miss Purdon was sitting in the outer office, typing some letters, when Ike Judson walked in and asked to see Father. He wore a dark, carefully pressed suit instead of his working clothes, and for a moment she didn't realize who he was; when she did, she tried to get an idea of what his business was out of him, but he refused to say anything except that he had to see Father. He didn't look as if he had any intention of leaving till he had, so she gave in finally and went into the inner office to talk to Father, who was on the phone long-distance to Fidelia.

"It's that Judson, Mr. Donlon," she said, when he hung up. "He says he *has* to see you—"

Father almost fell over the phone. "Who—Judson? I don't want to see him; tell him I'm—" Then he changed his mind suddenly and stopped and said: "No, wait a minute; I guess I'd better see him anyway—get this damn business settled. How does he look, Elizabeth?"

"Look—?" Miss Purdon was puzzled for a moment. "Why, he has on his Sunday-go-to-meeting clothes, if that's what you mean."

"It's not what I mean," Father said. "I mean does he look—?" He gave up all at once and said: "Never mind. I guess I'm borrowing trouble; I've got so damn much of it today that everything I see looks like more of it. Just send him in, Elizabeth, and I'll get this over with."

Miss Purdon went out to tell Judson, still a little puzzled by Father's behavior, but she was used enough to mornings when Father played Hamlet over nothing more serious than a toothache to go back to her work without wondering any more about it till she heard raised voices from behind the door. Or at least one raised voice— Father's—because Judson's was still only a stubborn, persistent monotone. She caught Ivor Kelly's name; she knew the story that linked him and Ila May Judson as well as anybody else, and it was at about that time that she decided she had finished her typing for the morning and started on some filing, so she would have a better chance of hearing what was going on. She wasn't very successful, though; once it seemed to her that Judson was quoting Scripture to Father, and after that she thought she heard Father say something about calling the police. But there wasn't time for her to decide whether she ought to be worried enough to do something, because just at that moment Lucille Hurley walked in.

Like all good secretaries, Miss Purdon didn't miss much of what went on in her employer's personal life. She had never been introduced to Mrs. Hurley, certainly, but she knew as much about her as I did—maybe more, because Father was considerably more careless about what went on in his office than about what went on in his home. So when Mrs. Hurley asked to see Father, Miss Purdon told her quite truthfully that Father was engaged, but she was also discreet enough to knock at the door of the inner office and let Father know at once who his latest caller was. She thought when she walked in that she had interrupted some kind of scene; both Father and Judson were on their feet, and Father looked white and incredulous, as if something had happened that he didn't quite believe.

At any rate, as soon as she came in the whole thing ended, because Judson, without saying a word, simply turned around and walked out of the office while she was telling Father who was outside. It took Father a minute to understand what she was saying—there was even a moment when she thought he intended to go after Judson and bring him back by force—but then he came to himself with a start, asked her with a hastily assumed carelessness if it wasn't time for her to go out to lunch, and told her to show Mrs. Hurley in. So that was the last she knew directly about what had happened, except that when she came back from lunch both Father and Mrs. Hurley were gone, and there was a two-line note from Father on her desk, informing her that he would be "out" for a couple of hours.

What happened in her absence between Father and Lucille Hurley never became public property, but I can reconstruct it pretty accurately now. In the first place, Mrs. Hurley's turning up at the office that morning hadn't been entirely unexpected to Father, because he'd sent a wire to her in Chicago on the night of the primaries, asking her—probably begging her, in the mood he was in—to come back to Queensport. When there wasn't any answer he phoned her late the next day, but by that time she had already left Chicago. She told me later that she'd thought of refusing to come—she'd had time to think about a good many things during those weeks in Chicago—but in the end she found herself on the train; there didn't seem to be anything else for her to do.

She came prepared, though, to give way to her own doubts and her own emotions for the first time since she had known Father; he noticed the change in her the moment she walked into his office that morning, and it threw him off what remaining balance he had left after his interview with Ike Judson. She must have walked almost literally into a storm of protestations, demands, and promises, and before she had time even to begin on her own troubles he was telling her his, up to and including his latest quarrel with me: "Do you realize she's even threatened to walk out of the house and marry that blackguard whenever he whistles for her? My God, a man works hard all his life, he builds up a business out of nothing, and what has he got in the end?—his friends turning against him, his daughter walking out on him to marry a man with a criminal charge hanging over him and nothing to give her but his own black name—"

She sat listening to him, feeling her own grievances growing less important at the sight of his panic—for it was literally panic that she saw in his eyes; he was upset to the point where he no longer seemed entirely responsible for what he was saying. Without being wise enough to formulate the thought exactly that even the fears and disappointments he was feeling would have to have come to some definite climax at that moment to have put him in such a state, she guessed that his behavior had something to do with the man who had left his office as she came in. But when she tried to ask him about it, he lost his control completely.

"Don't bother me with that; damn it, what business is it of yours? Do I have to account to you for every crackpot that walks in here?"

"You don't have to account to me for anything," she said. She got up, mustering her dignity, the resolutions she had brooded over during those weeks in Chicago. "I've had time to think things over, Pat," she said, "and I've made up my mind it was true what you said —that we ought to break it off now, while we're still young enough to make some other kind of life for ourselves—"

She would have gone on, but he had hold of both her arms now, shaking her, imploring her: "My God, not you too—not you too. Lucy, listen to me, I was worried when I said that, I had things on my mind—you don't realize the sort of things I had on my mind. But it's going to be just the way it always was now, just the two of us— can't you see, can't you see?" He glanced around the office in desperation. "I can't talk to you here. We'll go to your place—"

"I've given up the house." She felt her resolution going, and propped it up with weak expedients. "I'm at a hotel; we can't go there—"

"Why can't we? Why can't we? All right then—listen—we'll go to another hotel; I know a place—My God, can't you see I need you now?"

She gave in finally, seeing him frantic, almost weeping—thankful that there was no one in the outer office as they left, thankful that no one saw them get into his car and drive away furiously into the hot August noon. . . .

It was two hours later when he told her what had happened that morning, confessed it to her because he had to ask reassurance from someone.

"He had the idea I was double-crossing him—don't you see?" he said. "Can't you see how it was? Because I was the one who told him first that he ought to leave it up to the courts, and then I was the one who told him yesterday that the courts wouldn't do him any good—"

He walked up and down in the hot little room, pausing occasionally to glance at her anxiously.

"So if anybody was in any danger," he said, "it was me; if he really had the idea of shooting anybody, he'd have started on me, and afterward gone after Kelly—That makes sense, doesn't it? That makes good sense? I'd have looked like a damn fool, going to the police with a story like that—"

Mrs. Hurley looked at him; all at once she began to feel frightened.

"But you told him where he was, Pat—?"

"All right. I told him where he was." He turned on her suddenly, shouting it: "I told him where he was. But there's no harm in it; the fellow's just a crackpot. I tell you, he wasn't serious about it."

She didn't say anything. He came and sat down beside her on the bed.

"You believe me, don't you, Lucy? He wasn't serious about it. I wouldn't have told him if he'd been serious—"

She shook her head, still frightened. "Call the police now, Pat."

"Call—? Are you out of your mind? And have them after me to explain what I was doing all this while, that I let it go this long—?"

"Then go there yourself." She got up, speaking urgently. "You can go there yourself and see that everything's all right—"

She got him down to the car, her fear matching his now, and he drove her to her hotel, promising, when he left her there, to go straight on to the Hieronymus house. But he was waiting for the light at the intersection of Monroe and Henrico Streets when a radio in the doorway of an appliance store blared out the news, and after that, of course, there was no necessity for him to go anywhere at all. . . .

When I stopped the car before the Hieronymus house that afternoon there were half a dozen other automobiles already parked there; even before I saw that at least two of them were county police cars, I think I knew what I was going to find. A policeman stationed at the open front door barred the way inside to a small group of people on the front lawn; he was talking to a reporter who was writing earnestly in a small notebook. I ran up the steps.

"Can't come in here, miss," the policeman broke off to say to me. He shrugged back to the reporter. "This place is going to be a nut house in just about half an hour—more of 'em coming every minute—"

"But what's happened? Please—I've got to know—"

"You know as much as the rest of those people, don't you? Man's been killed—Now you run along—"

He stopped; I don't know how I looked, but the reporter stopped writing too and glanced at me.

"Hey, wait a minute," he said suddenly. "Aren't you the Donlon girl—Pat Donlon's daughter? What're you doing here?"

I didn't say anything; I don't think I could have if I'd wanted to. I felt as if I couldn't even breathe; the solid brick front of the house seemed to be wavering in front of me as if it were only its own reflection in moving water.

"Sure it is," the reporter's voice urged, from far away. "Betsy Donlon—that's who it is—"

"Betsy—?" This time the voice was familiar; somebody came forward out of the dimness of the hall behind the policeman. I recognized Kirby suddenly. "How did *you* get here? What the devil—?"

He took my arm; people seemed to be talking all at once, and out of the confusion I found myself sitting on a shrouded chair in a room inside the house, with Kirby asking anxiously: "Are you all right?"

"Kirby—was it Ivor?"

"You've got no business being here. You're white as a sheet—"

"Was it Ivor? Was it Ivor? Please, Kirby—"

"All right—yes. But you shouldn't be here—" A policeman came in and spoke to him. "She's all right, I think," Kirby said. "Listen, damn it—get out of here, will you, Mike? She hasn't got anything to do with this."

Another man came to the door and Kirby went over and spoke to him. I heard his earnest, rather angry voice, but it was like all the rest of it; it seemed to be happening somewhere far away, behind the words repeating themselves over and over in my head: *Man's been killed—Was it Ivor?—Yes.*

After a while Kirby came back, the man beside him.

"Listen, Betsy," he said, "this is Chief Murray. Do you think you can answer a couple of questions?"

"How'd you happen to come down here this afternoon, Miss Donlon?" the man asked. He was tall, ruddy, worried-looking; his face swam slowly toward me out of the dim background of the room.

"I wanted to see Ivor—" I said.

I knew I ought to have said more, but it all seemed so unimportant that I couldn't concentrate on it through those three lines of dialogue in my head: *Man's been killed—Was it Ivor?—Yes.* I heard Kirby saying something emphatically to his companion: "You can make a production out of this if you want to, Jim, but you know damn well how Pat Donlon's going to like that . . . not as if you didn't know what happened . . . nothing to do with it . . ." The words faded off into a blur of sound.

After a little I realized that the man had gone, and that Kirby was saying to me: "I'm going to drive you home."

"I want to know what happened—"

"I'll tell you what happened on the way. First you're getting out of here. Did you drive down? Where'd you leave your car?"

He got me to my feet and we went out a side door somewhere: I recognized the hall where I had stood with Ivor the night before as we went through. There was a bigger crowd outside now, a blur of curious faces as we walked to my car. Two or three men came up and spoke to Kirby. He opened the door of the car for me and then, when I was inside, walked a few steps away and talked to them rapidly for a few minutes. I sat there waiting. *Man's been killed—Was it Ivor?—Yes.* It wasn't till Kirby asked me for the keys that I realized he was back.

He told me what had happened as he drove me back to Fort Paris through the bright summer afternoon. He was the one who had walked in on it first, he said; he had driven down to the Hieronymus house around one o'clock to see Ivor, after having tried vainly, as I did later, to reach Father by phone. It was a fine day, and he had no good news to tell Ivor about a Dodd-Judson agreement to drop the charges against him, so he didn't hurry. Afterwards he remembered passing an oddly familiar-looking figure at a roadside bus stop near the house—a tall angular man in sober, dusty black, faceless for the moment because his back was turned, waiting patiently for transportation to take him up to town.

When he got to the house no one answered his ring. There were windows open, so he was fairly sure there was someone around, and he was just going down the steps again to try the back of the house when a grocery truck came up the drive and a woman whom he recognized as Hieronymus's cook got out with her arms full of groceries, thanked the driver, and came across the lawn to the house. She had a key, and they went into the house together. Inside the silent, shrouded hall Kirby looked around.

"Doesn't look as if he's here—"

"Try around the back. It's nice in the garden; that's where he was yesterday when I came."

He went out through the sunroom where Ivor and I had sat the night before. The woman was right. Ivor was in the garden; the screen door was still settling slowly to, with a quiet protest of hinges, when Kirby saw him lying beside a lilac bush at the foot of the lawn. In the hot breeze, as he hurried toward him, a black-printed leaflet floated slowly down the path at his feet; later he remembered the message upon it—*Be Sure Your Sins Will Find You Out.*

Afterward, of course, within a matter of minutes, there were urgent phone calls, a widening circle of consequences to spread rapidly through the quiet of the summer afternoon. Ivor, with three bullets in his chest, was alive, but hardly conscious; a hastily summoned doctor pronounced his verdict on the ebbing minutes of his life, and then allowed Kirby and an earnest county policeman to go inside—the latter to take advantage of those moments when it seemed that Ivor was aware of what was going on around him to press him conscientiously for a statement.

"If you could just tell me who did it, Mr. Kelly—"

But Ivor, though his eyes opened and rested on the two men, seemed uninterested in the problem of legal retribution; he tried to speak to them only once, and then it was something that began, "I wanted to—" and trailed off in a slight impatient movement of the head at his inability to complete the sentence.

Minutes afterward a priest arrived, and in a rapid ceremony Ivor was received again into the church he had had little to do with since the day his Welsh mother and his Irish father had quarrelled over the denominational jurisdiction of his soul. Kirby saw him once more before he died, but by that time there was no communication at all possible between him and the world he was rapidly leaving. What he had wanted—whether it had to do with me, or with something in that extraordinary and incandescent world that he had gone in search of so eagerly and never quite found—was lost in silence, and at twenty minutes before two on that summer afternoon Ivor Kelly's quest was over at last.

We were near Fort Paris by the time Kirby had told me this, and he finished the story quickly as he drove the rest of the way to the house. The Queensport police had picked Judson up five minutes after he had walked in the front door of his house on Barker Street; they found him in his dusty Sunday black, reading the Bible—"It's a damn queer thing," Kirby said bitterly, "how some people can't find anything in the word of God but the justification for their own cruelty." He had readily admitted that he had shot Ivor, and had furnished the police with the major details of what had happened— how he had taken a Williamsburg bus down to the Hieronymus house; how he had rung the doorbell, like Kirby, without response and then, going around the back of the house, had found Ivor in the garden; and how he had shot him, without allowing either of them time to say a word, with an ancient and carefully preserved Colt revolver that his grandfather had carried at Manassas and Sharpsburg.

We were at the house then; Kirby went inside with me. Aunt Bridgie had come home, and he gave her the situation in a few sentences while I went into the living room and sat down. I didn't even listen to what they were saying; the bullets that had ended Ivor's life seemed to have crashed into my own life as well, and I felt as if nothing would ever be important to me again. I sat there, feeling sick and numb, and after a little I heard Kirby saying to Aunt Bridgie: "You'd better take her upstairs and let her lie down. This has been a hell of a shock—"

Aunt Bridgie came over to me, but before she could do anything we heard Father's car in the drive; a minute later he came into the room. He looked startled, almost terrified, when he saw Kirby; if I hadn't stopped caring about anything, I might have wondered about that expression on his face, but I didn't at the moment. It was only

afterward that it came back to me, and that I realized what it was—
the look of a man who has come to his home as to a refuge against
the world and against himself, and who discovers suddenly that there
is no refuge for him even there.

Kirby spoke to him first. "I suppose you've heard what's happened," he said.

"Yes." Father came in and sat down heavily; he avoided looking at
either Kirby or me. "Hell of a note—"

"That's a mild way to put it."

"That fellow Judson must be out of his mind." Father took a deep
breath and plunged into something. "I saw him this morning, you
know, just before—He seemed calm enough then, a little edgy, that's
all—but you never know what's going on in a mind like that—"

"You didn't have any idea, then—?" Kirby said. He hesitated a
moment. "I mean—damn it, Pat, I know it's my fault for setting you
on Judson in the first place, but if you'd just been able to figure this
morning what he was likely to do—"

Father colored up violently. "Well, I didn't—that's all. My God,
I'm not a mind reader—"

"I know, I know. It's just that you can't help thinking, when something like this happens—"

Father looked at him defiantly. "He had it coming to him, anyway.
If it was *your* daughter—"

"Wait a minute," Kirby interrupted him. "You haven't heard, then
—the Judson girl's finally gotten around to telling the truth about this
business. She was at home when the police picked Judson up; I
guess it took something like that to scare it out of her. The father
of that baby she's going to have is a kid by the name of Bert Jackson—
works in a gas station, when he's working—"

He broke off; Father, looking stunned, had gotten up abruptly and
walked away across the room.

"I don't believe it," he said. His ruddy face looked suddenly ashen.
"Why, my God, what kind of little bitch—"

"It's true, all right," Kirby said. "Judson made some threats when
he learned the girl was pregnant, enough to give her a good idea that
her boy friend would have a pretty short time to live if her father
ever found out who he was—so when Judson came across that picture
of Ivor and jumped to conclusions about it, she let him go on thinking
Ivor was the man. Her reasoning about the whole business isn't any

too clear, but she seems to have figured that Judson wouldn't dare do anything drastic to anyone as important as Ivor."

Father turned around excitedly. "But it doesn't make sense! Holy God, didn't she realize she was turning this whole state upside down—?"

"She was looking out for Number One," Kirby said. "It's an old American custom; you ought to know all about that."

Father looked at him furiously. "Now, listen, Kirby—"

"All right," Kirby interrupted him. "All right. All right. You don't have to say it: you're no worse than the next fellow, and neither am I, and neither is Ila May Judson." He got up and started toward the door, turning at the threshold to finish his thought. "The only thing is, did it ever occur to you that because we were all so damn busy using Ivor to insure our own futures, he's ended up with no future at all that anybody can see from here? Maybe that makes him just unlucky, but it still doesn't pin any medals on us."

He went out to the hall. I followed him; there was something else I still had to know, something I couldn't ask him in front of Aunt Bridgie and Father.

"Kirby—" I said.

"Yes?"

I stood there; I didn't know how to say it.

"You were there when—when—" I took a long breath and started again. "He didn't say anything about me?"

"He didn't have time. We wouldn't even know how it happened if that damn Judson hadn't told us—" He stopped, looking at me. "You got into something way over your head this time, didn't you?" he said. "Why the hell do you have to be mixed up in this?"

I just stood there.

"I was in love with him," I said. "Isn't that reason enough? And he was in love with me; just last night it looked as if we might work things out—"

Kirby shook his head incredulously. "He told you that?"

"Yes."

I hadn't cried before that—you can be too numb when something like that hits you even to have any tears—but I began to cry then; I leaned my arms on the newel and put my head down. Kirby came over.

"Betsy, listen—" He turned me around; he insisted on my hearing him. "This is bad enough without your tearing yourself to pieces because something isn't going to happen that never could have happened anyway. Ivor was all through; he knew that—all he was trying to do was to put on a fine show on the way to wherever it was he was going. He couldn't have believed in the sun's rising the next morning except out of politeness—"

I turned away, sobbing. "It isn't true. He believed in us—in our being happy together—"

"Then you managed to work a small miracle—but it couldn't have lasted. I went through that campaign with him, Betsy; if he had half a dozen years to live he was lucky, and he knew it—he wasn't the kind of guy who kids himself about something like that. And he'd stopped caring about it; if you made him think he did, you gave him something to go out with, anyway, because the only damn thing in the world he ever wanted was something or somebody worth everything he could try to give—"

It wasn't much, but I wanted to believe that; if I could, it would make things a little easier. Aunt Bridgie came out from the living room.

"Kirby—I thought you'd gone." She looked at me in alarm. "What's the matter with Betsy?"

"The same thing that's the matter with the rest of us," Kirby said. "Why don't you make her go to bed, Bridgie? She's had about enough for one day."

"I'm all right."

But I couldn't stop crying, now that I had begun. I heard Kirby and Aunt Bridgie talking, and then Aunt Bridgie had her arm around me and was bringing me upstairs to my room. At twenty you're lucky; you can still cry yourself to sleep. I did, that night, and when you're asleep there isn't anything to remember—anyway, for a while. But there was always going to be tomorrow, and the day after that, and the day after that. . . .

XII

MONDAY morning. The funeral was at ten, but by eight o'clock the crowd had already begun to gather outside the cathedral; when the cortege arrived, the windows and doorways of the old brick houses opposite were thronged with faces, and the police were having difficulty in maintaining their lines against the dense surging mass of people in the street. Martha and I, waiting our turn to enter the church, watched the long stream of decorously solemn figures debouch from the shining black limousines drawn up before the curb— the governor, three ex-governors, two United States senators, half a dozen congressmen, the mayor of Queensport, innumerable lesser dignitaries and officials: every politician in the state, it seemed, was there.

"There's only one thing I'm sorry about," Martha said. "Ivor would have loved this; it's a pity he can't be here to see it. Every damn pious hypocrite in this state who turned his back on him when he needed him gathered together here in their best bibs and tuckers for a public exhibition of their grief—"

I didn't say anything. I knew the best I was going to be able to do that morning was to get through with it; I didn't have any feelings to spare for bitterness or anger. I looked out the window of the car, watching the line of mourners slowly climb the cathedral steps and enter the high arched doors that were drawn back now on their massive iron hinges. There was Ed Dodd: the crowd, recognizing him, surged forward with a sudden murmur of disapproval, and he mounted the steps a little more nimbly, the color rising in his broad face. He and his followers had been issuing pious statements of horror ever since the Judson girl had placed them in the highly embarrassing political situation of having won an election through the persecution of an innocent man, but apparently their repentance had come too late. The newspapers agreed that if Ivor could have been resurrected from the dead before the November elections, he could have taken the governorship from them without the slightest difficulty, and, though there was no danger that the miracle would occur, there was another kind of miracle that seemed less improbable—a Republican victory in November.

Martha was watching the crowd in the street.

"Come to see the show," she commented cynically. "Mr. Ivor Kelly, the ex-congressman, will now do his celebrated act of disappearing underground; be the last to see him before he goes—"

"Martha, how *can* you—?"

"It's easy; I just think what Ivor would have said himself. He never took all this public excitement seriously, you know, even when he was trying his damnedest to get it; it just seemed to him like the proper thing to go with the kind of life he wanted to have. Like the Roman triumphs: you didn't win wars because you wanted a triumph —you got the triumphs because you'd won the wars."

It was our turn to join the long procession up the steps of the cathedral now; minutes later, coming out of the bright mid-morning sunlight into the taper-lit hush of the cathedral, I saw the coffin lonely in the aisle before the altar. . . . Martha took hold of my arm.

"Look, you don't have to go through with this—"

"I want to. I'm going to. Only, Martha—it's so awful—I can't believe he's dead, I can't. It's as if we were all pretending, or acting— putting on some horrible kind of play—"

"Not a play—a Roman triumph. The biggest triumph of Ivor Kelly's life. This time the boy's really made it; an inauguration is minor league alongside of a turnout like this."

She looked around at civic leaders carefully ranked in high-backed carved pews at the front of the church, the Tyler Dewarrs looking dedicated to the high cause of their own immaculate consciences, Harvey Whiteley glummer, having been recognized and hissed by the crowd as he had come up the cathedral steps. Apparently everybody was anxious to be on the side of righteousness, now that Ila May Judson had made it perfectly plain which side that was.

"Everybody's here but Pat," Martha whispered to me. "What's the matter with him—has he decided to give up politics? This band wagon's big enough even for him to climb on."

"He said he wasn't feeling very well this morning."

"Neither is Ed Dodd, but he managed to make it. Pat may have been right at that, though; Judas has always been a little less popular than Pontius Pilate, and those weren't exactly friendly greetings Ed got just now from that crowd out there."

The church was filled to overflowing now; behind the pews reserved for the funeral party, and in the smaller chapels on either side of the nave, every available place was occupied, and people stood in long attentive lines against the walls. The solemn requiem high mass began; the bishop, the two assisting priests, the white-robed acolytes, moved through the somber ritual. Over the massed flowers about the coffin the organ rolled, thundering against the summer-morning brilliance of the stained-glass windows, rocking louder or fainter with the ground swell of the noises of the densely packed crowd inside and outside the cathedral. In the organ loft a choir sang: *Dies irae, dies illa—day of wrath—*

The bishop, who was officiating, was a stern ruddy German who made no concessions to the worldly importance of the occasion; a requiem mass was a matter of the solemn relinquishment of a soul to its Maker, not an occasion for graceful phrase-making. The politicians looked relieved that there was no eulogy; their interest was in seeing Ivor safely underground as quickly and decorously as possible, and any appeal to the emotions involved in the facts of his unequal battle with politics and fate was strictly to be avoided, from their point of view. Even now, from the vestibule beyond the inner doors of the cathedral and from the street outside, you could hear the restless murmur of the crowd, shut off from the expectation of any further spectacle till the doors of the church should open again. I glanced at Martha; she was kneeling beside me, her eyes fixed on the altar, as if she were accusing God with the same bitter cynicism she had turned on the solemn ranks of politicians and Important Personages before her. She saw me look at her and turned to whisper something to me rapidly.

"This is just the beginning—"

"What—?"

"This is just the beginning—"

I didn't know what she meant, and she didn't explain; she turned her eyes again to the altar. The mass drew to a close; the bishop laid aside his chasuble and maniple, put on the black cope, and went to the entrance of the sanctuary, where the bier waited, solitary, for the final absolution to be pronounced over it. Above us the choir sang

[205]

somberly: *Libera me, Domine, de morte aeterna—from eternal death —from eternal death—*

The acolytes brought incense and holy water; the bishop's voice rang out strongly in the curiously challenging ancient cry; *"Pater noster—"* and then quietly repeated the remainder of the prayer. He was beginning the ceremony of passing around the bier, sprinkling it with holy water and incensing it, when there was a sudden tumult of sound behind us; startled, I looked around to see the doors of the vestibule flung open at the back of the church and the crowd surging through. The next instant a large stand on which rows of votive lights burned before a statue of the Infant Christ the King overturned with a crash, and there were screams and shouts of panic. On the surface of the crowd a policeman or two bobbed around like corks in a flood; then the stream overflowed, struggling up the aisle toward the bier, while a dozen Important Men half-rose in their pews and looked anxiously for the nearest exit.

The bishop strode down the aisle toward the crowd. He was so angry that for a few moments his words came in disconnected spirts, like liquid from a too-full bottle: "How *dare* you—breaking into a church—desecrating the house of God—no respect for your Maker or for the dead—"

The crowd pushed back; those in front, anxious to avoid that wrathful presence, turned around entirely and tried to burrow their way into the surging mass behind them, as if they had been pushed forward so far through no will of their own. The bishop saw a familiar face in the crowd.

"Officer Cooley—*who* is responsible for this outrage? I shall hold you personally to account if this—this mob—"

The policeman made a gesture of acquiescence, of despair—but he was as powerless to get the crowd out as he had been a few moments before to prevent them from coming in.

"Father—your Reverence—" he whispered hoarsely, looking piteously at all the Important Personages before him.

The mayor, who was not a Catholic, and who looked stricken with the twin ideas that he ought to do something and that whatever he might do might be considered sacrilegious in such a place, stood up, whispered something furiously to the governor, who sat beside him —and sat down again.

"Passing the buck," Martha whispered to me. She looked alert and rather vengeful, as if she were enjoying this. "Ten to one the governor will now try to make a speech, and ten to one he'll start out: 'Friends—'"

The governor stood up, said, "Friends—" into the clamor, said it again, and then beckoned, frustrated, to the nearest policeman, who, almost sobbing, tried to struggle through the crowd to him.

"I can't help it, your Reverence—your Honor—There's too many of them—"

The bishop had control of his wrath now; his voice rang out suddenly, like an officer's on parade, through the cathedral.

"Now — I — want — this — disgraceful — exhibition — stopped — and I want those doors closed—"

He advanced down the aisle, the crowd, not surprisingly, somehow managing to contract itself before him; he looked as if he would have marched straight through it, or over it, like a Juggernaut, if it hadn't. By this time the police outside had apparently begun to get some control over the situation there, because the pressure at the doors had relaxed enough to allow some of the crowd inside the cathedral to escape into the outer vestibule. There was a sudden energetic effort on the part of ushers and police inside, a panic-stricken rush of stragglers as they saw themselves being deserted by their comrades—and the great doors of the cathedral swung firmly into place. Then the bishop marched back up the aisle and returned to the ceremony of committing Ivor Kelly to his Maker.

I imagine he was the only one in the cathedral, though, who had a very clear idea of what was going on; the distracted faces of the Important Personages who had come to bury Caesar, not to praise him, announced a sudden worried comprehension of the fact that it might be politically expedient to lay on the praise a little more vigorously and to go a little easier on the burying. Martha sat there with the faintest hint of a grim smile on her face, but she didn't say anything; she was watching those rows of faces in the pews before her, each one trying to compose itself enough to convince its neighbors that it really wasn't upset at all.

Then it was over: the congregation joined the bishop in praying for the repose of the soul of Ivor Kelly—perhaps with some secret petitions added for their own present health—and the pallbearers began their somber march down the aisle toward the door of the cathedral. We inside could hear the sudden wave of sound—half a sigh and half a cheer—that greeted their appearance on the steps outside. Later we learned that there had been a renewed rush against the police lines at that moment that had succeeded in breaking through temporarily in several places, so that the coffin had had to be placed in the hearse quickly, to prevent it from being actually surrounded and jostled. Some of the crowd had brought flowers, bruised and draggled now in the crush, which they threw on the coffin as it passed; the petals—white and scarlet and yellow and bright pink—scattered gaily, like confetti, over the gray bier. And above the moving, murmuring mass of humanity a huge campaign poster of Ivor swung in the August sunlight; he seemed to look down gravely on the excited throng, accepting the tribute of their emotion as he had accepted it in life—as if he had only happened to be there while all this was going on.

By the time we got outside, the situation was completely out of hand. The hearse was inching slowly through a solid mass of people in the street, with the drivers of the lead cars in the procession behind still trying vainly to move away from the curb. I stood at the top of the cathedral steps with Martha, looking down at the straining blue backs of the policemen working at clearing a way to the waiting cars, at the upturned faces following with their eyes the progress of the hearse, some of them—the women—frankly weeping, all intent, concentrated, lost in the drama of the moment. I turned to Martha.

"But why—?" I began.

She shrugged, watching the scene below with an ironic little smile.

"Because he's safely dead," she said. "Because they don't have to worry any more about living up to what he wanted of them, or about his living up to what they wanted of him. Because they're always happier with a legend than with a man—"

She broke off, looking around for Ed Dodd, whose place in the procession was unaccountably vacant.

"Gone out the side door, I suppose," she said, "to attend a funeral of his own, with himself as the political corpse. Now he knows what it means when it says in the Bible that the Lord gives, and the Lord takes away—"

The black limousines were moving slowly now; we found ourselves swept down the steps and bundled into one of them, along with three or four frightened-looking men whom Martha knew, and who turned out to be state officials from down in Fidelia. They all talked in low voices, as if they thought they made themselves less conspicuous that way, and when the car shuddered from some sudden impact of the crowd against it they looked firmly and palely at one another, apparently determined not to be the first to show alarm.

"It's bound to be more peaceful at the cemetery," Martha consoled them. "Why don't you just relax and think about the lovely peaceful four years *you*'re going to have after next November? Ivor will have nothing on you boys."

Nobody was in the mood to appreciate that—and, as a matter of fact, it wasn't much more peaceful at the cemetery when we finally got there. There was a traffic jam at the gates, because apparently all the people who hadn't been at the cathedral had gone out there to be on hand when the cortege arrived, and when we finally got inside there was a rush to the graveside in which several women fainted and an elderly man was almost pushed into the open grave. I think we were all a little hysterical by that time, except the bishop, who stood there, solid and bareheaded in the August sunlight, repeating the prayers for the dead in a strong clear voice: "Eternal rest grant unto him, O Lord, and let perpetual light shine upon him. May his soul, and the souls of all the faithful departed, rest in peace." I tried to think that it was Ivor I was saying good-by to, but none of it was real; it seemed that I would only have to turn around and he would be there at my elbow, watching this ceremony with the same grave politeness with which he had watched so many others during his life.

Afterwards the bishop, in a sudden unorthodox gesture of his own, spoke directly and sternly to the crowd.

"The way to show your respect for the dead," he said, "is by showing respect, not by turning a funeral into a spectacle—a carnival, without either decency or restraint. If you are here to honor this man, you can do it by behaving in a way more befitting a solemn occasion, and if it is idle curiosity that has brought you here, you can take your shame to yourselves for having no more regard for what is due to this place and to the dead—"

Kirby came over to Martha and me. He looked tired and grim.

"That's over," he said. "My God, what a morning. Any resemblance to a funeral is purely coincidental; this whole thing's been more like one of Ivor's campaign appearances—one back in the good old days."

"Well, at least this is one time when nobody's started to sing 'Has Anybody Here Seen Kelly?'" Martha said.

She began to cry all at once, biting her lips and trying to keep back the tears. Kirby looked at her.

"For God's sake, Marty, don't you start—" he said.

"I'm not. I don't give a damn. We're all going to be dead in another fifty or sixty years." She took out her handkerchief and dried her eyes angrily. "Anyway," she said, "they'll remember him. That's what he wanted—to be remembered, to be some sort of damn legend for them to tell their grandchildren about. Well, he will be now—a lot more than if he'd just been elected governor and sat there in that mansion down in Fidelia for four years like a couple of dozen other politicians before him, that nobody could even tell you the names of now—"

The empty hearse was edging its way through the crowd toward the cemetery gates. A group of people came up to Kirby and began talking to him earnestly about "some kind of memorial for Ivor—of course there'd be no difficulty in getting contributions." I recognized Mrs. Hirsch's diamond-stabbed black-satin bosom in the center of an august political circle. Martha took my arm.

"I'm going to take you home."

"I'm perfectly all right."

"Of course you are. But I'm going to take you home, just the same."

We walked back to the car, going away; the whole scene, under the cheerful sun—the quiet, white-monumented grass invaded and trampled now by the crowd, the long line of black limousines, the flowers around the grave—seemed like a bright nightmare, grotesque and frozen even in the August heat. Somebody said positively, almost in my ear: "He could have been a great man—"

"Oh, my God," Martha said.

"A great man—"

There was a campaign banner wavering somewhere up ahead against the noonday sky, floating over the trampled turf and the old white headstones. Martha looked at it, her lips twisted in a mirthless smile.

"A great man," she said. "A dead great man. That's what they want. So they can make him over into their own image and likeness, only a little bigger than life, and then set him up somewhere on a pedestal where they can admire him without a chance of their ever finding out that the admiration isn't mutual. Well, he wasn't a great man; he was just a boy who reached for the moon and ended up with a first-class serving of moldy rat bait. And all the banners and the speeches and the expensive memorials can't change that now, no matter how hard they try—"

She got into the car.

"Anyway, it's over now," she said. "It's over for him, and it's over for us, and it's over for them, even if they don't know it yet, because all they have left is something they've made up for themselves. So we can close the books, all of us, and go on from there—"

But there was one thing left that I had to find out before I could close the books on what had happened. The look I had seen on Father's face on the day of Ivor's death, when he had come into the house and found Kirby there—a look of terror, or guilt, rather than of surprise—was one of the things that had led me to it, but it wasn't the only one. There were others—Miss Purdon's testimony at the inquest, for example—that had made me even surer that there really was something there for me to find out. I seemed to be the only one who felt that way; the official consensus of the police and the newspapers, after hearing Father's story of what had happened between him and Judson on the morning of Ivor's death, was that Father had been a Good Samaritan whose laudable intentions had backfired through no fault of his own. But you know how it is—you have something there in the back of your mind, and you know it's there; the only thing is, you've never brought it out and taken a good look at it, because you know if you do you'll see something you don't want to believe you will ever have to see in this world.

That was the way it was with me, but the time finally came when I knew I was going to have to take that good look, no matter how much I wasn't going to like what I had to see. So three days after the funeral I located Lucille Hurley at her Corioli hotel and asked her to have lunch with me. She was surprised, but not surprised enough, by my asking her; I suppose I realized then that if I'd been hanging on to any hope that there really wasn't going to be anything for me to look at, I'd better let go of it for good. And I was right, because half an hour after I walked into the restaurant where she was waiting for me the whole thing was there on the table between us, and she was crying and I was sitting there feeling that, no matter what else I ever did, I could never go home again.

"He didn't really *know* anything was going to happen," Mrs. Hurley said. She was pleading with me then, trying to take back something she couldn't take back, or at least to make it sound a little better than it was. "He was just afraid it might—and then when I came in, I suppose it put it out of his mind for a while; he was so worried about what was going to happen to us. We hadn't even seen each other for weeks, you know—and it just put it out of his mind—"

I didn't say anything.

"You understand how it was?" she pleaded with me. "He never really knew anything—and as soon as he'd had time to think about it and talk it over with me, he realized he ought to do something; he was on his way to warn Mr. Kelly when he heard—"

There still wasn't anything to say; how could I tell her that all the explanations in the world couldn't alter the fact that Father had loaded that gun himself and put it into Ike Judson's hands when he had told him where Ivor was that morning?

She looked at me humbly. "I know how you feel," she said. "You were in love with him; I know how it is—And I feel as if I were to blame for it somehow, too; if I hadn't walked in just when I did, things might have turned out differently."

"Yes," I said. "And they might have turned out differently too if I hadn't talked to Father about marrying Ivor, or if Kirby hadn't asked Father to try to get Judson to drop the case, or if Ed Dodd hadn't wanted to be governor, or if Ila May Judson hadn't gone out one night last spring when she ought to have stayed at home. We're all in it, one way or another, aren't we?"

I was sorry for her; she knew what Father was, and what he had done, but it didn't help her; she would be there for him to come back to long after everyone else had seen him and judged him and walked out on him. Well, I was walking out myself now, apparently along with a good many other people who had read the political handwriting on the wall, and I couldn't begrudge him anything that Lucille Hurley could give him. I was walking out because there are things you can't condone unless you want to share, yourself, in the deed, and Ivor's death was a deed I couldn't bring myself to share in. Not consciously, at any rate—for it seemed, as I had said to Lucille Hurley, that I had had my unwitting part too in the chain of events that had set Ivor and Ike Judson face to face in the garden of the Hieronymus house that August day.

But what Father had done he had done in the knowledge, however unadmitted or disguised, of its consequences, and if I had been one of his chief reasons for doing it, it had still been without my consent—a consent I couldn't give even now, when it was too late for it to make any difference to anyone. So I said good-by to Lucille Hurley and walked out into the August afternoon with my new knowledge and my new independence, and I felt as alone in the world as anyone can feel who has just lost a father without even having the good things of the past all clear and fine to remember him by.

Later that day I phoned Kirby, and we had dinner together in a quiet restaurant out on the La Fayette Pike. I had told him it was about getting a job; I wanted to know if he would help me find something right away. Of course he asked questions, so I gave him the story—not all of it, but enough for him to be able to put two and two together and figure out why I felt I had to begin doing things for myself. I didn't know how he was taking it; he just sat there looking at me across the table as if he didn't quite know how to start going about believing something that he realized now he ought to have believed long before.

"But she said Pat didn't know—" he said at last, as if he were arguing it out more with himself than with me. "Judson never actually told him what he was going to do—"

"No," I said. "He never actually told him."

"He just saw how easy it would be if he let Judson—how it would solve that whole problem of you and Ivor—Or maybe he didn't even see it; maybe he just acted that way because that's the way he's learned to act in a lifetime of doing the easiest thing, the thing that will infallibly benefit him, no matter what happens to the next fellow. It's sheer instinct—"

"Yes."

"And that's why he didn't want to know," Kirby went on, spelling it out for himself, "because if he had known, if he'd brought it out into the light, he'd have had to do something to stop it. So he just convinced himself that everything was going to be all right—you can't blame a man for not trying to stop something from happening when he's convinced it isn't going to happen anyway, whether he does anything about it or not. He had it all figured out so he couldn't help but win."

"Yes," I said again.

"Only now it turns out that he didn't win anyway." Kirby looked at me. "Because you're going to get out—"

"I have to. I couldn't go on living there now."

He shook his head. "Pat's going to have something to say about that, isn't he? You're not twenty-one yet—"

"I will be, next June. If I have to go away somewhere till then, I will—but I can't stay in that house now; if I did, I'd feel as if I'd helped to kill Ivor too—"

All at once I was crying; I sat there while the candles on the table

[213]

grew blurred and crooked, and the wall behind Kirby faded off. Kirby looked at me angrily.

"You had no business being mixed up in any of this."

"I'm glad I was. I wouldn't have had it any different, even if—even if I'd known—You said I gave him something to believe in; it isn't very much, but if it was anything at all—"

"It's enough that I'd give every damn thing I own to have it myself," Kirby said. Then he stopped and said: "All right. I'll try to find you that job. I guess you've got a right to it—and if Pat puts up any arguments, he can argue with me."

It was still early when we finished dinner. I had my car, and after I'd left Kirby I turned it toward the Williamsburg Pike and drove down to the Hieronymus house and stopped before it, looking at the dark bulk in the darkness. It was the best place I knew to say good-by to something I could never really say good-by to; there hadn't been many places that weren't too complicated with other people and other things to belong just to Ivor and me.

After a while I walked around to the garden at the back, hearing a dog barking lonesomely somewhere down the road, seeing the trees and house soft and vague under a rising mist. It was almost fall; the summer was nearly over. Standing there, I tried to imagine what Ivor had felt at that last moment when he had seen Judson come round the corner of the house, seen the glint of the gun in the August sunlight—not fear, certainly, perhaps not even regret, or regret only for me, because there were so many things now that I would have to find out for myself, things he had learned through too much success and too much failure. Perhaps it had been only one last extraordinary thing to him, to end the adventures of the boy who had wanted to take extraordinary chances so that extraordinary things would happen to him. . . .

"Never let it bother you," Father had said to me once, "if other people seem to get all the glory in life. Remember it's not always the kid everybody is watching who gets the brass ring and the free ride on the merry-go-round." Well, Ivor hadn't lived his life on that theory; if he had lost the brass ring and the free ride, it had never troubled him. What he had wanted was the bright, insubstantial thing, the glory, which is never quite good enough when you grasp it, but is all we have to dream on for our finest dreams. If it had eluded him, or destroyed him, he had had the excitement of a Cortez or a Balboa in searching for it—a fabulous treasure that existed, like theirs, in the mind a thousand times more glittering than any earthly treasure could ever be—and in the end he had found the wisdom of the disillusioned, which is never so wise as when it admits that what it knows is not the final answer after all. Perhaps there had even been something more, the something he had tried to communicate to me that last night—the knowledge that, whatever happened, he was able to come to terms with it and still go on living with it and the remnants of his dreams. . . .

It was late when I went back to the car. I drove up to Queensport to Martha's place, and asked her if she could put me up for the night.